THE HAUNTING OF DANSBURY PLOT

KRISTEN HOUGHTON

First published by Skylight-NYC Publishers, LLC 2023

Teeth, the Haunting of Dansbury Plot Copyright © 2023 by Kristen Houghton

ISBN 978-1-7324166-9-7

Library of Congress Cataloguing-in-Publication Data
Houghton, Kristen
Teeth: A Civil War Story, mystery/horror novel/Kristen Houghton-1st. ed.
1. Chris Hopper, Will Hopper, Kevin Lingle (Fictitious characters)-Fiction 2. residents of Township of Dansbury 3. Horror 4. Coming of age 5. horror mystery 6. Dansbury's Plot

Criminal Element, an imprint of Skylight-NYC Publishers, LLC
175 Fifth Avenue
New York, NY 10010
Skylight-NYC Publishers.com
skylight-nyc@outlook.com

Cover by 2Hopper Production & Design Studio
in association with KH Koehler Design

Skylight-NYC
PUBLISHERS

Contents

Books by Kristen Houghton

CRIME and MYSTERY

CATE HARLOW PRIVATE INVESTIGATION series
For I Have Sinned
Grave Misgivings
Unrepentant: Pray for Us Sinners
Do Unto Others
The Hawaiian Word for Murder

FANTASY

THE TEDDY JAMESON CHRONICLES
Welcome to Hell, Teddy Jameson
Leaving Hell with the Angel of Redemption (coming in 2023)

HISTORICAL ROMANCE
The Anchoress: A Romantic Tale of Terror

ANTHOLOGY
No Woman Diets Alone-There's Always a Man Behind Her Eating a Doughnut
And Then I'll Be Happy! Stop Sabotaging Your Happiness and Put Your Own Life First

YOUNG ADULT NOVELLA
Remember, Hetty?
Lilith Angel a YA fantasy series

Dedication

For all the authors who inspired a "child unlike the others"—thank you!

chapter

1

"There was a war goin' on, you know? War is a terrible thing for anyone to have to go through. All kinds of—what you call 'em, Jonesey?—*atrocities* happen and people do bad things. People can be forced to do some awful things that they wouldn't ordinary do. And that's what happened during the Civil War, what those southerners call the war of 'Northern Aggression'. Some folks did a terrible thing there during the war, forcing others to make terrible choices too, and the score's gotta be settled. Gotta be settled soon. Been too long."

Old Man Hobart knows about things like that. I've heard him talk about stuff like that a zillion times. This time he's talking about Dansbury Plot.

Nothing grows on Dansbury Plot—almost everybody simply calls it The Plot—where it sits on the very edge of the Township of Bridge Crossing, across a really wide street from the Little League fields. It's a square of land about the size of two town blocks and it is barren and dry and dead-looking. Everything for miles around our town is green and flowery pretty much all year long, even during the kinda mild winters we have here in Bridge Crossing, Delaware, but not Dansbury Plot. I mean even with the little bit of snow we get, there'll be winter flowers poking up all over. And talking about the snow—there's *never* been any snow on The Plot. Not ever. Snow on everywhere else but not there. It just looks dead and brown when everywhere

7

else has a nice little cover of snow. What does that tell you about Dansbury Plot, huh?

A lot of scary stories have been told about The Plot and stuff that's happened. Little kids call it 'Bury-the-Dead-Dan's Plot' but won't go anywhere near it, not ever. Even animals keep clear of it. Hell, if a mouse was being chased by a cat, it would go clean out of its way and take a chance on getting caught rather than run across Dansbury Plot.

And speaking of cats, dogs too, they don't go anywhere *near* that place. If dogs are outside their house they'll stand a good distance away from The Plot, just shivering and sometimes they'll raise their heads and howl a kind of unearthly howl at nothing anyone can see. Cats, jeez, well, cats get their backs up and hiss if they're even *facing* in that direction. And you never ever see birds flying around there either. Me, I hate the fact that my bedroom window faces towards Bury-the-Dead-Dan's Plot almost as much as I hate Billy Sarlewski. Billy almost got me to step foot on that cursed plot of land. No fooling, he really almost did.

One day, last week, he made up a stupid game with blindfolds and stuff that included a prize for the winner. The prize was five whole bucks and ice cream. Billy's got the money to do stuff like that. He's got more money, and a lot more fat, than me and my friends because his mom is the Mrs. S of *Mrs. S's Simply Sensational Homemade Cookies*. I don't usually call people *fat* or bad names or anything like that. I'm not a mean guy, but my Grand-Dad says that someone like Billy brings out the worst in another kid because he is always trying to hurt someone. I hate Billy Sarlewski and I refuse to eat his mother's famous cookies even if the chocolate macadamia nut ones are the best I ever tasted. I won't ever eat them again. I swore that I wouldn't eat them after what Billy did to me.

Anyway, that day, we were all standing around the Little League field, which is across from The Plot, ignoring that dead piece of land *and* Billy. We pretend that The Plot's not there, the same as we do Billy.

But, so that day we were shooting the bull, trying to come up with cool nicknames for ourselves, if and when, we ever got to be big league ball players. One of the guys is named Sal Minella and he said he'd maybe like to be called *Salmonella* 'cause his batting average would be so good, the opposing team would throw up whenever he came to bat'. It *was* kinda a cool name, I guess.

We were really ignoring Billy because he is a big pain and mean to boot, when, to get us to notice him, he suddenly asks if anyone wants to win five dollars and an ice cream sundae. It seems he had made up a new game on the spot. He called it 'Trust' and the rule was one kid got to be blind-folded—he'd be the 'blind man'—and led around by another kid called the 'leader'. Billy swore nobody was going to be led towards Dansbury Plot.

"You're just going to be led around the ball field and out into the street that leads toward town to show how much trust you have in the guy leading you around."

We had to trust our 'leader' to watch for traffic and shit. The blind man who was the most trusting would win. He showed us the five-dollar bill and told us he himself would pay for the sundae. He was going to be the judge, of course.

So we each took a turn as the leader and led our blind man around the field and across the street. Well, we sure got bored with that game fast. But Billy said nobody won and we had to keep playing until someone did. Most of us wanted to go down to the pastry shop to get a lemon ice but Billy would have none of it. He said he had a *new* game and he got our interest by upping the reward to ten dollars, a banana split, *and* a pair of his sister Ellen's underpants for both the leader and his blindman.

Ellen was seventeen and really pretty. At twelve-years-old, me and my friends didn't know a whole lot about sex and stuff but Billy's sister was probably the reason a lot of us first began to think about it. She wore her private school uniform skirts really short and once, when she bent over to pick up a book she dropped on the street, we caught a glimpse of her white underpants. To actually own a pair would be unbelievable. Billy was a real pig.

The game was still called Trust but now it involved having your leader take you as close to Bury-the-Dead-Dan's Plot as he dared. Of course no one was going to actually *step* on The Plot he said, just get real close to it. The team that got the closest was the winner.

So the first two to go were Joey Coles and Bradley Galardi. Joey led Brad as near to the Plot as he dared which wasn't very close at all. The second two were Sal Minella and Steven Luty. Sal led Stevie closer than Joey had led Brad, but then Stevie took off his blindfold and both of them ran like hell back to our ball field. My best friend Kevin Lingle absolutely refused to have anyone lead him by The Plot and said that he didn't give a damn about the money or the banana split, or Ellen's underpants. And no one had better call him chicken or his older brother would beat the crap out of them.

I was the only one left.

Billy looked at me, smiled his stupid fat smile, and put his hands together like an Olympic diver. I knew what he meant by that gesture. The incident at the pool last summer. His smile and that gesture meant that he would bet that I would chicken out like I did last year about diving off the high dive at the town pool. Boy, I'll never forget that day.

* * *

We had all been diving off the lower board and been pretty proud of ourselves. Most of us did fairly decent dives with the exception of Billy who always belly-flopped. He just couldn't get the hang of it. After diving for about an hour we were tired and sitting on the side of the pool watching the high school kids go off the high board. A lot of them were on the school swim team and they were doing some really sweet dives. Kev said that he was glad we weren't going off of *that* board—it was way too high, and the other guys agreed.

Except for me.

I still don't know why I said what I did. I know I should always think before I say things, but most times I don't. I sure didn't think that day because, to be honest, I am not a big fan of heights. I mean I'm great at climbing trees but I never climb all the way up either. But I opened my big mouth and said to Kev, "I bet I could do it if I wanted. It's not that high. It looks easy."

I was lying back, looking up at the board and relaxing in the sun. I didn't see Billy's face. Billy was never one to miss an opportunity to humiliate someone else. It sure took the spotlight off of *him* when he could embarrass another guy. He said I didn't have the guts to go off the high board. He said that I was just blowing air out of my hole.

Kev asked Billy why didn't *he* go and dive the high board or didn't *he* have the guts *himself*. Good ol' Kev. He's not the bravest when it comes to diving and all but he fears no one because of his big brother Jeremy. Jeremy will kick anybody's ass for Kev.

Billy didn't get pissed or anything, he just told Kev that for him it wasn't a matter of having guts, it was that he hadn't *mastered* the lower board yet. Billy got that word *mastered* from his father who was always talking about how 'learning a sport is mastering it'.

His father is a lazy slob, who lives off his wife's cookie business and had probably never mastered any sport ever, unless stuffing your mouth full of food was a sport. He's a lot older than Billy's mom and he says he's *retired* although my Grand-Dad said Mr. Sarlewski never worked a day in his life. He lived with his parents until he was forty-five and lived off their money 'cause he said he was 'taking care of them.' They died in their house a few days apart, both of them weak and skinny like they weren't taken care of at all. My Grand-Mom said it's a load of bull he was taking care of them—more like taking care he got their money.

"That man never gave a damn about his parents. He was waiting for those poor people to die." She says she feels sorry for his wife. "Poor woman. She started her cookie business in her own kitchen, trying different recipes until she got everything just right. She worked hard to make it a success.

Sarlewski sniffed around and smelled money. He married her, doesn't do anything to help, but acts as if he owns the business. A completely shameless man with no morals at all."

Anyway, Billy went on to say that since *I* had said that *I* could do it if *I* wanted to, *I* now had to do it or *I* was a gutless chicken-shit. When he said that, all the guys looked at me. Being called a gutless chicken-shit in front of your friends is serious stuff when you're a kid. Five minutes passed before Kev asked me in a sort of whisper if I really thought I could do it. I looked over at Billy and he was talking to some high school jocks who were friends of his sister. They only ever talk to him because they all have the hots for Ellen. He was pointing to me and then the high dive and the jocks started laughing. I knew I had to take the challenge. I also knew that, in the future, I'd better learn to keep my mouth shut around Billy Sarlewski.

I got up and slowly walked to the ladder even though my knees were shaking so much I thought they would collapse under me. I grabbed hold of the sides of the ladder and began to climb, but halfway up the steps to the high dive platform I froze, I just froze. I couldn't move! My feet refused to keep going and all I could do was keep staring down at the pool, which looked like it was three thousand miles away. I couldn't get my hands off the sides of the ladder I was so scared. It was like they were glued to it. Two lifeguards had to come pry my hands off of the damned thing and help me down the steps.

I was bawling like a baby by the time they got me down. Billy saw the whole thing and laughed his ass off as the lifeguards were helping me. I hated him. Every day for a month after that high dive humiliation, he had made that gesture with his hands and clucked like a chicken whenever he saw me.

* * *

My face got red just thinking about last summer and I reached for the blindfold. Billy said *he* would be my leader since the others had all had their turns and Kevin wouldn't play the 'game.' Kev gave him the finger and said, "Screw you, Sarlewski!"

My heart was pounding but I let that bastard lead me across the street. I was counting the steps I was taking and I could feel the breeze blowing on the back of my neck. I could hear the kids talking on the ball field as Billy led me farther. He spun me around and I thought he was going to take me back to the ball field. I was walking easily thinking it was over but then I heard Kev yell out, "Hey, they did it! Holy crap! They did it!" and I lifted my blindfold. We were the closest! Ellen's underpants were mine!

I was turning to give a victory wave to the guys when I felt a hard shove on my back and I fell forward towards The Plot. I twisted my body to the side and landed with my hands on some really sharp rocks just an inch or so from that horrible barren ground. My left hand, my pitching hand, was cut and bleeding. I got up and Billy shoved me again and I did one of those arm swaying, rocking motions to keep my balance. The toe of one of my sneakers was just touching the Plot and my hands were about a half of a foot above that dead looking earth! I was gonna fall on The Plot! Lucky for me, Joey and Kev ran over to help me.

They leaned forward and grabbed my arms to pull me back and that's when I heard it. A sound, like a click, or a snap. I couldn't figure out what it was, but it was a definite sound. It was a familiar sound, too. I knew I'd heard it before.

We started running back towards the ball field and when I got there, I collapsed on the grass and looked around for Billy, but he was gone. Brad said he saw Billy running as fast as his fat legs could go heading back towards town because he probably thought I was going to kill him if I caught him.

But I couldn't even breathe let alone kill that creep. I put my head down on my knees and thought about that sound. It was a weird sound all right.

It wasn't until later that night when I was getting ready for bed that a memory came back to me. I remembered where I had heard that sound before, that weird snapping sound!

Two weeks ago at my grandparents' house, I'd heard that same sound.

My Grand-Dad was taking these big juicy steaks out to the deck to barbecue. The plate was piled high and one of the steaks was kind of hanging over the edge, dripping a little blood. As he walked to the grill his tough little cocker spaniel Kirby, jumped up high and tried to grab the steak. My Grand-Mom called out, "Watch out for Kirby!" and my Grand-Dad swung the plate higher just in time to avoid Kirby grabbing one. The dog missed getting the steak and we all heard Kirby's jaws close with a snapping click as his teeth hit hard on nothing but air.

That was the same sound I'd heard at The Plot. A snap of teeth like the sound Kirby made trying to grab the steak.

Except there was no dog at Dansbury Plot.

chapter

2

A few days later I was down at Old Man Hobart's pet shop. He doesn't really sell any animals, not even rabbits at Easter time, just food and stuff for dogs, cats, gerbils, and birds. And he doesn't really sell a lot of that either. He makes a living because he owns the building which, besides his pet shop, has *Lingle's Bike Shop*, the *Hair We Are Salon*, and the *Happy Teeth* dentist's office with its big sign that says, 'Healthy Teeth Are Happy Teeth'. They all have to pay him rent so it doesn't make a bit of difference if he sells anything or not. Me and Kev think he's richer than God.

Anyway, I was down at Hobart's because I first went to Lingle's Bike Shop looking for Kev, and his dad told me he had gone over to the pet shop to buy some straw for his white rat, Louie-Louie. Kevin's not all that clean a kid, but he is a fanatic about changing the straw in Louie-Louie's cage. Boy, he loves that rat. So I walked the few feet to the pet store to meet up with him.

Most people come into the pet shop just to hang around. The old guys come in because Old Man Hobart always has coffee going and doughnuts put out. They like to eat while they sit and gossip and stuff. The old guys don't have anything to do anyway and Hobart likes to sit and talk with them about the old days. They're kinda like an audience for him. All the grown-ups call him Hobart—I've never heard anyone say his first name. I mean, I know he *has* to have a *first* name but I don't know what it is and neither does Kev. Kids like me go to Hobart's to get free doughnuts and because, sometimes, he's got some really interesting stories to tell. He's old as dirt and knows a lot about stuff, I'll give him that.

Hobart keeps the place open from nine a.m. until six p.m. every single day except Sunday. His friend, Jonesey, this derelict type of guy who sleeps for free in the back room of the shop, helps out by 'checking the stock', buying the doughnuts, and making the coffee. He's all right, too, except he very rarely says anything. I guess Hobart does the talking for both of them.

About Jonesey. My Grand-Dad says I shouldn't call him a derelict because he's just a sad old man. He says he's a very intelligent man who never had the money to go to college. He read a lot and he's what my Grand-Dad calls a self-educated man.

When he was twenty-five, Jonesey became an electrician and set up shop in a small apartment. People said he was fair with his prices and never cheated anyone. He had an awful childhood and that's why he was always very quiet. His only friend was Mr. Hobart all through childhood and on into his adult years.

His wife Elizabeth was the town librarian. Jonesey was some kind of marathon reader or something back then—anyway he really liked to read. They met when he attended a meeting for a book club she was starting at the library. She was pretty and outgoing so nobody understood how they ever fell in love, but they did and they got married after knowing each other for about a year. They had no kids, just each other and they were happy just to be together.

His electrician business really took off and they bought a house with an office in back for Jonesey. When they were married for thirteen years his wife got some disease called ALS and died after being sick for five years. Jonesey loved her so much, he closed his business and took care of her himself until the day she died.

The day his wife was buried, Mr. Elbert Daniel Mervin Jones—Jonesey's real name—left their house and took to wandering the town, not eating, using the gas station's toilet when he had to pee or do the other thing, and sleeping at night on his wife's new grave.

Once one of the most polite guys around, he became nasty when folks tried to help him. Nothing anybody could say had any effect on him. He even told Pastor Darnell of the Presbyterian Church to go to hell when the pastor tried to get him out of his sadness and recited that old saying, "God giveth and God taketh away." Rumor has it that Jonesey told him to "Taketh your crabby wife, Mrs.-Big-Shit-I'm-the-Pastor's-Wife Darnell, while you still have the balls and cock to do it." Boy I would've loved to have been there when

Jonesey said that!

People began to avoid him and said he was becoming the town scandal. Some of the regulars at the pet shop told Mr. Hobart that Pastor Darnell was going around saying that Jonesey should be put away. Like in a nuthouse for crazy people.

Old Man Hobart felt really sorry for his lifelong friend, whom he had called Jonesey ever since they were in elementary school together, and he didn't want to see him put in some loony bin or anything. So one rainy night he went up to the town cemetery on his own and tried to persuade Jonesey to go home.

Instead of telling Mr. Hobart off like he had done to everyone else who had tried to help him, Jonesey began to cry. He said he couldn't ever go into that house knowing he would never see his wife Elizabeth there ever again. He just wouldn't ever go there, not ever.

Jonesey was skinny and exhausted and his eyes were red and swollen from crying. He told Old Man Hobart he just wanted to die, too. Hobart sat with him all night in the rain and somehow convinced his friend that he just wasn't ready for dying and that he should sleep in a room in the back of the pet shop if he felt he couldn't go back home. He told him it would kind of be like when they were in the sixth grade together and the Hobart family had that old tree house in their back yard. Jonesey always stayed there when his father got stinking drunk and tried to beat up on him.

What really got through to Jonesey though, was something Old Man Hobart said after he mentioned the back room of the pet shop. He used to say the same thing whenever Jonesey ran away from home and hid in the tree house to escape his drunk old man—

"You'll be safe with me, Jonesey. You can stay as long as you want."

Jonesey went with Mr. Hobart over to the pet shop that night and he sure must feel safe 'cause he's been there for the past thirty years.

I saw Kevin sitting inside the pet shop eating a doughnut. Jonesey was bringing him a glass of milk and when he saw me come in he went over to where the milk and coffee were and got me a glass of milk too. Then he motioned to the doughnut box and I went and got a Boston crème. Jonesey smiled his sad smile and nodded his head at me. He's always been nice to me even though he doesn't talk very much. I know he likes me and the other guys who come into the shop. Except for Billy. I think he hates Billy because that creep makes faces at Jonesey through the window and calls him a nut-case and a weirdo whenever he sees him outside the pet shop. Of course, coward that he is, Billy always runs away before Jonesey can react. But then, I don't think Jonesey could ever hurt anybody, not even Billy.

Anyway, me and Kev are sitting there drinking ice cold milk, eating our second doughnut, and listening to the old guys talk, or as one of them says, 'shoot the breeze'. It was a nice thing to be doing on a warm spring day. The old guys' voices were a pleasant, distant hum. We don't pay much attention to them and they don't pay much to us except to ask how our parents are and stuff. Mostly they ignore us and we like it that way.

"Shooting the breeze," I say out loud for no particular reason. I like the sound of certain words and expressions and like to know where they came from—like how did people start to use them and all. I even bought a brand-new notebook last year and printed 'Important Words and Phrases to Remember' on the cover. I write new words and expressions in it that I hear so I can read them over and over again. So I say, "Shooting the breeze" a couple of times and then ask Kev how he thinks that expression came to be used.

"It means talkin', I think." He mumbles this because his mouth is full of jelly doughnut and milk. Kev drops the 'g' ending on a lot of words.

"Duh! I know *that*, I just wondered where it got started is all. Jeez, you're dribbling on yourself, Kev!"

"It's Civil War slang." Both of us turned in surprise. Jonesey was talking to us!

I couldn't think of anything to say, it was so rare that Jonesey spoke to anyone, but Kev said, "It's *that* old? I mean people said it *way* back *then*? In the Civil War? Wow!"

For answer Jonesey nodded and turning his attention to me, he spoke again.

"You go ask your Grand-Dad. He'll tell you. Knows everything about the Civil War history, your Grand-Dad does. Teaches the periods of the Civil War and Reconstruction in his American history classes at the local community college. He knows everything about that time. Knows all the lingo from back then too."

"What's—?" begins Kev and I know he's gonna ask what the word lingo means. I tell him the word means slang just like Jonesey said and then I explain it even more.

"Kinda like when you say something is 'sweet' when you really mean that it's great. Or when your brother Jeremy told that umpire at his last baseball game to 'chill out'. He was telling him to calm down. Get it?"

Kev thinks about it for a minute and then say, "Yeah, got it my man. Sweet!" He high-fives me and tells me that my Grand-Dad must be the smartest guy in the whole world knowing all that 'lingo stuff'.

I'm thinking of buying Kev a dictionary next year before school starts.

Jonesey didn't say anything else after he talked about my grandfather, just went back to pouring coffee and opening up a fresh box of doughnuts that Old Man Hobart had just brought in. I guess he had used up all his talking for the day.

Me and Kev continued eating and listening to the buzz of voices around us.

"—not gonna build nothing on it. A score's got to be settled first." Old Man Hobart was settling into his favorite chair by the window and talking to the old-timers.

"I don't know about that Hobart. You get some of those real estate people, those developers coming in, you'd be surprised at what they can do. I want people to invest in a type of mini mall."

Billy's father, Mr. Sarlewski, was talking. I turned toward him surprised—I didn't even see him come in. My Grand-Dad calls him an opinionated anal perforation which is a fancy way of saying asshole. Mr. Sarlewski always thinks his is the only opinion that counts.

"And *I'm* tellin' *you*, Sarlewski, nothing is going to happen. Let 'em try. There's a debt. Got to be paid, score's got to be settled."

"Listen, Hobart, Dansbury Plot *can,* and, *will* be dug up and developed. I heard that young man, Mark Colbert, from that new real estate place on Brook Avenue, say it's prime land for some nice, new businesses. Nothing too fancy, he said, and they'd keep the buildings' height to no more than two stories. Maybe put in a small park with benches and a fountain. He says all that land is going to waste and should be developed and that the revenues from those businesses will lower our property taxes."

Some of the men are nodding, agreeing with Mr. Sarlewski.

"I might invest in a storefront there myself. Been telling my wife we should get a bigger place for our cookie business."

Me and Kev almost choke when he says 'our business' like *he* had anything to do with it except live off of his wife's profits. Kevin laughs so hard he spits milk through his nose.

Old Man Hobart gets up from his chair snorting with laughter. He points a finger, one by one, at each of the men sitting there and drinking his coffee.

"All of you are damn fools if you listen to that Mark Colbert. He's not from around here. He don't know about The Plot. Nothing will be put there until the score is settled."

"What score are you talking about? It's just some land where there was once a jail or something during the Civil War. If people were held in that jail once upon a time, well, they must've done something to deserve it. Damn criminals. Shit, the land's just sitting there. There's no score to settle. I don't believe in anything like that anyway."

Mr. Sarlewski was standing there with his legs wide apart trying to look like he was some big deal authority but all he looked like was a much older version of his mean, rotten son. You could tell who Billy took after, boy, oh, boy!

I was listening really hard to what the old guys were saying. We had all heard the different stories—legends my Grand-Dad calls them—about The Plot. Some said there had been a jail on it, some that there had been a hospital on it for dying soldiers in the Civil War. My Grand-Dad says it was probably a holding camp for Yankee prisoners-of-war before they were shipped south to real prisons. Thing is, nobody knows for sure. No one knows who even owns it any more. No one can even *find* records on it. The only sure thing is that it is there and it is a creepy, dead-looking piece of land where nothing grows and nothing lives.

The conversation is getting pretty loud and some of the guys are cursing. Old Man Hobart notices me and Kev and tells us that we'd better go on home. There's liable to be fireworks going off inside his store, he tells us. He says we shouldn't be hearing all the cursing because we have virgin ears. Ha! Me and Kev can curse with the best of them if we wanted. We just don't want our parents to know is all, so we don't curse in front of grown-ups. We each grab another doughnut and leave.

* * *

"School's out, Chris," says Kev as we walk towards our homes. "I guess you'll be goin' to your grandparents' house."

He sounds really down. Even though my grandparents only live across town, it's not like he'll only be two houses down from me like we are now. We're best friends and all. Every summer, I spend all of July with my grandparents but *this* year I'm going there right after the last day of school. I'll be there all summer.

"Yeah, my parents are going to Hawai'i for *two whole months*. It's their fifteenth wedding anniversary."

"Wow! Hawai'i?! Wow! Don't *you* want to go, too?"

'Hell no, they're gonna be busy, you know like being romantic and stuff. *I* don't want to go—I'll be bored nuts!"

I don't tell him that my parents are trying to 'save their marriage'. That's what my mom told me. She said that sometimes couples grow apart and have to 'reconnect'. She said that it's really important for her and my dad to take time to get back together and that they need this time alone. I know that my dad sleeps in the spare room in the basement now. He says it's because his snoring keeps my mom up. That's a crock right there. I never heard my dad snore when he falls asleep in front of the television. I know what real snoring sounds like. Whenever me and Kev stay overnight at each other's houses, I hear Kev snoring like crazy and, believe me, his snores could break glass!

Anyway, my parents pretend that nothing's really, *really* wrong but sometimes I hear my mom cry at night and that upsets me a lot. My dad's still living in the house and everything, so I guess I'm luckier than my friend Brad whose dad left him and his mom last year and Brad hasn't seen him since. That's gotta suck.

I stop talking and Kev doesn't say anything else but I know that he knows the real reason my mom and dad are going on a two-month trip. He's my best friend. He'll let me tell a kinda fib and pretend that he believes me. That's what best friends do. We share a lot of secrets too so, as best friends go, Kevin Lingle is the best around.

I also know he wishes he had grandparents like mine who live close by. His live half way across the country and he sees them maybe once a year.

"Anyway," I continue, "I get to spend all summer with my Grand-Dad and do all kinds of great stuff. And you know my Grand-Mom is the best cook in the whole wide world. She's gonna be in New York for an entire month for her author and book review thing, but she'll leave a bunch of good stuff in the freezer for us to heat up and eat. It'll be great! My Grand-Dad says we're gonna 'batch it', just us two guys." I suddenly get a great idea. "Hey, listen, Kev, I'll ask them if you can stay over a couple of nights or even a week, okay? I mean I've got my own room there and it's got twin beds. Plenty of room. I'll ask them today."

"Yeah?! All right!"

Kev loves my grandparents! They're what he calls 'young grammies' even though they're like in their sixties. I think that's because they both still work. My Grand-Dad is a history professor and my Grand-Mom runs a small bookstore they bought a few years ago. They're not fat like some other grandparents, they play tennis, and he thinks my grandfather tells the best stories in the world.

"We can go to all the celebrations and the fair for the Fourth of July together and eat all the free hot dogs we can eat! What a great summer this is gonna be!" Kev is dancing around, he's so happy.

We make plans to go play ball tomorrow and I go home to call my Grand-Dad. We shoot the breeze for a while, me and my grandfather, and I even ask him about the expression. He says Jonesey is absolutely right—it *is* from the Civil War time. He tells me what he calls the 'origin of the phrase'.

"The story goes, my inquisitive grandson, that a colonel came upon a group of young soldiers, called Johnny Rebs."

The confederates were called that, he explains, because the North said they were rebelling against the United States, so they were rebels or rebs.

"Anyway they were fooling around at camp after dark shooting bottles and tin plates, making a lot of noise when they should have been quiet because the Yankees might be nearby. The colonel told them to stop their racket and said the only shooting they should be doing was 'shooting the breeze,' in order words, talking."

God, my Grand-Dad is the best! He knows everything!

"Hey Grand-Dad? Was there like a prison or something on The Plot during the Civil War? Old Man, um, sorry, I mean *Mr.* Hobart kinda said there was."

"Yes, I believe there was a holding camp for Union soldiers captured by the Confederates. The south did have a camp in Delaware. I don't know a lot about it and I am surprised that there really aren't any records down at the town hall about that. It would be interesting to get copies and show them to the students in one of my classes, but, to answer your question, yes, Mr. Hobart is correct."

We talk a little more and I hear Kirby barking like crazy in the background. My grandfather tells me he sees a squirrel in the yard. Kirby loves to chase squirrels even if he never catches them. Before we hang up I ask him about Kev staying over and he tells me, if his parents say it's okay, Kev can stay as long as he likes.

"He can stay for a whole month if he wants. It'll be just us men and lots of good food left by one very good cook."

Ha! I hang up on Kirby's barking his fool head off.

I repeat the words Johnny Rebs just to hear the sound of it and then write it and 'shooting the breeze' into my special notebook. Like I said, I like the sound of certain words and expressions. Johnny Rebs, Johnny Rebs. I laugh and imagine Kirby barking at Johnny Rebs making all that racket.

* * *

That night I dream of Kirby. In my dream not only can Kirby bark, he can also talk. But the talking is strange 'cause his mouth never moves, but I can still hear him talking. I'm walking with someone who has hold of my right hand. I think it's my grandfather, but Kirby says, "This is not who you think it is. Let go of his hand before it's too late."

Then Kirby goes into a barking frenzy like he always does when he's excited. The person holding my hand turns towards me and I hear a snapping sound. I can't see his face. It's like he's a shadow or something. He bends down towards me and I hear another snap.

I yell out for Kirby to stop trying to grab the steak, but he says it's dripping, the blood is dripping, drip-drip-drip, onto the deck floor and he wants the meat. I look down and there *is* blood but I don't see any steak. I don't see any floor either. We're in a field. My left hand feels wet and when I look at it I see the drip-drip-drip of blood is coming from me! It's making wet spots on the dirt. As I stare at it, I hear another snap. I try to see who is with me. Where is this guy's face? Snap! Snap! Blood, drip-drip-drip, dripping! No, No. Kirby! You can't eat my hand!

"*I* don't want to eat your hand, dumb-ass! I want steak! *That* wants your hand!"

Drip-drip-drip. Snap! Snap! Not my pitching hand, no!

"Tasted it you see. Tasted your blood, drip-drip-drip, your dripping blood."

"Kirby? Kirby! What are you talking about? Please don't eat my hand, that's my pitching hand!"

Drip-drip-drip, dripping. My blood? Whose blood? Kirby?

"T-a-s-t-e-d your blood. Not me. Where's my steak?"

Snap! Snap! Snap! I wake up. Snap! What the hell is that noise? Snap! I lie awake too scared to even call out for my Mom and Dad. Omigod, I'm going to die. Under the thin sheet I touch my left hand with my right. It doesn't feel wet. I touch all my fingers and then the palm of my hand. I feel the scab smack in the center of my palm. It's taking a long time to heal and itches a little but I don't scratch it, God no. I don't want it to bleed.

Snap! I jump and fearfully turn my head towards the sound. Snap! Snap! I almost laugh but I start to cry instead. The snapping sound is the shade smacking against the windowsill. The wind is kicking up. I hear thunder in the distance and the snap of the shade when the wind blows against my window. We're probably going to have a storm.

No way do I go back to sleep.

chapter

3

Me and Kev are playing a game of catch on the Little League field. He catches because he's the best damn catcher around. Everyone wants him on their team, no kidding. He can stay in a catcher's squat for hours, he's that good.

I'm pitching like a crazy man. I'm pretty good too. The only sound is the rhythmic pop when the ball hits the pockets of our gloves. It is probably the sweetest sound in the world and I don't think of anything but lobbing the ball to Kev and waiting for him to return it to me. Game of catch, pure and simple.

I feel a burning sensation in the palm of my left hand. Its sweaty and I notice the constant pitching of the ball has worn some of the scab away. The salt from the sweat is what makes it burn. It's not bleeding though, thank God.

"Let's stop for a while, okay Kev? I got soda and chips in my backpack."

"Yeah, okay. It's gettin' hotter now, anyway."

I wonder if I should tell Kevin about my dream. I mean we're best friends and all and I know he won't make fun of me being scared. The only thing is, if I tell him the dream, I have to tell him about the sound I heard out by The Plot.

"Hey, Kevin."

We're sitting on the bleachers munching baked Lays potato chips and he looks at me funny because I only ever call him Kev.

"Hey, did you ever have a nightmare that was kind of stupid, like with a talking dog or something?"

"Well, yeah, kind of, but not with a talkin' dog. It was a human *person,* but it didn't have a human head." Kev nods his own head at me.

"Yeah? Like what did it have for a head?"

"Listen, remember our English teacher, 'the Parrot?' We always called Mrs. Higgins the parrot because of that big hooked nose she had. Remember her from fifth grade?"

"Yeah! I remember her." I swallow and take a swig of soda from one of the cans I brought with me. "What about her?"

"I had a terrible dream about her right after this one day when she's screamin' at me in class. Remember how she was yellin' at me like that? Like a crazy lady? All because I didn't do my homework?"

"You never did your homework in her class, Kev! That's why she was always yelling at you. She got tired of always asking you why you didn't do it."

"Are you gonna listen to my dream or what?"

"Yeah, yeah, go ahead. You had a dream about her yelling."

"And it was pretty scary! In the dream she made me stay after school to do my homework. After everybody was gone it was just her and me in the class room and I was doin' my vocabulary definitions. I had my head down and everythin' and when she asked me if I was finished, I looked up at her desk and almost died because of how she looked! Instead of a human head she had a giant parrot's head, all green and blue feathers and with this humongous sharp beak, razor sharp!"

"Wow!"

"Yeah, wow is right. Scary! So, she gets up from her desk and comes over to me to check my homework. She says it's all wrong and then she starts peckin' me with her beak and yellin' at me! And you know how in a really bad nightmare you sometimes tell yourself that you're only sleepin'? I kept tellin' myself that, but it didn't work. I was being pecked to death by the Parrot! She's chasin' me around the room peckin' at my head and stuff. She's gonna kill me but I can't wake up!"

"What happened?"

"What do you mean, what happened? She was tryin' to kill me!"

"Did you wake up before you died in the dream or what?"

"You know what? I did wake up just as her beak was goin' for my eyes! And when I woke up it was pitch dark and for a minute I thought she *did* get my eyes 'cause I couldn't see! I was sweatin' like a madman and the sweat was drippin' down my face so I thought my eyeballs were bleedin'! It took my mom and dad an hour to get me to stop screamin'!"

23

We're quiet for a while, thinking about Mrs. Higgins aka the Parrot. Then I get up to throw away my trash and, without looking at him, I tell Kev about my dream and about the sound I heard the day we played Trust. I feel kinda funny telling him about the snap sound like I made it up or something.

I tell him everything, my hand bleeding and all and when I finish telling him, I turn around and look at him. He's finishing his chips and looking out at the Plot.

"Well? What do you think about my dream?"

"Kirby really was talkin'? I mean, what did his voice *sound* like!"

"Kev!"

"What? I wonder what Louie-Louie would sound like if he could talk."

"Kev, didn't you hear anything *else* I said? Like about the snap and my hand and everything I just told you?"

"Sure I did. Don't get so nutty. Let me think. Are you *sure* you heard a snappin' sound? Really?"

"Honest to God."

"And your hand was cut?"

"Yeah."

"Did you maybe—bleed on The Plot?"

"I don't know. Why?"

"'Cause maybe there was some super large bug or somethin' that was on the ground or maybe it was like that plant thing we learned about in science, you know, it grabs live stuff that comes near it and eats them—what's it called?"

"Venus Flytrap, and there was nothing on the ground that I could see, nothing lives there anyway, no bugs, nothing. Anyway I never heard of a *snapping* bug."

"I think they have snappin' bugs in the Amazon."

"Hey, Crap-for-Brains, we're not in the Amazon!" I sigh.

Kev's my best friend and stuff but he lives in some really weird world that is unreal. Sometimes he's no real help at all. He just looks at me kinda hurt and all—he hates it when I call him Crap-for-Brains. God, he can drive me nuts!

But, like I told you, he is my best friend. He always sticks up for me against Sarlewski, so I tell him he can stay the entire month of July at my grandparents' house if he wants and if his parents say okay.

"All r-i-g-h-t!! Can I bring Louie-Louie? I *gotta* bring Louie-Louie, he'll be lost without me."

"I guess. Just keep him in his cage. I don't know how my grandmother feels about rats in her house. Okay?"

"You got it, my man!" He high-fives me. We start to pick up our gloves to go play another game of catch and Kev say, "You know what that snappin' sound maybe was?"

"What?"

He looks really serious, not like himself at all. His eyes look old, like the eyes of the men down at Old Man Hobart's. He kinda scares me.

"Maybe the ground was—this sounds stupid so don't you even laugh, okay?—but maybe the ground was, you know, hungry or somethin'."

Believe me, I'm not laughing.

4

Two days later, I'm waving goodbye to my mom and dad at the departure gate at the airport. My Grand-Dad hugs my dad, who's his son, then hugs my mom, and tells them everything will work out. My mom hugs my Grand-Dad really tight and says thank you. She tells me that she'll call once a week and that my Grand-Dad knows the places where they're staying so if I need to call her, it's okay. Then she cries and hugs me so tight I almost cry and barf up breakfast at the same time. Grown-ups are way too emotional.

It's my second trip to the airport that week. My Grand-Mom left for New York four days ago for her book review trip. The night before she left, she and my Grand-Dad talked about my mom and dad when they thought I was busy watching television. I heard everything they said, especially, "But don't let Chris worry about anything. Hopefully this trip will help the marriage."

Before she got on the plane my grandmother asked me if I wanted to go along with her to the Big Apple to sit with her while she reviews books and authors. She says she just might have an extra ticket hidden in her luggage if I say yes. Or, and I see her wink at my Grand-Dad, do I want to hang out with an absent-minded history professor who just might want to go exploring for artifacts by the old quarry and go swimming every day.

"So what'll be, Christopher?" asks my Grand-Mom. Oh man! They both start laughing because they know what I'll say. Swimming every single summer day and going to that great old quarry where I might find Indian arrowheads is my choice. My grandparents are real jokers, all right!

That night while me, my Grand-Dad, and Kirby, are settling down in front of the TV to watch the Yankee game, I tell my Grand-Dad about what Sarlewski said down at Old Man Hobart's and what Hobart said about The Plot. "What did Old Man, I mean Mr. Hobart, mean about 'settling a score', Grand-Dad?"

He passes me a bowl of hot buttered popcorn and a bottle of cream soda and gets one for himself before he answers. He calls this our game food. Kirby plops as near to me as he can get because he loves popcorn. He won't bark or anything, he'll just stare at you 'til you give him some.

My Grand-Dad asks if I know what settling a score means? I tell him of course I do, it's getting even.

"Not exactly. It *is* getting even but it's a little more sophisticated than that. It means that a wrong must be righted, more or less. That someone must pay for a damage or hurt done. Do you understand what I'm saying?"

"Yeah, I think so. Like when Billy Sarlewski smashed up Kev's science project because he was jealous that Kev won first prize. Kev's brother Jeremy told me and Kev he was gonna get even with Sarlewski and *he* went and smashed *Billy's* project. Like that? Is that settling a score?"

"Well, I guess you and Kevin thought it was. More like 'an eye for an eye and a tooth for a tooth', I would say. Biblical and violent. Momentary satisfaction."

I'm surprised that he quoted something from the Bible. He doesn't ever go to church or anything, just on special occasions like somebody's wedding or if someone dies or something. And about the Bible, he says it's just the history of a people mixed with their religious beliefs and mythology.

"Well, what *is* settling a score, then if it's not getting even?" I ask him.

"It is a form of restitution for harm done. It is an Old West saying that has to do with playing cards. If you lost the game the money score was settled and you were made to pay."

"It doesn't have to do with smashing another guy?"

"I'm sure that happened sometimes, probably most times, but that's not what it should mean. Do you understand?"

"I think so." I try to think about what he said about card games and stuff and the conversation at Hobart's, but the game starts and I'm distracted.

We watch the game. The innings are really long and in the middle of the fifth I find I can't keep my eyes open. It's been a long day. I've been up since five-thirty in the morning. I stretch my mouth into a gigantic yawn and give Kirby the last few pieces that are in the bowl and then give him the bowl to lick.

"Good ol' Kirby. You love popcorn, doncha?" I stroke his soft fur and nod off.

Next thing I know I'm outside in the dark and Kirby is right there with me. We're just walking along so's Kirby can do his business. It's hot and there's a sound of thunder.

"C'mon, Kirby. It's gonna rain. Hurry up, already. How many bushes do you have to pee on anyway!"

"As many as I *want* to pee on." He's talking again but not moving his mouth! He goes to lift his leg but then smells something in the air. His fur is standing up on the ruff of his neck and he is sniffing the air like crazy.

"It's here!" he says to me. He throws his head way back and howls and that makes the hair on *my* neck stand up. He turns back to me and his eyes look strange. The night is so black but I know Kirby sees something out there. I can't see it but I feel it. Kirby stops howling and cocks his head like he hears something. I listen too, keeping so still my body aches.

"What is it, Kirby?" I whisper.

"Shhh. I can hear it. Listen."

"Hear what? Kirby? I don't…." And then I *do* hear it. Snap! Omigod! I *see* something, too!

A dark something is moving towards us and I hear that snapping sound again. Kirby turns to me and looks scared.

"Get away from here!" he says and goes into a shrieking howl.

But I can't move; it's like when I was at the diving board and my hands felt stuck to the ladder but this time it's my feet that feel glued to the ground.

"Don't wait, go!" shouts Kirby. "Don't bleed, don't bleed! There isn't any steak! Run!"

I tell him that I can't move and he bites my ankle hard. The pain unglues my feet and we both race back towards the house

"You bit me, you little shit!" I scream at Kirby as we run.

"Better me than those!" He looks behind him. "*They* don't want steak. Don't bleed, don't bleed! Run, run!"

The awful sound of snapping follows us. Snap! Snap! Jesus Christ, Kirby, help me!

"Don't bleed!"

"Is my ankle bleeding? Kirby, did you make my ankle bleed?"

"…bleed…bleed…don't…bleed…..*bleed*….."

"…*Feed* your hungry man. Make him a Taste-T Steak sandwich tonight!"

I almost jump out of my skin, the commercial shocks the hell out of me. It's dark and I'm alone in the living room. Where's my Grand-Dad? Where is Kirby? Sleep is still in my head and I feel woozy. I try to get up off the couch and fall on the floor. My ankle! I can't feel my ankle! Is it there? I touch it but I don't feel anything wet and sticky like blood. No blood. Whew! My ankle is

28

just asleep, just pins-and-needles.

Where is everybody? I'm turning over to get up when I feel something touch me and I scream! It's Kirby sniffing my leg.

"Hey? Little Man, you okay?" My Grand-Dad goes to lower the TV. "Sorry about that. I just took Kirby out. He really had to pee! Damn commercials. They condense the sound to make them loud to get your attention and then —" He looks at me. "Why are you on the floor?" He helps me up and then calls Kirby who has run back to the kitchen door. I follow him, stomping on the floor, trying to get rid of the numbness in my ankle.

"Kirby, come on boy. It's okay. What's the matter with you? Is there a possum out there or what?"

I look over to where Kirby is standing in the kitchen, staring out the screen door into the backyard.

"Kirby!" He turns when my grandfather calls him again and looks straight at me. I swear he looks scared like in my dream.

"Something is spooking that dog. I just hope it's not a skunk. Remember last summer when Kirby got sprayed? The house smelled like skunk for a month! Your grandmother went around lighting incense and spraying that horrible cherry spray and—what's the matter? Are you okay, Christopher?"

I'm looking at Kirby who is standing in front of the door with his legs planted stiffly apart like he does when he sees a strange dog coming near him. The ruff on the back of his neck is up and I hear a very low warning growl. My grandfather goes over to move Kirby away and shuts the door.

"Let it go, Kirbs. You're no match for whatever is out there."

I know he means a skunk but boy, truer words were never spoken. Whatever is out there is more dangerous than any stupid skunk. I go upstairs and fall into bed exhausted.

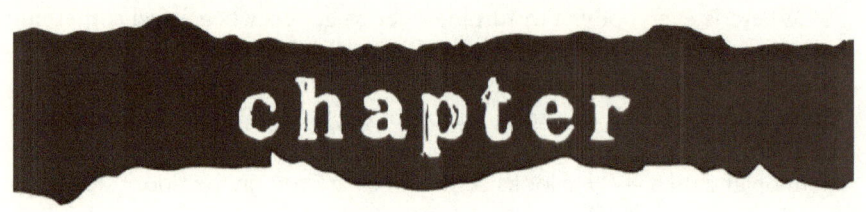

chapter

5

"Christopher? Chris! C'mon down here. Let's eat and get an early start to the day. Your buddy and his distinguished pet will be here before you know it. It's almost eight o'clock!"

I'm struggling out of a foggy sleep. I know I had a dream or something but I can't remember it. I hear my Grand-Dad calling me and hear Kirby barking out on the deck. I feel like I did when I had the flu last year, ache-y and cold. My head hurts and the memory of the dream is just at the back of my eyeballs. What did I dream? Shaking the sleep out of my head, I go into the bathroom to pee and take a shower.

Breakfast is waiting for me when I shuffle downstairs to the deck. Kirby is chowing down in his favorite place and my Grand-Dad is sipping his coffee. I love eating outside on the deck in the summer.

"Hey, Kirby, look! It's Christopher all up and raring to go. What's up Little Man?"

I don't answer and my Grand-Dad feels my head like maybe I have a fever or something. He puts a plate of my favorite walnut and honey waffles in front of me and, as he pours me orange juice, he says, "Did that storm last night wake you up? Kept Kirby and me awake. I thought the shutters came off and were banging against the front door. What a noise! Kirby was cowering under the covers. All that banging. Funny thing though. I went out this morning and the shutters were just fine, not one came unhinged. No rain, but, man, what a wind! Christopher?"

I don't answer 'cause I'm looking down at my waffles and just now remembering some of my dream. Banging, there was banging in it. A loud thud, thud, thud. It was like the sound you heard on that old TV show, *The Munsters,* whenever anyone banged with that enormous knocker that was on their front door.

"Chris? Aren't you hungry? You're not sick, are you? I guess I fed you too much junk food last night what with the popcorn and soda after a big dinner. Hey, Chris?"

Before I can answer, the doorbell rings and we both jump a little. Kirby goes running to the door barking like he's this big guard dog or something and I stop trying to remember my dream.

It's Kev and his mother. She's got a suitcase and a beach bag and Kev's got Louie-Louie in his special travel cage. Travel cage! Like Louie-Louie is the pampered pet of some famous rock star or actor or somebody. Jeez! Kev comes in and we go up to my room with Louie-Louie and Kirby, while my grandfather and Kev's mother go get Kev's bike off the rack on Mrs. Lingle's car and then go 'shoot the breeze' over coffee on the deck.

* * *

Kev puts the rat cage up on the high dresser near an open window so Louie-Louie will have a view and so Kirby can't reach him. Ol' Kirbs is sniffing the bottom of the cage but he doesn't bark, just kinda whines a little. After awhile, he loses interest because he can't get to Louie-Louie, and he heads down the stairs.

"Well, Kevin," says my Grand-Dad who is now standing in the doorway of my room. "How are you and how is the famous white rodent with the double name?"

"I'm fine, sir." Kev is being all polite and stuff. "Thanks for lettin' me bring Louie-Louie."

"No problem, young man. If you let him out of the cage just make sure Chris's door is shut and Kirby is downstairs. We don't want any wrestling matches between dog and rat. And you are welcome, Kevin. It is a pleasure to have you and your furry friend stay with us." He smiles at Kevin then winks, "Just don't tell my wife."

"Yes, sir! I mean, no, sir! I mean thanks!!"

"I hope you're not too tired to go swimming today. Your Mom said you were up all night. Did the wind storm keep you up? I'm not surprised. It was a helluva stormy night. Well, never mind, you boys be ready in an hour. I want to get to the pool before all the umbrellas are taken. It's going to be hot today."

I help Kev unpack and we talk about how we're gonna race each other across the pool and stay the hell away from the diving boards. Kev tells me he was so excited about coming to stay here that he couldn't sleep and he stayed up all night playing craps with his brother. Then he looks at me and says, "Hey, Chris? What storm was your Grand-Dad talkin' about? It was so sticky-hot last night, there wasn't even a *breeze* blowin.' Me and Jeremy were sweatin' like pigs. There wasn't any storm last night."

* * *

By the time we get to the pool, it's after eleven o'clock and there's pretty much of a crowd, mostly high school kids. There are some really old people—like a gazillion years old—sitting in the shaded area. They're probably in their nineties but they look ancient. These are people who call my grandfather *sonny*, 'cause they remember him when he was *my* age. They're nice though, they never bother anyone except to sometimes give one of us kids money to go get them a can of ice tea or a bottle of water. When the kids come back with it, whoever sent them usually says to keep the change. Last summer some guy with a big blob of white sun-block on his nose told me to "Keep the change, kid" after I got him a soda and I ended up with seven whole cents! Big spender, that guy. That's okay though, like I said, they just mostly sit in the shade, their legs fish belly white, watching other people swim and never bother anyone.

Me and Kev find a spot with one of the last umbrellas and dump our stuff under it before we race for the pool. It is hot! After we're in the pool and floating on our backs I look around for my Grand-Dad and see him making the rounds, talking to all the old people who call him 'sonny'. He's really polite and all and pretends he's interested in what the old guys have to say.

Kev asked my Grand-Dad about that once—why he listens so politely to the boring stuff old people have to say. My Grand-Dad told us that some people never have anybody who really listens to them, everyone just ignores them and that's sad.

"They're lonely, Kevin, that's all. They feel like they're not important, that no one cares what they have to say. If someone listens to them, even once in a while, it gives them a feeling of self-esteem, as if what they have to say matters, as if they're respected. Everyone deserves that. It doesn't cost me anything to listen to them but *they*, on the other hand, gain a lot by being allowed to be heard. Do you understand, Kevin?"

I don't know if Kev understood but I did. It's just being nice is all. Like my Grand-Dad.

After talking to the old guys my Grand-Dad settles in a lounger to read a book. A few minutes after he sits down I see the scary sight of Mr. Sarlewski in swim trunks going over to him. He just starts talking to my Grand-Dad without even saying hello first. I look around but don't see Billy anywhere.

Mr. Sarlewski's big, booming voice carries over to us and we hear him say something like he said down at Old Man Hobart's. That real estate thing on Dansbury Plot. Mr. Sarlewski is acting all phony sincere and stuff, calling my Grand-Dad by his first name and all.

"So what do you say, Will? There are *some* people in this town who respect you. What's your idea about what I just told you? I need to know if I can count on your support. Might be big bucks in this deal for both of us. You could move your little bookstore into a nice modern building in that mall."

He smiles a sneaky snake-like smile. I see my Grand-Dad smile back and shake his head.

"I, for one, don't want to see our little area become overdeveloped. We're a community with a nice small town atmosphere. I think new construction will ruin that and I have to say I'll vote against any proposal for it."

Mr. Sarlewski gets a mean look on his face. His friendly voice is gone. "You're as bad as Hobart. Except *he* doesn't want to build because he's scared of spooks out at Dansbury Plot. Always talking about how the land is cursed. Old kook."

"Well, you never know, Warren. There might be some truth in all his talk."

Kev nudges me and whispers, "*Warren?* His name is *Warren?* What a dork name!"

Then we hear Mr. Sarlewski say to my Grand-Dad, "So you won't stand behind this real estate idea?" He stands there impatiently with his legs spread out and his arms folded.

"No, sorry Warren." My Grand-Dad opens his book to show the conversation is over. Mr. Sarlewski's face gets all red and he stomps away.

Me and Kev laugh a little more about Mr. Sarlewski's first name, but the day is way too nice to think about him. We close our eyes as we're floating, talking about important stuff like whether we want to get the new jumbo chili dogs they're selling for lunch or whether it's better to get the double cheeseburger with onion rings like we always do.

Kev decides he'll stick with the cheeseburger and onion rings because, as he says, at least you know how the burgers and rings will fill you up. Maybe the jumbo dogs won't and then you'll have to get something else to eat.

So we're floating and talking when I feel myself yanked under water and held there. Someone's got my legs. I push hard at whoever it is but I can't get loose. My legs are locked between their legs and I feel their arms wrap tightly around my shoulders holding me under water. I think I'm going to drown if I have to hold my breath much longer! I am drowning! I struggle like crazy but whoever is holding me down won't let go. I'm gonna die!

Suddenly the arms around me let go and I'm free. I come up sputtering and gasping for breath. Kev's slapping me on the back and asking me if I'm okay. I'm wiping the water out of my face when I see Billy Sarlewski. He's standing in waist deep water laughing really loud and calling me a dipshit loser. "You can't dive and you can't swim either dipshit! You're a dipshit loser!"

I turn toward Sarlewski. "You lousy creep!" I scream, throwing myself at Billy. I get a good hold around his chest and slam my knee into his back. I try to drag him under but he starts screaming for help. Kev is yelling all the curse words he learned from his brother at Billy.

"Hey! What the hell are you doing to my son? I'll have you thrown out of this pool! I'm getting the lifeguard now! Let go of my son or I'll—"

"Or you'll what, Warren?" My Grand-Dad has run over to the pool edge and is now standing next to Mr. Sarlewski. His look of relief that I'm okay shows on his face. Then he turns to Mr. Sarlewski and says, "I believe my grandson is merely retaliating in kind to the unwarranted ruffian treatment accorded him by your son."

"What the hell did you say?" Mr. Sarlewski asks him. "You want to put that in English, *Pro-fess-or*?" He drags this last word out with a sneer, but my grandfather only smiles.

"It *was* English, Warren, but I'll clarify it in simpler terms for you. Billy held Chris underwater and my grandson is simply trying to do the same thing to him."

"Your grandson is roughing up my boy! He ought to be kicked out of the pool, barred from ever coming back. No one attacks Billy! Where the hell is the pool manager? I'm filing a complaint against your grandson right now."

"Your kid started it, mister." It's one of the old guys. "I saw the whole thing on my way back from the toilet. Your kid pulled the other boy under and held him there."

"You can't see anything, you old fart. You're as blind as a bat."

"Got enough sight to know a bully when I see one," the old man says standing there, not at all afraid of Mr. Sarlewski. Billy's father starts to say something else when two other old guys come over and tell him they saw Billy pull me under too. One of them says it's not the first time Billy has done this—he does it all the time to other kids—and maybe *he's* the one who should be barred from the pool.

Mr. Sarlewski's outnumbered and he knows it so when one of the lifeguards comes over to see why there's a crowd, Mr. Sarlewski starts saying things like, "Hell, they're just kids fooling around, first real day of summer vacation, no harm done," and a whole other bunch of crap. The lifeguard goes back to her station shaking her head. She knows what an asshole Mr. Sarlewski is.

All three of us, me, Kev, and that creep Billy, climb out of the pool. My Grand-Dad checks to make sure I'm all right then gives me and Kev money to go get two fresh lemonades. He tells us he wants to talk to Billy's father. I know he just wants us away from Billy who's standing behind his father and giving us the finger. My heart is racing like crazy. I want to smash Billy Sarlewski so bad.

* * *

We're drinking our lemonades down by the refreshment stand when Kev tells me how he couldn't get Billy to let go of my legs and shoulders no matter how much he grabbed at him.

"I grabbed him and punched at him but he wouldn't let go. I thought you were gonna drown, Chris. I was scared! Finally, I went under water and just sank my teeth into his big, old gut. I saw a wrestler do that on TV. It made Billy let you go all right! I hope I gave him that dog disease, you know, that hydro somethin'?"

"Hydrophobia?"

"Yeah! That's it! You think I gave it to him?"

I laugh a little but don't tell him that only a mad dog could do that. I don't want to hurt his feelings. I just mess up his hair and say, "Maybe." Good ol' Kev, my best friend!

When we come back to the pool, I see Mr. Sarlewski stalking over to where my Grand-Dad is sitting. Billy walks next to him. He's eating from a big bag of his mother's famous cookies, my used-to-be favorites. He shakes the bag at me and licks his lips. I want to punch him.

His father starts yelling at my Grand-Dad and waving a finger in his face.

"I want you to know that I'm taking Billy home. He feels like he's going to puke from the trauma he suffered here today. Your kid almost drowns him and then that Rat-Boy friend of his bites Billy. I called my wife. She says to take him to the emergency room at the hospital to have that bite checked out and that's what I'm going to do before I take him home."

I look at Billy's gut. There's just a red mark there, no broken skin. I guess

Kev didn't bite hard enough.

"My wife is almost hysterical about what could have happened to our boy."

Kev whispers to me that he wonders how hysterical Billy's mother would be if she knew that he's always trying to sell his sister's white underpants. Boy!

We hear my Grand-Dad say he's sorry if Mrs. Sarlewski is upset and then say, very nicely, that if Billy is nauseous maybe he shouldn't be eating an entire bag of cookies! That really pisses Mr. Sarlewski off.

"You know Will, I was going to forget that your brat grandson was trying to drown my kid and pretend it was just roughhousing. Maybe you and I could've remained on civil terms. But now I see where he gets his holier-than-thou streak. He gets it from *you*. Everyone knows you think you're better than everyone else, Mr. College Professor. I'm not surprised at your grandson's actions. He doesn't know about getting along with his peers. He spends too much time with you learning ancient history that's no use to anyone unless they're dead." His face is twisted in a nasty smirk. "From now on you tell Chris to watch his ass. No one messes with my son. And that goes for his friend Rat-Boy, too."

"Is that a threat, Warren? Because if it is I've got witnesses here who heard you say it."

My Grand-Dad turns to the old guys near them. They all nod their heads.

But my Grand-Dad isn't finished yet. He has something else to say to Sarlewski.

"You said my grandson takes after me. I like to think you're right. Chris has the same sense of fair-play as I do. Your son, on the other hand, lacks it and in that respect, Billy takes after *you*, Warren."

"Fuck you," says Warren Sarlewski and Billy turns around toward me and says, "Yeah, fuck you!" and gives the finger to me and Kev.

As they walk away, I hear one of the old guys say something about apples not falling far from trees.

chapter

6

We stay at the pool until four o'clock and then go home to feed Kirby and Louie-Louie. While we're upstairs taking showers and getting dressed, my Grand-Dad puts some of the frozen lasagna my Grand-Mom left, in the oven, and goes outside with Kirby to grill some fresh sausage.

I'm getting dressed when the phone rings. It's Mrs. Lingle wanting to talk to Kev. Billy's mom called her about Kev biting her son and she wants to know why and what happened.

I leave him alone in my room so he can talk to his mom. She sounded upset when I answered the phone and I don't think Kev wants me to hear her yelling at him.

I wander into my grandparents' bedroom and stand looking out the back windows and listening to the silence. The heat of the day is just hanging, no breeze at all and the humidity is so thick you can almost see it. There's a rumble of thunder from somewhere and a few streaks of lightening. I can smell the heavy scent of honeysuckle from the backyard.

Outside it looks like some old pictures I once saw at a museum. They were all yellow-y looking. My Grand-Dad called the color sepia tone and told me it was invented in 1850.

"The tint was the result of a chemical process that the photographer used in the darkroom to prevent the photograph from fading, Christopher. It was very popular back then. There are a lot of pictures from the Civil War that are that color."

I start thinking about Dansbury Plot and remember how it always looks yellow-y too. That's one of the reasons it's so damn spooky. Everything can be green and flowers and all, every place else around it, but The Plot just looks yellow and dry. Thinking about The Plot and everything, my hands start to sweat and get itchy. Without knowing that I'm doing it I scratch at my scab and feel it kinda smooshy and loose. I pick at it and it looks like red, raw hamburger meat. I keep staring at it—I can't stop looking at my scab and how it is breaking away from my skin. I've sure had scabs before but this one scares me. Red, raw, meat.

Kev's brother once ate some raw chopped meat. He mixed it with raw eggs and sliced onions and slapped it between two slices of rye. He called it a cannibal sandwich. Me and Kev were totally grossed-out over it. It was great though, seeing him eat it.

Remembering what Kev's brother did, I lick the scab and the skin around it. It has a salty copper penny taste and it's warm, almost hot. The spit on my tongue makes the raw skin in my palm burn a little bit.

From outside I can hear Kirby barking and for no reason at all, I feel scared. The thunder rumbles in the distance again and everything turns a darker yellow. I shiver. I want daylight to stay forever—I don't want the day to end and the night to come with any weird dreams.

* * *

After dinner, and a phone call from my mom and dad, me, Kev, and my Grand-Dad play a game of fetch with Kirby. The sky is still dark and the yellow light kinda makes it seem like we're in an old movie or something but we're having fun. Even Louie-Louie is outside, in his cage of course. Kev put him on the table where he can watch us. "I don't want him to feel left out," is what he says, so ol' Louie-Louie is what my Grand-Dad refers to as our 'fan in the grandstand'. All I know is every time Kirby goes running after the ball, Louie-Louie runs around in his wheel, just like he's playing too.

We're outside until almost 9:30 and we can still see some sunset on the clouds. Sitting on the deck finishing a chocolate ice cream bar, I say that this is my favorite time of the year because the days last so much longer.

"The summer days fade slowly into the summer nights," says my Grand-Dad, quoting some poem. *"Leaving a touch of sun to warm the moon."* He likes to quote poetry and stuff.

"That's nice," says Kev yawning. "Is it by some famous person or somethin'?"

"It is, Kevin, indeed, it is. But it was written by someone more special than famous. You know him all right. We all do. His name is Mr. Elbert Daniel Mervin Jones." My Grand-Dad smiles at me 'cause *he* knows *I* know who Elbert Daniel Mervin Jones is.

"Who is he?" Kev asks me. "Did we study him last year in Mrs. Rodan's lit. class?"

I just smile at my grandfather and he answers Kev.

"Well, Kevin," he says, "you know him better by the soubriquet or nickname of Jonesey."

"*Jonesey?!* Old Man Hobart's *Jonesy?* He can write poetry? Who knew! Wow!"

"Kevin, there are secret parts to every human being. Most of the times, we only see the superficial or surface part, the everyday part. That's what we allow others to see. But everyone has parts that are known only to themselves or a few other people, a part they don't share with the world. Jonesey is a poet. That's a part of him that he doesn't want to share with just everyone."

I think about that for a minute, the part about secrets and wonder what my secret part is. Then I ask, "If he's so secret, how come you know the poem, Grand-Dad?"

"Yeah, Mr. Hopper, how come? Did Jonesey want to share it with you?"

My Grand-Dad shakes his head and smiles. "No, as a matter of fact he didn't. Mrs. Hopper found a small notebook full of poems hidden in a secret drawer of an old desk she bought last year at that little antique store on Chester Street. Old desks were often built with hidden drawers to store women's jewelry. The store acquired—"

"Huh?" says Kev. My Grand-Dad ruffles Kev's hair and smiles.

"The word acquired, for want of a better definition Kevin, means 'got'. Anyway the antique store got the desk from the storage room at the old library. The Board of Directors at the library wanted to get rid of what they termed old and useless furniture. Really a shame because that desk is quite beautiful. Jonesey's wife Elizabeth was the town librarian many years ago so she may have kept the poems in that desk."

He smiles at me before he continues. "So, your grandmother bought the desk and found the notebook. The poetry in that notebook was all dedicated to 'Elizabeth Jones, my precious love, the sun to my moon.' It was signed 'All my love always in all ways, Elbert'"

"Wow!" says Kev again.

"I guess he really loved her," I say. "But if he's so secret a guy, how come he let you keep the poem? I mean you let him know that you found it, right?"

"Indeed we did let him know. Your grandmother even tried to get him to let us publish it for him but he didn't want that. He didn't want the book either. Jonesey told us that it would break his heart if he read any of those poems again. He said that we could keep the book if we didn't show it to anyone else. Nobody knew about the poems, and he wanted to keep it that way. He also said if we didn't want the book, he was just going to burn it, so we kept it. There are some remarkable poems in there. The one I quoted is my favorite."

"So only you and Grand-Mom know the secret, not even Hobart?"

"Only we two and Elizabeth. And now, of course you and Kevin who, I know, will not tell a soul. Correct assumption, boys?"

Me and Kev swear on our honor to keep the secret, cross our hearts, and spit.

The phone rings and when my Grand-Dad gets up to answer it, Kirby follows him inside.

While he's gone, Kev talks about how nobody in the whole world would ever believe that Jonesey was a poet. I say I guess you never really know someone even if you think you do. I always thought Jonesey was just a quiet guy without any thinking going on in his head. Boy was I wrong.

We're just sitting, talking about Jonesey and stuff, relaxing. I glance in the back window and see my Grand-Dad, with the phone to his ear, walking around the kitchen. The night is so quiet his voice carries and I hear him say to somebody, "Yes, that book came in yesterday. I'll bring it tomorrow. I had no idea you were a history buff," before he hangs up. Then he comes to the door and motions us to come in the house.

"It's ten-thirty, boys, but if you want to stay up a bit longer that's okay, just come on inside."

He comes out the door leading Kirby on a leash. I'm surprised. Kirby never runs anywhere, he's pretty good about staying with you when he goes out in the yard. He only ever chases squirrels and it's nighttime, so no self-respecting squirrel would be out. I guess he must have seen my surprise because my Grand-Dad gestures to the leash and says, looking out at the backyard in the night, "Just to be safe. You never know what's out there. Kirby's jumpy lately."

* * *

Despite my fear of bad dreams, I fall into a deep sleep. I even sleep through Kev's snoring which says a lot. But sometime around 2:00 AM I hear a weird sound. I can't figure out what it is. It's a whirring sound, very soft.

I don't wake Kev even though I want to. I know this sound. I heard it somewhere before so it's not scary. I sit up in bed and look around the room. Kev mutters something in his sleep and I catch the words, "Wheel. Now? Supposed to be sleepin' shhhhhhh! Jeez!"

The sound is coming from the bookcase near the window. My eyes look around the dark room and suddenly I can see what's making the sound. I jump because at first it looks like a ghost with red eyes but when my own eyes adjust more, I see it isn't a ghost at all.

It's Louie-Louie, his pink eyes glowing like marbles. He's spinning like a madman on his wheel, racing. Like he's trying to get away from something really bad.

chapter

7

Today, Kev decides that we need to do something more than go to the pool. He tells me this when he sees me grab my swim trunks. It's gonna be a hot day, I tell him. We should go to the pool.

"So, okay then, how about if we do this. We go to the pool and stay until twelve o'clock, if you want to, okay, Chris? Then we'll go see the new *Batman* movie in the afternoon. Joey and Brad are goin'. After the movie we can go out to eat at Dairy Barn. My treat. I got birthday money!"

I'm surprised when he says it will be his treat. Kev *never* uses his birthday money unless it's really important. He can make the twenty bucks his Aunt Cindy sends him every birthday last almost a whole year. And now he wants to spend it on me?

But I know what Kev is trying to do. He wants me to avoid the pool and Billy Sarlewski. The mornings are safe because Billy never gets there really early anyway.

"Did your Mom tell you not to go to the pool? Truth."

"Truth? She said maybe we should stay away from there for a couple of days."

"Because you bit Billy? Is that why? Truth."

"Truth. No, not because of that. I mean she was mad that I bit somebody and all but when I told her why, she was okay with it. My mom just thinks they'll try and start trouble if we're there. She also told me Mr. Sarlewski called my father at the bike shop and told him he was sendin' Billy's emergency room bill to our house."

"What'd your Dad say to him?"

"He said that when the bill comes he'll file it with all the other junk mail under bullshit. Oops, sorry, Mr. Hopper!"

My Grand-Dad is standing in the doorway of my room and he just laughs.

"Oh, I imagine the word bullshit is somewhat descriptive of the whole Sarlewski situation, and very apropos. Good for your father! Well, boys, what are you doing today?"

"Kev doesn't think we should spend all day at the pool. He wants to go to the movies and then out to eat at Dairy Barn in the afternoon."

Without being told, my Grand-Dad knows why and agrees. "Smart move Kevin. Best for us to let a few days go by without running into the Sarlewskis. Besides, if it is going to be as hot as the news says then you really don't want to be in the sun after noontime. And *I* have a few things to do down at the bookstore anyway, so I can't be at the pool all day. By the way, Kevin, your brother Jeremy is doing a great job helping out there but I need to check out a few things. After you boys leave the Dairy Barn, come on over."

"Wait! Grand-Dad, you're not afraid of Mr. Sarlewski, are you? You always tell me that we shouldn't let other people keep us from going places or doing what we want. If I try to avoid Billy, isn't that like letting him keep me from being at the pool and stuff? Doesn't that make me a coward or something?"

My grandfather walks over to the window and stands looking out at the front walk. He doesn't say anything for about five whole minutes, and me and Kev just kinda sit on the bed waiting. Finally, he turns around and rests against the window sill.

"You're absolutely right, Chris, I did tell you that you shouldn't ever feel that you can't do something or go somewhere because of another person. If you really want to stay at the pool when Billy is there, you should be able to do so. No one has the right to keep you from where you want to go. We're in a free country after all."

"So you're sayin' we *should* stay at the pool all day, Mr. Hopper?" asks Kev nervously. Boy, his Mom must've really scared him!

"Not exactly, Kevin."

"But," I start, "if I avoid the pool, Billy will think I'm a coward, he'll tell *everybody* at the pool and it'll be just like last—" I trail off but they both know what I mean. Last summer and the diving board.

"Chris, if you are going to be influenced by what people think then you will spend your entire life living for them and not for yourself. *That* is no way to live."

My Grand-Dad walks over to me and continues, "No one will think you're a coward, Chris, just because Billy says so. Keeping away from Billy doesn't make you afraid. I think it makes you smart. It shows that you're not willing to ruin a day in your life because of him. He's a mean, nasty little boy who will grow up to be a mean, nasty little man."

I'm pretty surprised that he said that. My grandfather is the type that never says anything bad about anyone. He turns his head away from me and stares out the window again for a long time.

Finally, Kev asks, "What's the matter Mr. Hopper? You okay?"

Kev's question makes my Grand-Dad turn, look at us and smile. "Oh, yes, yes, Kevin, just have something on my mind, that's all. Something to check out." He ruffles my hair and Kev's.

"What do you say we men go have a disgustingly big breakfast of bacon, eggs, and French toast? And if we're still hungry after that, there's some great peach pie I picked up at the farmer's market. Okay with you boys?"

Boy, nothing better than a huge breakfast with my Grand-Dad! He knows how to eat. We race each other downstairs with Kirby dancing ahead and barking, almost tripping all three of us.

Pool first, movies later—what a great day we're going to have!

chapter

8

"Listen, I never understand how come nobody ever seems to know that Bruce Wayne *is* Batman! It drives me crazy! How can you *not* know?!"

Another thing about Kev—besides being completely devoted to Louie-Louie, he is an absolute nut about anything to do with Batman.

Me, Brad, and Joey are listening to Kev talk about the movie. We're all down at Dairy Barn getting their famous zoupy dogs which are foot-long hot dogs smothered in chili, onions, and mustard. They drip all over so you kinda have to hold them over a paper plate to eat them and then scoop up whatever drops with your fingers. If you mix ketchup with it, it looks like you're scooping up blood and guts.

"Maybe you only *think* everyone should know Batman and Bruce Wayne are the same guy because *you* know it. But you only *know* it because you're watching the movie. Otherwise, you wouldn't know it either." Brad pronounces this as if, duh-h-h, how dumb can you be?

But Kev insists that anyone who had a brain, even if they weren't watching the movie, would know. He gets all excited about this stuff as if it were real. Turning to me he says,

"Want another zoupy?"

He's already bought me popcorn at the movie, and now two sodas, cheese fries plus the zoupy. I'm stuffed. I shake my head no and we go back to talking about Batman and Bruce Wayne. Kev and Brad are really into it.

I'm licking the last of the chili from the plate and my fingers when I notice Joey looking at me.

"What?" I say.

"Nothing."

"C'mon, Joey, what is it?"

"Nothing, just, just that—I heard about the pool. Wow!"

I squirm. That slimy Sarlewski. Now I have to go through another whole summer of people thinking I'm a chicken. Maybe I shouldn't have listened to my Grand-Dad. I should have stayed at the pool *all day* today so nobody would think I was afraid of Billy. He probably bragged that I left early so I wouldn't run into *him* and his stupid father.

I start to tell Joey that whatever Billy said was a lie but stop when I see him grinning at me. "*Now* what? You think it's funny? What? I almost drowned!"

"Chris! Me and Brad heard about how your grandfather stood up to that old fart Mr. Sarlewski! That was so great! Nobody really tells him off except Old Man Hobart and he's not afraid of anyone! I mean, Mr. Hopper seems so like, you know, like, kinda like one of those real polite guys or something, the ones you see in those artsy-fartsy movies. I mean your grandfather is a *teacher*, not a wrestler or anything. Who knew he was so tough? Hey, no offense, or anything, Chris! But, man to back down Mr. Sarlewski? And just with words! Boy!"

Kev joins in with, "Yeah, wow, you should've seen him. I thought Mr. Hopper was gonna pop Billy's father in the face!"

I think about how my Grand-Dad did back down Billy's Dad. I don't ever think of him as tough or anything, he's just my Grand-Dad. He's smart, he tells great stories, and he knows just about where every expression anybody ever said comes from. I got my fascination with words and stuff from him. When my Dad was real busy getting his investment business going and hardly ever home, my Grand-Dad taught me how to play baseball. I spend a lot of time with my Grand-Dad. We get along great. He understands a lot of stuff and I can tell him things I can't tell anyone else.

"Did he, Chris?" Brad is talking to me.

"Huh?"

"Did he almost slug Mr. Sarlewski?"

I look at Brad and Joey who are waiting to hear that Will Hopper, my grandfather, almost punched out Billy's Dad. Then I look at Kev who's doing kung fu moves. Kev makes his eyes big and nods his head giving me a 'say yes, puh-leeze!' look.

46

"Yeah," I finally say. "I think he would've if Mr. Sarlewski didn't turn chicken-shit and leave the pool!"

I know it's a lie—my grandfather probably hasn't gotten into a fist fight since he was my age—but, it's okay. I like the look in their eyes that tells me they're impressed. Someone finally stood up to Mr. Simply Sensational Cookies. Good ol' Will Hopper, my Grand-Dad. I'm about to tell Joey that my Grand-Dad is a *professor*, not just a teacher, but he's talking.

"—The Plot and my Uncle Harry said *no way*."

"What did you say about Dansbury Plot?" I ask him.

"I *said*, Mr. Sarlewski is going around town trying to get people to buy shares in some real estate thing he wants to build on Bury-the-Dead-Dan's Plot and when he asked my uncle Harry, my uncle said no way because he thinks The Plot is haunted."

"Yeah!" chimes in Brad. "Mr. Sarlewski was down at the bakery doing the same thing. He was talking up a storm about The Plot! He's asking people to invest money to build stores and stuff there. Some people were actually listening to him, though. He's getting people thinking that they can make a lot of money putting up new buildings there. It's spooky. Who'd want to shop *there*? You'd have to be crazy to go on The Plot."

We walk out of Dairy Barn still talking about The Plot and Brad and Joey both have some weird stories about things they say really *did* happen at the Plot. Joey tells us how his uncle says it's haunted by weird sounds and Brad chimes in with something that happened there about a hundred years ago. How some four-year-old girl went missing near The Plot and when they found her she was bitten all over her body by some wild animal or something and how she never talked again her whole life long and just stared straight ahead with bugged out, terrified eyes.

"She died at about like *two hundred years old* and you could still see the deep scars from the teeth marks on her shriveled-up old lady body, honest!"

Kev looks at me when Brad says that about teeth but he doesn't tell Brad or Joey about what I heard when I almost fell onto The Plot or about my dream. I know he's dying to, but best friends keep secrets for each other and Kev takes that real serious.

The sky is getting yellow again and the clouds look real heavy. The air smells funny too, like an old, moldy building. Joey asks us if we want to go bike riding but I tell him we're going over to the book store.

Before they go Joey turns to me and says, "Hey, Chris? Tell Mr. Hopper I'm glad he told off Billy's father. He's the man!"

"Yeah, me too!" Brad smiles as they walk away. "*The* Man!"

* * *

The sign above my grandparents' store says *The Willin' Cate Book Store* and there're black cut out figures of a lady and a man on the sign. My Grand-Dad told me the figures are supposed to be a lady and gentleman from the time during the 1890s and that those were the kind of clothes they wore back then.

On the sign, the lady is bending toward the man lifting her skirts just above her shoes and the man is looking at her ankles. I don't get what the sign means—I just know my grandparents' names are William and Catherine. My Grand-Mom, though, just laughs about the sign and says she and my Grand-Dad are bawdy people.

I looked up the word bawdy and the dictionary said that the word meant, 'dealing with sexual matters in a comical way; humorously indecent', but I still don't get what that has to do with the sign. My Grand-Dad explained that the sign was kinda bawdy because no decent woman back then in the 1890s would show her ankles to a man. Ankles? That's kinda dumb. What's sexy about ankles?

Kev's brother Jeremy is standing behind the counter reading a comic book and drinking a can of soda when we walk in. I don't see anyone else in the store. Jeremy sees me looking around.

"Your grandfather's upstairs," he tells me. "He says he's researching something for Old Man Hobart. The old guy came over late in the morning."

"Old Man Hobart came here?" Hobart almost never leaves his store for anything except to go a few doors down to buy doughnuts. "Is he upstairs now?"

"No, not anymore. He left around one o'clock. They were upstairs for about two hours. He said he had to ask your grandfather something about a war. Man, I love your Grand-Dad. I'm going to make sure I get to be in Professor Hopper's class when I go to college next year. Your grandfather is the best." He puts the comic book back under the counter. "Hey, you guys eat yet?"

Kev tells him we had zoupies and Jeremy gets Kev in a mock strangle hold because we didn't bring him any, then he gives Kev the rest of his soda. Boy, it must be great to have an older brother.

Me and Kev climb the really cool spiral staircase to the room upstairs. My Grand-Dad is so deep in reading some book that he doesn't even hear us come in the room. He actually jumps when Kev yells out, "Hey, Mr. H!" but he turns and smiles at us and says, "Hey yourself, Kevin Lingle!"

I walk over and look at the book he's reading. It's got this big long title, *Andersonville and the Infamous Prisoner of War Camps of the Civil War.*

"What's 'in-fay-mous' mean?" Kev is looking over my shoulder. "Does that mean somethin' is like famous or somethin?"

My grandfather closes the book and says, "It's pronounced *infamous*, Kevin and yes it does relate to the word famous but it means to be famous or well-known for something vile and evil. For something terrible." He sighs.

Putting a bookmark in the book he lays it on his desk. "So, tell me boys, how was the movie? Batman beat the bad guys?"

"Of course he did! I mean, who ever heard of the *bad guys* beatin' *Batman*?! Hey, Mr. Hopper? You're smart and everythin'. Maybe you can answer me this. How come nobody seems to know that Batman and Bruce Wayne are the same guy? You'd think any idiot would know that, right? I mean—" Kev goes into a long detailed argument of his favorite topic. My Grand-Dad listens to him like this is the most important thing he's heard all day.

While they're talking, I open the book on my Grand-Dad's desk to the place he marked. I see the words "prisoners, brutality" before my Grand-Dad comes over and closes the book. He shakes his head at me and tells me, "This book is too disturbing for young minds, Chris" before taking it over to a locked cabinet. He also tells me the book is for Mr. Hobart and he wants to keep it in good condition for him. I don't understand that. Usually he lets me read anything I want and then he'll explain what I don't understand. Once he let me handle and read a book that was over one hundred years old! He wasn't worried about keeping *that* one in good condition 'cause he knows that I'm always really careful with books. I don't bend pages like some people do to bookmark them and I never drink soda or anything when I'm reading so nothing gets spilled on them and damages them. I'm really extra careful with books.

I watch him lock the cabinet and put the key in his pocket. What's going on? I want to ask him but he walks over to Kev and they begin debating how Batman can keep his Bruce Wayne identity secret and how nobody even guesses. He's laughing and smiling with Kev but when he looks at the cabinet, he looks sad, like he read something depressing. Finally, Kev stops talking and my Grand-Dad picks up his car keys.

"I'm going to be out for a while, Chris. You and Kev stay here and help out Jeremy. I'll be back around 6:00 and then we'll go home."

"Where you going, Grand-Dad?"

"Oh, just some business I have to take care of. You and Kevin would be—how do you put it, Chris? You both would be 'bored nuts.' Besides, Jeremy could use a little help here."

We kinda don't say yes right away and he offers to pay us. "I'll give you ten dollars a piece if you help him stack the new books that came in yesterday."

"All right!!" yells Kev. Money is another thing that makes him happy. I don't say anything because something's not right. I just know it. I help around the store a lot and I do it because I like to be there. Kev helps out sometimes too, and never gets paid. He does it just to hear my Grand-Dad tell stories. So why is my Grand-Dad willing to pay me, us, to help Jeremy? Then I think that it's like he's not so much paying us to help stack books but more like he's paying us to stay in the store and not go with him.

But Kev is dancing around like a lunatic and telling me that, with the ten dollars, he'll be able to buy Louie-Louie a new water bottle and a cover for his cage. That rat! He mock punches me and I push him away annoyed.

"God, he's just a rat! You know that don't you?" I feel sorry as soon as I say it. I don't know why I got so mad.

"Don't ever say that, okay Chris? Don't ever say that. Louie-Louie is just a really special pet. We have a connection."

Kev looks so serious that I tell him I'm sorry, I didn't mean it, not really. Sometimes I forgot how much Louie-Louie means to Kevin.

Halfway down the spiral staircase, I turn and see my Grand-Dad taking the book out of the cabinet and putting it in a paper bag. He looks at me for just a second and what I see reminds me of what I saw in a wildlife documentary.

An antelope had escaped a hungry lion by swimming a river and was looking back at the lion bringing down another member of the herd. It was a look of disbelief.

* * *

Later that afternoon, while we're taking a break from stacking books, Kev and Jeremy go sit outside to drink lemonade and eat chips. I tell them I'll be right out and then go to the area of the store that sells encyclopedias to look up the Andersonville Civil War prison camp.

From February 1864 until the end of the American Civil War (1861-65) in April 1865, Andersonville, Georgia, served as the site of a notorious Confederate military prison. The prison at Andersonville was the South's largest prison for captured Union soldiers and known for its unhealthy conditions, cruelty, and high death rate. In all, approximately 13,000 Union prisoners perished at Andersonville.

There are pictures on the page of some soldiers who look like the walking dead. Their bones jut out and their eyes are hollow and desperate-looking. The pictures scare me and I don't want to read anymore. I close the encyclopedia and feel sick.

Maybe my Grand-Dad's right. Some things *are* too disturbing for young minds.

My young mind sure feels disturbed right now.

chapter

9

It's almost seven and we're waiting for my Grand-Dad. Jeremy's on the phone with his girlfriend. She's brand-new, Kev tells me.

"Is she pretty like the last one?"

"*I* don't know, I *guess* so. They all look alike to me. Hey Chris? When is your Grand-Dad gonna get here? Louie-Louie isn't used to havin' to wait for dinner."

There are three things that mean the world to Kev. Batman, zombies—and the one that means the most to him—Louie-Louie, his pet rat.

About Louie-Louie. Kevin found Louie-Louie in a box on the front steps of Old Man Hobart's one rainy Memorial Day weekend when he went with his Dad to the bike shop.

The reason Kev went near the box was because he saw it move and he was curious. When he looked inside he saw a white rat, scared and skinny as hell. He was probably someone's pet and maybe their mom got freaked out having a rat in the house or something so they just dropped him off at the pet store figuring Hobart would take care of him the way he takes care of any stray animals he finds near his store. He and Jonesey are nice that way.

But whoever left the rat there probably didn't remember that it was a four-day holiday week-end and Hobart's would be closed.

Anyway, it was raining pretty bad and the box was getting soaked so Kev put Louie-Louie inside his jacket and took him inside his father's bike shop. He didn't know what to feed him so he just gave him a little bit of a half eaten candy bar he had in his pocket.

Later that day he made a bed for him from some old rags his father had in the shop. He took him home and his father bought nuts and seeds from the grocery store for Louie-Louie. Mr. Lingle had an old bird cage and they put the rags in the bottom of it so the rat would be comfortable. He said that if the rat lived, Kev could keep him and they'd buy a brand-new cage for him at Hobart's next week. Kev stayed up most of the night taking care of Louie-Louie, hand feeding him the food his father got plus the rest of the candy bar. The rat could only eat a little at a time but Kev was real patient.

Besides the regular rodent food Kev gets from Hobart's, Louie-Louie always eats a little bit of a candy bar Kev saves from his lunch. It got so that the rat will only eat if Kev feeds him. His father, his brother, and even his mother might put food in the cage but unless Louie-Louie sees Kev, he won't eat. And to this day he always looks for that candy Kev keeps for him—he's got a real sweet tooth, that rat. So I guess Kev became Louie-Louie's mother in a way, he loves him that much.

Once when we were buying rodent food at the pet store, Jonesey told Kev that he had saved Louie-Louie's life and that now Kevin and the rat shared a special connection, a bond. So that's the story of Louie-Louie for what it's worth. Rat and boy have a real connection.

"Chris?"

"Yeah?"

"We going soon? I mean, Louie-Louie usually eats before seven."

"Yeah, Kirby too," I tell him. I'm worried about that look my Grand-Dad had on his face but I don't tell Kev or his brother.

Jeremy locks up and then he and Kev follow me outside. I tell Jeremy he doesn't have to wait with us but he says it's no problem. He's not going out until eight. So the three of us wait there on the front porch of *The Willin' Cate Book Store* just talking together.

"I hope it rains tonight after batting practice." Jeremy is looking at the sky. "There's a lot of thunder lately, but no rain. Everything is so hazy and sticky. It's really weird. You'd think with all the thunder we'd have a ton of rain. All we get are lightning storms, though. Especially over The Plot."

"The Plot?"

"Yeah, it's strange. I mean we're pretty *near* The Plot but the lightning *never* comes over the ball field. We're in the state play-offs so we *have* to play a game tomorrow. I just want it to rain to cool off the ground a little bit and get rid of the lightning storms. There's so much lightning over The Plot that the batters have a real hard time seeing the ball. It's spooky that the lightning only stays over that piece of land, like some weird horror movie or Stephen King book."

Me and Kev don't say anything, just look at each other. In the distance we hear thunder and someone's dog barking each time the thunder rolls. It's after seven already.

At seven-fifteen my Grand-Dad's car pulls up and he gets out. He walks up to us with a faraway look on his face. He looks just like he does after teaching a class about some old stuff everyone has forgotten. He's sweating from the heat. The paper bag with that book is gone. I guess he gave it to Old Man Hobart.

"You boys ready to go? I'm sorry I'm late, but I forgot the time. I was so busy talking with—well never mind. We'll order pizza, okay with you two? Jeremy, you're certainly welcome to come eat with us. And, thank you for staying with the boys." He sighs a really deep sigh.

Jeremy says no thanks to the pizza, he has to get home because he's going out with his friends after batting practice and they'll probably eat something later. He asks for a ride home though.

* * *

After we drop Jeremy off, we head over to Scaglione's Pizza Palace and order a sausage and pepperoni pie, plus mozzarella sticks, a meatball hero, and a gigantic antipasto to go.

"Just so I can truthfully say we had salad every night if anyone asks. The antipasto does have lettuce in it you know," my Grand-Dad says with a wink. He looks like himself again as he laughs and jokes with Mario the owner of the pizza place.

And I would say there was nothing wrong with him except that when I ask him if he gave the book on Andersonville to Old Man Hobart, he just sighs deeply and nods yes.

That book must have some really horrible stuff in it, like more horrible than what was in the encyclopedia. Who'd want to read a book like that if it's so gross?

chapter

10

"What makes lightnin' storms?" Kev is talking through his second slice of pizza.

"Oh, atmospheric pressure, instability, convection and—"

"Huh?! Mr. Hopper, can you make it simple, please?!"

"Simple, hmmmm. Well, Kevin, it—"

"Like how come there might be lightnin' in one spot but not in another spot right near it? Why does that happen?"

"Well, mainly it is caused—"

"But why would the lightnin' just flash over one spot, just one, and no other place near it? How come?"

"If it's only over one spot, let's say the ocean, then—"

"Not the *ocean*! This doesn't have *anythin'* to do with the ocean! This is real land stuff, so how come it would happen?" Kevin stops talking and waits. "C'mon, Mr. Hopper! You know everythin' about everythin'! Why aren't you talkin'?"

I tap him on the shoulder. "Because you won't give him a chance. Jeez, Kev!"

My Grand-Dad has a little smile on his face as he asks Kev if he'll let him finish what he started to say. Kev nods, his mouth full.

"When the hot air is—"

"So why does it only happen over Dansbury Plot?"

"Lightning?" My Grand-Dad puts down his slice of pizza.

"Yeah, I'm scared for my brother."

I explain to my Grand-Dad what Jeremy told us about The Plot, and the lightning storms there. He listens without saying anything, then he asks, "Jeremy says this is happening *only* over Dansbury Plot? *Not* over the ball field or the street or anywhere else?"

"Just over Bury-the-Dead-Dan's Plot," Kev tells him.

"Why, Grand-Dad? I mean, why *would* that happen."

"Hey, Mr. Hopper, is that what's called a *phenomenal*?"

"Phenome-*non*, Kevin, and if it is only happening over one section of land, I guess that would be the word for it."

"Yeah, but, Grand-Dad, *only* over The Plot? That place is spooky enough! Anything could happen there!"

"Is somethin' going to happen to Jeremy?" asks Kev suddenly, looking scared. My Grand-Dad pauses to think before he answers.

"I wouldn't worry about him being on the *ball field* itself, if that's what you're concerned about. He and his team mates should just steer clear of Dansbury Plot."

"Why? Are they gonna get killed or somethin' or eaten by some crazy weird animals with humongous teeth like that little girl Brad told us about." He looks at me. "Remember, Chris? Brad said she never talked again and she had all those teeth marks on her shriveled up old lady body, all that spooky supernatural stuff!"

Kev goes real crazy, getting up and accidentally spilling milk all over the floor. He can't stop—he's all hyper. Kirby starts barking and jumping up and down trying to grab Kev's slice of pizza.

"Kevin, Kevin! Calm down. Take a deep breath. Nothing is going to happen to Jeremy, nothing."

"But you *said*! You *said* they should stay away from the Plot! You said!"

He's almost crying and my Grand-Dad gets up and puts an arm around him, telling him it's okay.

"You said!" Kev gets the last sentence out with a gasp because now he's hiccupping from getting himself all excited.

"I *said* they should just stay away from The Plot because of the danger of being struck by *lightning* not because of anything else. There may be some natural particles on that land that attract the dry lightning. It's a *natural* reaction, not a *super*natural one, Kevin. And, Chris?" He looks at me when he asks this. "What in the world is Kevin talking about? What little girl, what marks?"

I tell him what Joey and Brad said about The Plot, everything from Mr. Sarlewski trying to get people to invest in buying shares of The Plot to the strange noises that Joey's uncle said are heard at The Plot, to the story of the lost little girl bitten all over her body. I ask him if he ever heard about the little girl, like is it in history books or whatever.

"It wouldn't be in history books in schools necessarily because it's more of what's called local lore. The local myths and stories of one small town wouldn't be included in books used by multiple state school systems. *I've* never heard of it but I know who may have. If anyone knows strange stories about this town it would be Mr. Hobart. He's practically a walking book of anything that has ever happened here. I've heard him tell a lot of stories, but that is one I've never heard. I'll talk to him tomorrow and ask him. All of us will go to see him."

"So you're sayin' somethin' *could* happen to my brother? Like if he went over by The Plot?" Kev has calmed down but he still looks scared.

"Kevin, Jeremy's not an idiot. Give him some credit. He's not going over to Dansbury Plot to stand there and see if lightning will strike him. Don't worry about it. It's my understanding that no one goes there anyway."

"So he's safe on the ball field?"

"Yes, he is. Don't worry. Now let's clean this spill."

I grab my Grand-Dad's arm as he turns to grab some paper towels and ask, "Are we safe *here*, Grand-Dad?"

"Here?"

"Yeah, here, you know, *here*, 'cause the other night you put a leash on Kirbs and you never leash him! Like, is the back yard safe?"

"The back yard?! Chris, of course the back yard is safe!" Me and Kev are looking at him so he takes a deep breath and continues slowly, "And I only put a leash on Kirby because I heard there were skunks around. There's no other reason. Why would there be?"

"Truth, Mr. Hopper?" says Kev.

"Yes, Kevin, truth." He jokingly crosses his heart and his eyes making us laugh.

My Grand-Dad goes to wipe up the mess Kev made. While he's cleaning it, I'm thinking about The Plot, how it's been here forever, how everybody knows about it and we all take it for granted. How kids in Bridge Crossing feel that if you just leave it alone, you'll be okay. People pass it every day—always on the other side of the street—and it's just there. Places are built around it, but never right smack next to it.

Then I think how there must be a million balls from all the games played on the Little League fields that were hit onto it, but that nobody ever goes to find them. The way the coaches or the umpires always just throw out a new ball to the pitcher when the old one goes over onto The Plot instead of sending some kid to get it. Come to think of it, if you looked at Dansbury Plot you never *saw* the balls anyway, so where did they all go? I don't know one person who ever said they had a ball from The Plot. And that's weird because most kids who like baseball want to get as many balls as they can 'cause we're always losing them.

I think about how dead looking Dansbury Plot is and how I bet even Mr. Sarlewski never stepped foot on it. He's probably waiting for somebody else to go over there, like that real estate guy, to see if it's safe before *he* actually walks on it.

Then I remember really clear, that snapping sound and my weird dreams about Kirby. And—I don't want to even *think* about this—but I remember Kev asking me did I maybe bleed on The Plot when I cut my hand on a sharp rock after Billy pushed me. And how Kev said that maybe the Plot was hungry.

I'm thinking all this stuff so I don't pay any attention to Kirby. He's standing by the back door really quiet, with his fur up. I pet him and he whines a little.

"I think Kirby has to go out, Grand-Dad. Want me to take him?"

He says yes and me and Kev go out the back door. It smells funny outside, like hamburgers left too long on the barbecue. Kirby sniffs the air and I hear a low growl. He isn't doing anything, just standing there all stiff-legged. I tell him to come on Kirbs, hurry up, but he just stands still, not moving.

"Hey, Chris. I know how to make Kirby go. I saw it on this jungle thing on TV. If you pee on a bush or something, an animal will go over and pee too. Go ahead, try it."

"Listen, Kev, that is the dumbest thing you ever said. I am not going to pee on a bush."

"It's not so dumb. Remember when we went campin' with my Dad and Jeremy? We peed outside then."

"Of course we did! We were sleeping in a tent. There were no bathrooms. That's different."

"What about that jungle show? Are you sayin' they were lyin'? Try it! I betcha Kirby will pee right after you."

"You go pee on a bush! I'm not going to do that, jeez!"

After sniffing the air for about a million minutes, Kirby finally does what we came outside for him to do but he does it in a weird way, like he's afraid something's going to jump out of the bushes at him while he's peeing.

We go back in the house and the phone's ringing. My Grand-Dad asks one of us to answer it because he's busy cleaning up and Kev beats me to it. Two minutes later Kev turns to me and yells, "It hit it! Lightnin'! Chris! Lightnin' hit Bury-the-Dead-Dan's Plot. Jeremy saw it! Lightnin' hit The Plot!! Hey, Mr. Hopper! Lightnin' hit The Plot!"

chapter

11

Kev is begging my Grand-Dad to let us go to the field right away but he won't let us go alone. He's coming with us.

"It'll be dark by the time you're on your way home and I don't want you boys out alone, walking on the streets in the dark. I'm responsible for the two of you so *I'm* coming or *you're* not going. And we're taking my car. Give me a minute, will you, Kevin? My keys are upstairs."

I just look at him. Bridge Crossing is about the safest place in the whole world. Like we have no real crime or anything. I mean, I guess anything can happen anywhere but it's much less likely to happen here. It's not like we hang out really late or anything but there have been times when me, Kev, Brad, and Joey have walked home when it was *almost* dark.

When my Grand-Dad comes down the stairs, me and Kev race out to the car, Kev yelling for my grandfather to hurry up. The night is hotter than even just an hour ago and when I take a deep breath, my nose burns a little. The air smells worse than it did before. Like a smell of food that went bad.

* * *

At the Little League Field, we see Jeremy and his friends. Kev's father and mother are there too. They're all looking across at The Plot where a thin curling stream of smoke is rising up from the ground.

Kev runs over to his brother to find out all about what happened. I hang back a little to listen to the grown-ups talk but nobody knows exactly what happened. Kev is motioning me over to where the older kids are. As I walk over I see boys and girls talking and looking at The Plot. One girl is all over Jeremy, hugging him really hard, pretending like she's scared. Maybe I'm wrong, maybe she really is scared.

I walk over to Kev and he pulls me by the arm away from the others. I thought Jeremy and his friends were having batting practice but when I mention this to Kev he gives me a smart-ass look, like he knows something I don't and can't wait to tell me.

"Hey, Chris," whispers Kev, "You know what this place *is*? It's a make-out place. You know, *make-out*? Like what Cindy Nunziato wanted to do with you at her birthday party last year? Gross! Jeremy and the guys bring their girlfriends here to do stuff, you know kissin' and all that gross touchy feely crap. They were makin' out in the dugout. Yuck! I don't know if I ever want to even sit in there again!"

"So what happened? Did Jeremy really see it or was he too busy doing stuff with his girlfriend?" I'm really sarcastic. I don't care about anything else but that lightning over The Plot.

"No, he saw it all right. He was checkin' the street just to see if a car was comin' down the road. He was worried that his baseball coach might be checkin' up on him and the guys.

If the coach knew that they weren't practicin' the night before a play-off game, they'd be in big trouble. That's when he saw it. Man! He said it was like a fireworks thing. A big crash of thunder and then, Bam! A streak of lightnin' hit The Plot! Jeremy said they all jumped and ran to the edge of the baseball field but all that was there was that weird smoke curl going up. Then another humongous crash and *another* lightnin' bolt hits The Plot!! All the girls were screamin' and the guys were all yellin'. Jeremy ran to the clubhouse but it was locked so he broke a window to use the phone inside to call my parents and then me."

People are still talking, but mostly, they're all looking at The Plot. Nothing is happening there though, just that curl of smoke going from the ground straight up to the dark cloudy sky. One of the girls says they should go home. I turn and see that it's Ellen Sarlewski talking. She's standing with the other kids. Boy, she is really pretty. I think about her white underpants and how Billy is always trying to sell them. He's a lousy brother.

Me and Kev walk over to the corner of the Little League field to get a closer look at The Plot, but not too close. Not too close. It's creepy. There's smoke going up to a sky that looks dark and yellow. There are no friendly puffy clouds like you see in books or movies, just a heavy, blanket of clouds that are blocking the moon and the stars.

I'm busy looking at The Plot—and listening hard for any weird snapping sounds. I'm blocking out all the other noise and straining so hard to hear that I don't know someone has come up behind me until he speaks. At the sound of his voice, I jump a mile.

"Debt's about to come due. Like I said, got to be paid."

It's Old Man Hobart standing behind me with Jonesey right next to him. Like I said, he practically never goes anywhere so for him to be here is kinda scary and also important.

Old Man Hobart walks over to the edge of the field to get a good look at Dansbury Plot. Jonesey stays by us and gives us a smile of hello then turns to my Grand-Dad who's walking over.

"Hot out tonight, huh, Jonesey?" says my Grand-Dad. Jonsesy just smiles again and together they walk over by Old Man Hobart. We watch the three of them talking, or at least my Grand-Dad and Hobart are talking. I only hear Jonesey say a few words but I can't catch what they are because he's kinda mumbling. Then I hear Hobart say, "Might like to ask Jonesey about that" and I see my Grand-Dad nod. Jonesey just stands looking at The Plot.

"Hey, Chris? Are we gonna go home soon?"

Now that there's nothing much to see, and he knows Jeremy's okay, Kev wants to go.

"Louie-Louie doesn't like bein' alone at night. You know, there's always somebody home at night at my house. Can we go soon?"

"He's got Kirby for company," I say, but Kev says Kirby's not the same as 'human people'.

"Well, we gotta wait for my Grand-Dad. If he wouldn't let us walk here alone he sure isn't going to let us walk home alone. He's busy talking to Old Man Hobart and Jonesey so we gotta wait."

We look over to where my Grand-Dad and Hobart are talking and I see Jonesey shaking his head and pointing at The Plot. They seem to be really involved in what they're talking about. Everybody else on the baseball field has gone to sit in the bleachers. I hear some of the guys making ghost-like sounds and the girls pretending like they're shrieking, then I hear muffled laughing. Kev says the guys are probably copping a feel. That's how it is when you have an older brother—you learn all about stuff to do with girls.

Old Man Hobart and my Grand-Dad are walking back to where we're standing. My Grand-Dad asks if me and Kev would like to stop by that new ice cream place on the way home. He doesn't have to ask us twice, boy! Kev asks if he can get a small cup of vanilla ice cream for Louie-Louie and my Grand-Dad laughs and says sure, why not?

Jonsesy comes over when we're in the car and smiles a good-bye to us, then leans down and whispers something to my grandfather. Then he does something strange—he shakes hands with my Grand-Dad and reaches in the back to shake hands with me and Kev! It's strange because I've never, ever seen him do that. Most men do shake hands, even women, but not Jonesey. It's almost like he never wanted to touch another human being. I stare at my hand as if somebody famous just shook it.

Suddenly Kev grabs my arm and tells me to turn around and look out the back window of the car. I look up towards the night sky and see that same curl of smoke going up to the dark clouds.

"No, Chris, not at the sky! Look! Just above the ground. Do you see those sparks over Bury-the-Dead-Dan's Plot?"

I look back and see tiny little blue sparks are just floating over the Plot. It reminds me of when a tree fell on a power wire outside of the school last year. My entire class ran over to the windows and watched the sparks from the wire crackle and spit like a living thing. The air above The Plot looks like that.

"Chris? You think that maybe there's a live wire buried under The Plot? It sure sparks like it's live! Right, Chris?"

Kev's all excited. My Grand-Dad and Jonesey turn and look back at The Plot too. Before I can answer Kev, Jonesey surprises me by saying—

"No, Kevin, there's nothing alive on Dansbury Plot, nothing alive at all."

chapter

12

Every Friday afternoon, around four o'clock, you will see fresh flowers on the grave of Elizabeth Ann Jones. They are small bunches of whatever is growing wild behind Hobart's pet store. In the spring and summer there are roses and daisies, and sometimes a blue flower my Grand-Mom calls hydrangea. In the autumn, there're mums, and winter is mostly some green stuff with red berries on them. But no matter what the weather is, at any time of the year, on Fridays, her husband Elbert Daniel Mervin Jones never forgets to put fresh flowers on her grave.

I saw him once when me and Kev were biking over to town to meet Joey and Brad at the bike shop. Jonesey was going up the hill to the graveyard carrying flowers wrapped in ribbon, a cloth sack, and a blue pot. I was curious so we biked around the hill and kinda followed him.

We weren't spying on him or anything, the way that creep Billy does with people. We were just interested in what he was doing. I mean I figured the flowers were for his wife, but I wanted to know what the sack had in it. It was a pretty big sack. Kev thought that maybe Jonesey had gone wacko again and was going to dig up his wife's bones or something because he missed her so much. I told Kev *he* was the one who was wacko, not Jonesey, to even think something like that. He looked at me and shot back that he saw an old movie on TV with Vincent Price where some guy, who was crazy with grief, dug up his girlfriend's bones and carried them around in a sack. If you ask me, he watches way too much television and I told him so.

Anyway, we're biking around, hoping that Jonesey didn't think we were looking at him and we see him take the blue pot over to where there's a spigot and fill it up with well water. Then he goes back, puts the flowers in the blue pot, and places it on the ground to the right of his wife's headstone. He takes a lot of time arranging the flowers until they sit looking really nice and full in the pot.

So, I'm circling near the top of the hill—Kev was still down near the bottom—and I stop and make believe I'm looking at the glorious view of Mendelsohn's gas station, just in case Jonesey happens to look up and see me.

I watch as Jonesey opens the sack and takes out a white tablecloth, a thermos, two mugs, and two doughnuts. He puts the tablecloth on the ground in front of the headstone, then he pours something hot from the thermos into *both* mugs and puts one right next to the flowers. Next he carefully unwraps one of the doughnuts and places it on its wrapper, next to the mug. *Then* he reaches into the sack again and takes out a book.

I watch him sit against the left side of the headstone, take a sip from his mug, a bite from his doughnut, and then begin to read out loud. Kev finally makes it up the hill and pulls up next to me. I motion him to be quiet. Jonesey was reading a story and I knew I'd heard it. But, no, that wasn't right—I hadn't heard it, I *saw* it.

I was at Joey's house and his mom was watching an old movie on TV. I remembered the names of the characters because they were really different—not so much the girl's name, Catherine, that's my Grand-Mom's name—but the guy's name was really different, really kinda strange. His name was Heathcliff. I had never heard that name before.

Now I was hearing Jonesey talk about Catherine and Heathcliff to his dead wife! He stopped and asked Elizabeth—like she was sitting next to him and everything—if she remembered them talking about maybe visiting the wild moors mentioned in the book and how she had said that love never dies and how Catherine and Heathcliff would always be together.

"Just like us, Beth. You are always inside me, always."

I was fascinated by the way he was talking to somebody who wasn't there for him to see. He went on talking for a few minutes, sipping from the mug, and then he placed the back of his head on the stone like it was a soft pillow instead of hard granite, and closed his eyes. The book lay open on his leg.

I pointed down the hill so Kev would know that we should leave. I took one backward look at Jonesey. With the flowers and the thermos and mugs, it looked like someone was having a picnic. I mean if it wasn't a graveyard, it would be a nice place to sit and read and have something to drink and eat.

Much later I found out that Jonesey and his wife used to have tea every afternoon at four and read out loud to each other. On nice days they had their tea outside. Elizabeth loved flowers and there were always flowers in a blue vase on a white table cloth wherever they had their tea, indoors or out. It's what people call a tradition, I guess.

Jonesey kept the tradition by going up to her grave every Friday, pretending they were having tea together again. I guess he does it on a Friday because that's the day he misses her the most of any day of the week. Elizabeth died on a Friday.

I watch Jonesey open his eyes, get up, and take the blue pot filled with the flowers she loves, the mug of tea and the doughnut, and place them on the white cloth right in front of her grave. He sits back down facing the headstone and finishes his own tea. I guess in a way, they're still having tea together, even though she's dead.

I never told anyone about seeing Jonesey at that graveyard and what he was doing, not even my Grand-Dad. I kinda felt it was a private thing he was doing and I even felt bad that I had seen it.

chapter

13

There must be about twenty people at Hobart's Pet Store the next morning when me and Kev arrive with my Grand-Dad. I count 8 empty boxes of doughnuts in the trash and the smell of coffee is really heavy when you open the door, like the pot's been going for hours. The old-timers are there and also some people dressed in suits that I've never seen.

"Wow, Chris, everybody must be here because of the lightnin' last night at The Plot. I guess they all want to talk about it. Boy, are those guys, over there, news reporters? Wow!"

But it turns out that Kev is wrong about why all these people are here. They aren't here because of lightning over The Plot, they're here because of Warren Sarlewski and some real estate guy. One of the old guys from the pool is talking to my Grand-Dad and he tells him that there was some sort of informal meeting at the bank with Sarlewski and a bunch of real estate people.

Everyone is talking about how Mr. Sarlewski is pushing the town council to declare Dansbury Plot an 'abandoned property' and reclaim it for the town. Anyway, he told people, taxes haven't been paid on The Plot in who-knows-how-long. There are no records, no owner on the tax rolls, nothing. He said that unless the township can find out exactly who owns The

Plot and get them to pay back taxes, it should be sold by the town back to itself for the sum of one dollar.

"'The Township of Bridge Crossing has eminent domain rights to that property and can sell it if they choose to do so. It's an abandoned eyesore that can be put to good use in updating our town.'"

That's what the old guy says Mr. Sarlewski told the people at the tax office. My Grand-Dad laughs when Old Man Hobart, who overheard the conversation, snorts and says that Sarlewski wouldn't know the words 'eminent domain' let alone what they mean, if the words crawled up his ass!

"That puffed up loudmouth toad probably got the words from that young out-of-towner, that real estate fella, Mark Colbert, the guy standing over by the door. He might know how to talk that fancy real estate legal shit, but he knows nothing about Bridge Crossing. Shouldn't tell people who have lived here all their lives what to do. Should leave Dansbury Plot alone, if he's as smart as he thinks he is. Just leave it the hell alone."

Kev taps my Grand-Dad on the shoulder and asks him what 'Emma's Aunt Domain' means. "And anyhow, who's Emma and why is Mr. Sarlewski talking about her aunt? What's that got to do with Dansbury Plot? I don't get it."

Last year the school nurse told Kev's parents that he should get his ears checked by a doctor because a teacher thought he might have a hearing problem. The teacher told the nurse, "He always messes up words, and a lot of times I have to call his name more than once before he answers me in class."

His mom took him to get checked by some ear specialist but there was absolutely nothing wrong with his hearing. I think Kev just hears what he wants to hear and has a lousy vocabulary. He's not a big reader. Also, he daydreams a lot so he hardly ever listens to the teachers.

"To begin with," says my Grand-Dad, "it's pronounced em-in-ent, Kevin, *e-m-i-n-e-n-t*. And it has nothing to do with anyone named Emma or an aunt." He smiles at Kev. "Simply put, eminent domain rights refer to the right of a government—in this case the Township of Bridge Crossing—to take over private property for public use. So what Mr. Sarlewski meant when he said that the Township of Bridge Crossing has eminent domain rights on Dansbury Plot, only means that the town can seize the property because the land was owned by the town before it was sold to someone named Dansbury."

"Huh?" Kev scratches his head in confusion but my Grand-Dad is infinitely patient with him.

"All that legalese really means is that the town could own it—The Plot—again. If that ever did happen, they could do anything they wanted to do with the property."

I repeat the words 'eminent domain' to myself. What cool words! These are words I'm gonna write down in my notebook when I get back to my Grand-Dad's house.

Jonesey motions us over by the coffee pot, gives us two glazed doughnuts and pours cups of coffee for my Grand-Dad and himself. I think about him pouring tea into mugs the day I saw him in the graveyard. Having tea with his dead wife.

We sit and listen to what everybody is saying, some guys talking at once, or interrupting each other to get a word in. The suit people aren't reporters, they're real estate people and one of the women is a banker. They're talking about how the land on the Plot is definitely worth money and that it should be developed commercially.

Old Man Hobart lets the talk go on for about another half hour and then tells everyone, in a loud voice, that they have to leave because he and Jonesey have to do inventory. People are reluctantly leaving and we're getting up to go when Hobart stops us. We stand back and let the stragglers pass us.

"You and the boys can stay, Will. I just need to get all that foolish jabber out of here. Sit down, have another cup, it's about time we had an intelligent person in this shop."

We sit, me, Kev, and the three men, eating brownies and talking about whether the New York Yankees have decent enough pitching this year to make it to the World Series.

Suddenly Old Man Hobart pushes his chair against the wall so that he's balanced on the chair's back legs and looks at my Grand-Dad.

"So, Will, what really brings you in here today? And don't tell me it's Jonesey's coffee!"

* * *

Old Man Hobart wasn't always old. Maybe that sounds like a stupid thing to say but it's true. When you're a kid, old people just seem like they were *always* old. Anyone over thirty is an old person to a twelve-year-old kid.

It's hard to imagine Old Man Hobart as a young man, let alone think of him as a kid *my* age. I know Jonesey was his best friend ever since they were in elementary school together but somehow I can't see them as older versions of my best friend Kev and me. Are *we* going to be like Jonesey and Old Man Hobart when we get old? They've been friends forever. Hobart even talks for Jonesey, sometimes. I don't want Kev ever talking for me but that would probably be the way it would be 'cause Kev's a big mouth and I'm quieter, but not so quiet as Jonesey.

I just can't picture them doing the things me and Kev do though—riding bikes, going swimming, playing baseball, whispered talks about what his brother tells him about girls, or cutting a class on a hot spring day. I don't see them doing any of those things, but they must have, right?

Anyway, after Mr. Hobart asked my grandfather the real reason he came to see him in the store, my Grand-Dad turned to me and Kev and said, "Why don't you tell Mr. Hobart and Jonesey what Brad said about the little girl who was found with bite marks on her body? Go on, Chris. You heard it first-hand."

I repeated the word 'first-hand' a few times to myself because the words sound really cool, and then I told them everything about what Brad said. I even told the part about the bugged out eyes and how you could still see the scars on her body when she died and while I told them, Kev acted out the parts, like a mime. When I was finished Hobart and Jonesey just looked at each other.

"Well? Have you ever heard of this story or is it just someone's great imagination for a good spooky tale told on Hallowe'en?" My Grand-Dad got up to pour himself another cup of coffee and waited for Hobart to answer.

Jonesey got the milk from the cooler for the coffee and nodded at Old Man Hobart who seemed to be waiting to start.

"It does make a damned good story, doesn't it? The kind you can tell around a campfire, but yes, it is true. At least as true as a story told by a senile old man can be said to be true. My Great-Uncle told me this story and *he* heard it from his grandfather who heard it from *his* own father. You remember the ravings of my Great-Uncle Pete, don't you, Jonesey?"

Kev looked at Jonesey who smiled in his sad way and shook his head yes.

"Uncle Pete was a man who was a little too fond of his liquor and when in his cups, so to speak, told some fantastic tales. Now he had always been a storyteller, that's a fact. He traveled all over the world as a merchant seaman and we loved to hear him tell fanciful stories about genies and mermaids, and whatnot. We knew they weren't real, of course. But a few years before he died, some of the stories he told were downright macabre. Even more than that, they were like to scare the bejesus and living hell out of you."

"What's maca—ma-ca—, that 'M' word mean?" asks Kev.

"Ma-ca-bre. It means to portray human injury or death in such a way as to inspire shock or horror," says my Grand-Dad.

"Huh?! Jeez, I'm only twelve! Can you make it simple?"

"Sorry, Kevin, it means grim and gruesome. Is that a better explanation?"

"Yeah, way better, Mr. Hopper!"

"Anyway," continues Old Man Hobart, "a year before he died he said he 'knew things' and the stories became more and more filled with horror. They weren't stories told to amuse children any more, no sir, now they were tales worthy of the fearsome writings of an Edgar Allen Poe." He moves in his seat. "He was living in a small house on the edge of town and we— Jonesey and me—used to bike over to visit him, about once a week." He looks at me and Kev and says, "We were around your age then and we'd bike all over hell and creation if we'd a mind to."

I try really hard to picture the two of them my age and in a way I can. Almost, anyway.

"The local doctor told my mother that Uncle Pete was just old and senile and didn't know what he was saying. That was a nice way of saying he was crazy as a loon. But Uncle Pete, well, he was her uncle, her mother's kid brother after all, and she cared for him. But I heard doc privately tell my father that Pete's mind was lost from all the years of drinking hard liquor and putting God knew what else into his body. The old doctor thought that it was maybe opium or some other shit Pete had picked up on his travels to the Orient that had damaged his brain, who knew?"

Old Man Hobart paused and drank his coffee, then continued.

"He got so bad that my saintly mother persuaded my old man to let her put Uncle Pete in the spare bedroom. It was right next to mine and I could hear Pete blabberin' most every night. My mother told me to just let him talk, he wasn't hurting anyone, and don't pay any attention to what he says.

"One night, my parents were at a bowling awards dinner and Jonesey was staying over to keep me company. Around 11:00 at night, we heard Uncle Pete yelling something over and over again. Well, we went into his room and he sees us and starts saying, 'I have to tell, I have to tell!!' and motioning us to sit on the foot of the bed. Then he says that this story was passed down for generations and he can't die without passing it on to someone in the family. Me and Jonesey were the only ones there, so he passed his story to us." Hobart sighs. "Funny thing was that once we sat down and he had our attention, he wasn't yelling anymore. He was calm and—normal."

"'I want to tell you about little Cecelia,' Old Pete says real calm.'"

Hobart pauses again and looks at Jonesey as if he needs to know that he and his best friend heard exactly the same story. Jonesey nods at him to go on.

Hobart heaves his body around on the chair, sighs again and says, "This is the story Uncle Pete told us that night, the story of a little lost girl named Cecelia."

chapter

14

"It was in the late 1800s—about 1875 I believe—at a big Fourth of July celebration right here in Bridge Crossing, that something strange happened. There was a town picnic and people were having a good time relaxing on the green, what we now call the town square over by the park. There were wild berries growing near the old park. Today, it's just part of the biking paths, all black-top macadam over them, but back then, and even when we were kids, right Jonesey? those berries were there for the taking. The trouble was that the berries were mixed in with thorny bramble bushes so if you went in, and you weren't careful, you got scratched up pretty good." He sips more coffee.

"Uncle Pete said somebody, some new young man, just come to town with his wife, thought it would be nice to take the children berry picking. All the little ones went too, as young as four years old. That was the age of little Cecelia.

"Sometime during the berry picking the little girl went missing. The man and his wife searched all over the berry patch and the surrounding field but couldn't find her. They went back to the picnic area hoping Cecelia would be back by her parents, but she wasn't. A search party was formed and they went out looking for her, searching the fields and the woods but no one found her, not even a trace. No bonnet, no tatters from ripped clothing, no shoes, nothing at all."

Jonesey coughs quietly and looks at Hobart who continues. "The girl's father, with a hysterical wife on his hands, pointed an accusing finger at the newcomer in town. The man was carted off to the police station where the constable kept at him all night long trying to get him to admit that he had something to do with Cecelia's disappearance but the man stood his ground. He had never been alone with Cecelia—he and his wife had been there together with all the children the entire time. He didn't know how Cecelia could have gotten away from the group without someone seeing her."

More coffee sipping.

"The man's wife was questioned separately by the constable's assistant and her story was the same as her husband's. She said they were all together, never anyone alone and the last time she had seen Cecelia, the little girl was picking berries with the others. She made a statement, too. She said, 'We were coming back to the picnic. Some of the children were complaining about being scratched up from the brambles. I was gathering them all around me and everyone was there but that sweet little girl. No one knows when she left our group, no one.' She was pretty hysterical herself.

"Anyway, no charges were brought against the man or his wife. The children were all brought to their homes with the women, and the men went out again to see if they could find Cecelia. Search parties were out late into the night looking for her but there was no sign. It was almost as if she stepped off the earth and vanished into nowhere."

Old Man Hobart shifted in his seat and was quiet. After drinking three cups of milk, I had to pee really badly, but I didn't want to miss what he had to say. I just held the pee in tight.

Kev was on his third brownie and he kept his eyes on Old Man Hobart like he was watching someone in a movie.

"Weeks went by and still no Cecelia. Then one night late, her mother looked out her back door and saw what she thought was a pile of clothes in the yard. She thought that maybe the clothes had blown into her yard from someone's laundry line. It had been pretty windy lately and she went out to see. Next thing her husband hears her screaming and looks out to see her holding the pile of clothes. Only it wasn't clothes, it was their daughter, Cecelia! She was wearing the dress she had worn on the day she went missing—a pretty dress with yellow and pink flowers on it—and she was as limp as if she were dead. He sent his oldest boy to go get the doctor and went and carried his little girl into the house, his wife screaming and crying and holding on to Cecelia for dear life.

"The doctor came and examined that poor child. Her clothes were ripped and she had scratches all over her hands and face. Those scratches were from the bramble bushes. But when they undressed her, the mother began to scream all over again. There were bite marks all over her body, her arms and legs, her belly, chest, and back like some wild animal had attacked her. The bites were swollen and red and crusted over with dried blood. The odor coming from them smelled real bad. The doctor took some swab samples of the wounds. Then they put her in a tub of warm soapy water and later the old doctor put some type of antiseptic ointment on all the bites but they pretty much remained hot and swollen. The smell stayed with her too, like rotten eggs. All this time she just stared straight ahead and didn't move or make a sound.

"Well, Cecelia's father was all for going out and hunting whatever animal had done this to his baby right then and there but the doc stopped him cold. He said that those weren't the marks of neither canine nor feline teeth, nor any wild or domesticated animal from these parts. 'Look at 'em, he said. 'Look at how small and even they are. No long canines like a big wildcat or wolf has. No, they're small, smooth. I know it sounds crazy but they appear to me to be human bites, and it also appears to have been done by more than just one set of teeth. The bites are distinctly different.'

"Cecelia's father looked closely and it turned his stomach. They *did* look like human teeth marks. The doctor told him not to talk about it because he wanted a friend of his, some fella from a university, to take a look. So Cecelia's father agreed and he told his wife to do the same. No talking to anybody about anything. She was so frightened that she swore she wouldn't tell a soul about Cecelia."

Old Man Hobart gets up to stretch his bad leg and then sits down heavily, the chair creaking. "Well, the doc's friend was an anthropology professor. He came within a few days of getting doc's telegram and spent three days examining little Cecelia and checking, under a microscope, those samples the doctor took from the wounds. He concluded they were definitely human teeth marks made by more than over twenty different sets of teeth. And he said something else."

Hobart pauses again and looks at each of us, one by one. By that look I know he's got something important to say. "That university fella told them that if he wasn't a rational God-fearing man, he would say that whoever had made those marks wasn't a living creature. The swab samples showed dead, decayed matter."

I feel like a snake is slithering up my spine. I look at Kev who's just staring at Old Man Hobart, his mouth open and his eyes terrified-looking.

"You want to know who that anthropology fella was? He was Uncle Pete's great-grandfather. An ancestor of mine then. He'd been to some strange places around the world—guess Pete inherited his wanderlust from his great-grandfather.

"In some of the places the prof traveled he heard stories of how the dead come back. How a person maybe died cruelly at the hands of someone else and they can't rest until they get some kind of revenge. Most of the times he took it in a scholarly way, you know, he saw them as just local legends of primitive people.

'But there was one story that came from a country as civilized as our own. That country was England. He heard it on one of his travels over there. Weird story too, if I recollect it. Seems there was a king, Henry II who had imprisoned a mother and her son for treason. He left them in a dungeon to starve to death. Well, when the guards went in to get rid of the dead bodies, they found evidence that the mother had eaten her own son's arm and part of his leg and they said he wasn't quite dead when she'd done it. And her cheek had a bite taken out of it too, probably by the son before she got to him."

Kev makes a fake retching sound and goes, "Gross!"

"And here's the kicker to this story," continues Hobart. "Whenever new prisoners were placed in that cell where the mother and son had turned cannibal, they would scream in agony all night long. The guards swore that when they would go in the next morning there would be teeth marks all over the prisoners' bodies and they weren't the marks of any animal. No sir! It was like the starving dead were returning for fresh meat."

I feel cold all over just hearing Old Man Hobart say this.

"Anyways, getting back to the story about Cecelia, the professor and the doc decided between them that the best thing all of them could do in the circumstances would be to keep everything secret. Only Cecelia, her family, and the two of them would ever know. The girl's parents were advised to put out a story that Cecelia fell and hit her head and got amnesia and that was that. They were never to tell anyone about what they had found on her body."

Muttering "God-damned arthritis," Hobart gets up slowly and walks stiffly around the store before returning to his chair and continuing the story.

"Now I don't know, maybe someone did tell, else how would anyone else know about it? Maybe someone in the family told because a secret like that is hard to keep. The poor mother died ten years later, and the father followed her by two. The care of Cecelia was left to the two boys. When the older boy married, his wife lasted about three months in taking care of Cecelia and couldn't take it any more. She told Cecelia's brother that he had to place his sister in some type of asylum otherwise she would leave him. So the poor brother did what his wife wanted and Cecelia was put in a convent place for the rest of her life. Lived to 104, she did, never speaking a word, just staring straight-ahead."

Old Man Hobart stretches his bad leg and grimaces. "That's Uncle Pete's tale and I didn't know whether to believe it or not. Pete died two weeks after tellin' me and Jonesey. As for me, I never told anybody about what Pete said, but, dammit something like that, well, who knows who might have talked about it? One of her brothers or the oldest brother's wife, no telling what tales *she* had to tell about Cecelia. Maybe one of the nuns at the asylum told. We'll probably never know."

Everybody is real quiet and then Kev asks him where did he think those teeth marks on Cecelia's body came from? Old Man Hobart points a finger at Kev as if to keep him in his seat while he answers the question.

"Kevin Lingle, there's a lot of things in this world that don't make sense when you look at them logically. Most people are afraid of saying that they believe in ghosts because once they say it, they're admitting that there's a supernatural force outside their control and they don't like that idea. Some people only want to believe in good supernatural beings, like angels because that's nice and safe. Now me, I'm an old man and I'm afraid, just like anybody else, of what can be said to be evil things in this world—I'd be a damned fool not to be. I don't want to believe, no sir!

"But I tell you, I've heard stories that terrified my dreams. Heard old rumors of haunted tunnels that were dug under the town itself that made me afraid to go out at night when I was a kid. I've passed by places where I quicken my steps because I felt a presence that scared the shit out of me. That's called instinct or a sixth sense, every animal has it. And we're damn fools if we don't heed that sixth sense!"

He looks at Jonesey, but he's staring down at his hands. He looks really upset about something.

"Now, those teeth marks on that poor little girl? Something terrified that child so that she never spoke another word her entire life. And that part about the marks being made by something dead? Why would Uncle Pete's Great-Grand-Daddy say a thing like that if he didn't believe it was true? He was a man of science, from all accounts, and science deals in fact. Legends and myths about different cultures, he dismissed them all during his long career except one, the story he heard in England. He wrote a couple books about legends, published 'em in the early 1900's. All his stuff was academic, put out by the university press where he taught I guess. But he wrote one other book before he died, too. Used a *nom de plume*, a pen name, for that last one. You know how these professor types are."

He winks at my Grand-Dad who smiles and walks over to get a doughnut.

"He was an anthropology professor, hmmm. If he had his work published by a university press, it shouldn't be too hard to locate, nom de plume or not. If you remember that name, I'll be happy to see what I can find out."

"Bathclift or Bathclif, I believe it was," says Old Man Hobart.

My Grand-Dad turns suddenly with a surprised look and bumps into Jonesey who's putting on a fresh pot of coffee making him almost drop the pot.

"You okay, Will?" asks Old Man Hobart looking at my Grand-Dad.

"Yes, I'm fine. Just haven't been sleeping well lately. The heat and all."

I get up to go pee. As I'm coming out of the bathroom I hear Hobart say to my Grand-Dad, "I read a few of his books, Will, that ancestor of mine. All of 'em were on the legends of different peoples. Too scholarly for my tastes. Read 'em because I was a bit proud to have an author in my family, but I never found any other book he wrote. Always wondered if that last one he wrote, the one with the nom de plume, was about the cannibalism in that English dungeon."

Old Man Hobart downs his last cup of coffee and says he has to stretch his old legs a bit and take a walk up and down the block. He tells Jonesey to watch the store.

"Will, while you're checking out that name I gave you, can you find out if there are any other books on legends and such from around here? From quiet old Bridge Crossing?"

My Grand-Dad nods yes.

"Good. Maybe the story of Cecelia is somehow connected to a legend or some other strange happening here," says Old Man Hobart limping more and more as he walks us to the front of the store. "Maybe there were stranger things that went on here than we know."

Professor Will Hopper looks at Old Man Hobart for a few seconds then responds,

"Let's hope not."

chapter

15

A s soon as we start walking towards home I decide to ask my grandfather about the book he won't let me see.

"Hey, Grand-Dad? What's in that old book, that Andersonville book, that you say is too disturbing for young minds? What's so bad about it?"

"Yeah, like wow, Mr. Hopper, does it have sex and all that kinda gross stuff?"

My Grand-Dad looks at Kevin and then begins to laugh. He laughs until he has to lean against a tree to catch his breath and wipe his eyes.

"Oh, Kevin, Kevin, you are truly a gem!" He laughs again. "If only there was something as innocent as sex in it!"

We stand there waiting for his laughing fit to stop. Then I ask him why he won't even let me *see* the book. "Is it a horror story, 'cause if it is I've read *those* kind before. I've read all kinds of scary stuff so no big deal."

He turns all serious. "Boys this book is *truly* a book of horrors, but not like a horror book with monsters that you know are only some writer's imagination. Scary as those are, we know they're not really true. No, this book details the horrible, inhumane acts done *by* humanity *to* humanity. War crimes, cruel and unusual punishments meted out, for no other reason than that one person had the so-called authority over others less fortunate.

Horrific acts of cruelty that resulted in unbearable hardship and torture. The monsters in *this* book were real people. Andersonville actually existed."

"But if the book is so bad why are you keeping it, and why did Old Man…, I mean, Mr. Hobart want to read it with you? Does he like stuff like that? Like is he a weirdo or something?"

He smiles a bit at me asking if Mr. Hobart is a weirdo. "No weirder than any other man I know. He's looking for some information and he had me order the book last month. It's about the Civil War and, since that era of American history is my teaching specialty, he thought we could discuss what he's looking for."

"But don't you already know everything about the Civil War and stuff, Mr. Hopper? What's so different about this book."

"Kevin, no one knows *everything* about any one topic. You discover new information all the time. This book is shocking to me because it details how sadistic"—he stops and explains the word sadistic to Kev—"how sadistic a few prisoner-of-war camp wardens acted during the Civil War. I strongly feel you and Chris should not read it. It would give you nightmares and they would be the worst kind of nightmares because what you read isn't imagination at all, it is absolutely true, it actually happened."

We keep walking until we get to the Dairy Barn and we stop for some fresh-squeezed lemonade. The real estate guy who was at Old Man Hobart's is there with the banker having lunch. He nods at my Grand-Dad who nods back.

After we pay for the lemonade, we start walking home. We're about a block from home when Kev, who's been really quiet, slurps up the last of his drink.

"Mr. Hopper?"

"Yes, Kevin?"

"Do ghosts have teeth?"

* * *

"I don't understand it. About the teeth marks on that little girl, I mean. How could somethin' dead make teeth marks? So I'm thinkin' if what bit that little girl Cecelia were a bunch of ghosts, well, *do* they have teeth?"

I don't think my Grand-Dad knows how to answer Kev because he doesn't say anything at first, like he's thinking it over. Then he says with a laugh, "Kevin, that is a question to which I have no answer. I don't think I've ever really thought about the idea of ghosts having teeth."

Kev asks me if *I* think a ghost can have teeth and I tell him he's nuts.

"Jeez, Chris, didn't Old Man Hobart just tell us that the marks on that crazy girl were made by dead things? So, isn't a ghost a dead thing or what? That's why I want to know if ghosts have teeth!"

"To my knowledge, Kevin, I'd have to say no, but then my knowledge of ectoplasmic beings is somewhat limited."

"There you go again, Mr. Hopper, with those words! What the heck is an echoplastic being anyway?"

"It's ec-*to*-plas-*mic*, you doof," I say nudging him with my shoulder, "and it means ghosts! Don't you know anything?" Man I don't understand how somebody doesn't know words. It drives me crazy!

"Well not everyone is a brain when it comes to words, you know, Chris. If it means ghosts then just say ghosts. Jeez! You're the type of guy who, if you met a ghost, you'd say, hi, Mr. Echo-plastic-guy, open your mouth and show me your teeth.'"

We start mock shoving each other and showing our teeth in big, stupid grins. We're best friends and we never get mad at each other, even when we think the other one is a dumb-ass.

My Grand-Dad is smiling at us and the day's getting hot. He says that if we finish lunch early, he'll drive us over to the pool.

"As long as you promise not to bite anyone, Kevin," he jokes.

Kev says no problem as long as my Grand-Dad promises to find out if those 'echoplastic things' have teeth.

I feel really good as we're turning onto the block before my grandparents' house. I'm with my two favorite guys in the whole world. What can go wrong in my world?

chapter

16

All-in-all my day has been pretty near perfect. Hanging with Old Man Hobart and Jonesey and listening to that weird Cecelia story. Talking with my Grand-Dad and drinking lemonade. Busting on Kev for the way he says words. Going to the town pool and finding no Sarlewskis there. Perfect.

We spent two hours swimming and doing cannonballs at the deep-end of the pool and after that we stuffed ourselves with cheeseburgers and cokes. Then we had a big burping contest to see who could make it the loudest and longest. Kev won with his third burp. It was so loud and long that some woman told him he was "just disgusting" and that he should have better manners than that. That's when we *knew* who had the prize-winning burp.

Like I said, a perfect day.

When we come home from the pool, Kev goes upstairs to give Louie-Louie a snack and I take Kirby out back.

"Hey, Kirby, hey Kirbles, good dog!" I'm ruffling his fur while I'm sitting and waiting for Kev so we can go to the ball field. It's still early so we figure we can bike over, hit some balls and be back before supper. It's nice out except for that funny smell leftover from the other night.

"Hey, Chris? Wanna take Kirbs for a walk instead of bikin'? I gotta get more food for Louie-Louie at my house. We can hit some balls in my yard."

Kev is coming down the stairs with his catcher's mitt and his brother's old bat. "I asked your Grand-Dad and he says it's okay."

Kirby loves running after balls. He loves it more than playing fetch. I've never taken him to the field—I don't want him running near The Plot, no way!—but we've played ball in the yard and at Kev's house.

"I guess. Let me get his leash otherwise no squirrel in the neighborhood will be safe."

When Kirby sees me get his leash and my baseball stuff, he starts running around in circles. Crazy Kirbs! My Grand-Dad calls him Mr. Pinstripes 'cause he always says if Kirby was human he would probably be a great infielder for the Yankees.

We don't talk much while we're walking. Kirby is a pretty good walker and doesn't pull but he seems to stop at just about every tree and bush along the way. Funny thing is, he doesn't always pee.

"He's doin' the phantom pee," says Kev when Kirby stops for like the one-hundredth time. That makes me laugh and we start talking about people we know who might do a phantom pee. We come up with the names of teachers, the old guys at the pool, and even Old Man Hobart.

After I mention Old Man Hobart we both become quiet. I know I'm thinking about that story about that girl Cecelia, and what happened to her. Kev asks me if I believed that stuff about the teeth marks and dead things and Hobart's Great-Uncle Pete.

"I mean, do you think his uncle made it up, Chris? You think he said those things because he was crazy? Remember that lady who lived over by the bakery? 'Member how we were kinda scared of her and thought she was a witch? She was always saying weird things, telling people she was from another world and stuff. Once, when Brad skate-boarded too close to her lawn she told him, if he ever came near her property again, she would kill him just by looking at him."

"Yeah, but I think she just said those things to make us kids leave her alone. I saw her talking with my grandmother once and she was real normal. She even smiled at me! But Old Man Hobart's uncle? I don't know. I guess he could've been crazy."

I say that to Kev so he doesn't worry too much but I don't believe Old Man Hobart's uncle was crazy. I think crazy old Uncle Pete wasn't as crazy as the doctor and Old Man Hobart's father thought he was. Once my Grand-Dad told me that when people don't understand someone they're likely to say that person is nuts. He told me it was human nature to rationalize what you think is strange or different by labeling it crazy. Your mind has to make sense of stuff or you'd be worried all the time.

Nobody's home at the Lingle house so Kev takes the key from under a special fake rock in his mother's garden and opens the door. I think everybody in Bridge Crossing has a spare key hidden under a fake rock in their yard. I guess there's either nothing to steal in our houses or there are no real thieves in the town.

It's gotten hotter outside but it's cool inside the house. Kirby goes to lay down by the screen door where there's a just a hint of a breeze. Kev doesn't close the outside door, just clicks the lock on the screen which I always think doesn't make a whole lot of sense. We're so trusting here in Bridge Crossing but, seriously, if someone wanted to get into a house through a locked screen door, all they would have to have with them is something to cut the screen.

"It's too hot to play ball. I don't think Kirby should be running around," I tell Kev.

"Yeah. That's okay. I'm pooped. Wannna grab some comic books? I've got the newest Batman!"

So we decide that we'll read the comics, have some lemonade, and when Mrs. Lingle comes home she can drive us back to my grandparents' house. We feel beat from the whole long, perfect day.

Kev's pouring glasses of lemonade and getting two bags of chips. He puts them on the kitchen table, fills a bowl with ice cubes and water for Kirby and then sits down across from me.

"What do you think was so bad in that book, Chris? The one Old Man Hobart had your Grand-Dad order for him. I mean if it was a horror story, you know, me and you have seen really gross ones in the movies. So what exactly did he mean about it bein' too scary for us and stuff?"

I think about it for a minute. "Yeah, Kev, me and you have seen some really scary movies and I've read some totally cool horror stories but, like my Grand-Dad said, it's not the kind of horror stories we're used to seeing or reading about. He said it has to do with people being mean and cruel to other people. Real life horrible stuff. I guess he figures we'd have nightmares. But I'd still like to read it. How bad can it be, do you think?"

"I don't know, Chris, but, remember when we saw that zombie movie, *The Cursed Island* and the guy zombie did whatever his master told him to do? It scared me so much I was afraid to get up and go to the bathroom at night for a whole week!"

"But, see, that's what my Grand-Dad meant. The stuff in that movie isn't really real, there aren't any real zombies anyway. But the stuff in that book *is* real."

Kev is munching on his chips and he starts shaking his head at me. "No zombies?! There *are* too zombies. They come from that weird island, Tahate-i or somethin', you know which one. And they're as real as you and me. Honest!"

"The island is *Haiti* and there *are* no real zombies! It was a movie from someone's imagination. They made it up, Kev!"

"I don't know about that. There's this other movie that me and Jeremy watched really late one night. It was something that Jeremy called a cult classic and it was scary as hell."

I plug up my ears with my fingers and cross my eyes, like duh!

"No kiddin', Chris! Listen! The name of this movie was *The Night of the Living Dead* and it had these zombies called flesh-eaters and they wanted to eat real live human people and—"

I look at Kev who's going on and on about the movie but suddenly I don't hear him after he says the word flesh-eaters.

"Wait, Kev, stop."

"C'mon, Chris! You're not listenin'."

"No, no, I am. That part you said about flesh-eaters, what did you mean by that?"

"Huh?! What do you *think* I mean? You're supposed to be the word person. You don't know what flesh-eater means?!"

"No, yeah, I *do know* what it *means*. But I don't know about the movie. I never saw it."

Kev describes the movie which he says was in that 'old color' black and white and it sounds like a typical horror movie. The only thing different is that these dead people start coming out of their graves and have this crazy urge to eat live people.

"I wish I could see that movie," I say.

"You can! Jeremy copied it from Chiller Theatre, that spooky show that's on real late on Friday nights. Wanna watch it tonight? *Then* you'll believe in zombies. I can guarantee that, boy!"

We're finishing up the chips and lemonade when I hear Kirby let out a small, snuffled bark and see him wag his tail.

"Well, hello, Chris and son number two! What have you boys been up to?" Mrs. Lingle is at the screen door with a bag of groceries.

"Hi, Mrs. Lingle." I get up to open the door and take the bag in for her. She bends down to pet Kirby and tells Kev to get a breadstick for him.

"A breadstick won't hurt him," she says. "Just don't ever give him candy bars like Kev gives to Louie-Louie." She gives a joking frown to Kev and smiles at me.

Kev tells his Mom we were getting food for Louie-Louie and were going to play ball but it got too hot. He asks her for a ride back to my Grand-Dad's.

"Sure, let me put this stuff away and I'll be happy to drive you boys and Kirby."

While she's doing that we go up to the room Kev shares with his brother. Kev's side of the room is a major pigsty except where he keeps Louie-Louie's stuff. His clothes and games and about a million Batman comic books are all over the place, but his brother's side is clean and neat. Jeremy's bed is even made.

"Boy, Kev, doesn't Jeremy ever complain about the way your side of the room is such a mess?"

"Naw, we have a deal. He doesn't say anything about my side of the room and I don't tell my parents about the time I found him and one of his girlfriends in here."

"Were they *doin'* stuff?" I wish I had an older brother!

"I think they were about to, but I walked in. I was supposed to be at the orthodontist but I forgot my retainer and had to come home to get it. Boy, were they surprised! The girl actually screamed and called me a sneaky little shit! It was great!"

We get Louie-Louie's food first and then Kev digs through Jeremy's dresser looking for that zombie tape.

"Got it!" Kev holds up a box. "Let's go."

He turns and grins at me and says, "Zombie heaven here we come."

chapter

17

Mrs. Lingle does two things on the way to my Grand-Dad's— she drives and talks at the same time and does both of them pretty much just as fast. She is asking Kev if he's being good, causing any trouble, needs anything else from home, how's Louie-Louie, and what's Kev eating. Then she asks me how my Grand-Dad is, what have I heard from my parents and my Grand-Mom, how does Kirby like sharing a room with Louie-Louie, and if I noticed that Kev snores. Listening to her I know why Kev talks as fast as he does.

I tell her that my Grand-Dad is good, my mom and dad call once a week, that my Grand-Mom calls almost every other night, and that yes, I did notice that Kev snores. I told her Kirby sleeps in my grandparents' room but that he's seems okay when he's been in my bedroom with Louie-Louie. Whew!

I'm happy as anything when she drops us off at the house. Kirby jumps out as soon as I open the door. I guess he's happy to be away from all that non-stop yakking too.

My Grand-Dad comes outside as she's driving off and waves at her.

"Did you ask Mrs. Lingle if she'd like to come inside, Chris? Perhaps she'd have liked some iced tea."

I tell him, yeah, I did ask her, but that she said she couldn't 'cause she had things to do. I don't tell him that Kev told me *not* to ask his mother to come in because, as he put it, "She'll stay here for *hours* just talkin' and we'll never get to watch that movie! Anyway, it's almost time for me to feed Louie-Louie."

"Yeah, Kirby is probably hungry too. I'll see you outside in ten minutes, okay?"

"Make it twenty. Louie-Louie likes company when he eats."

Boy, does he love that rat!

While Kev is upstairs with Louie-Louie, my Grand-Dad takes me into the living room and asks me to sit down.

"Christopher, when your mom calls tonight, there's no reason to tell her or your dad about any of the things we've been talking about or heard at Hobart's store. It would only worry them and they've got some important things of their own to think through. The same goes for your grandmother. She's busy in New York City and that's where I want her to be right now. If the time comes when I think your parents and your Grand-Mom should know, I'll call them. For now, let your mom and dad just relax without having to worry about Bridge Crossing. All right?"

"Yes, sir. I won't say anything."

Relax without worrying about Bridge Crossing? Boy, maybe I should've gone to Hawai'i too!

Later, my Grand-Dad starts up the barbecue and me and Kev go inside to get the burgers. They're defrosting in the sink and I get a weird feeling looking at them all bloody and raw. I bring them outside and Kev brings out the buns and the ears of corn.

I watch the smoke from the barbecue rise towards the eerie yellow sky and hear a distant sound of thunder. I can't wait to watch that zombie movie tonight. I don't believe in zombies but the flesh-eater thing—now that's something else.

* * *

It's after nine-thirty and more than half a baseball game is over. I tell my Grand-Dad we're going upstairs to watch some zombie movie Kev brought from home.

"Is it that movie about some island with zombies running rampant? I remember seeing that quite some time ago. It's a little silly but it's fun."

A batter hits a high fly ball to center and my Grand-Dad's attention goes back to the game.

"Enjoy the movie" he says, eyes on the screen. "Want any popcorn or chips?" We mutter a quick, "no that's okay", and run up to my room. Kev pops the video in the VHS and we pile pillows on the floor to sit and watch.

This movie is nothing like *The Cursed Island*. That movie was just a bunch of actors doing cheap imitations of a Frankenstein monster. They walked all stiff and stuff and made moaning sounds and kept saying 'yes master, gombo, gombo' and stealing whatever their dumb-ass master told them to steal. It was a really stupid movie no matter how scared Kev says it made him. They didn't kill anybody—they just threw people into walls or the ocean. The people always got up to go after the zombies again. It was pretty lame.

But this movie is different. These zombies really eat people. They're like cannibals, they crave live human flesh. And the weird thing is that the live people, instead of getting together to kill the zombies start turning on each other. This old guy practically throws his own wife and daughter at the zombies just so they won't eat *him*! It turns out okay though because this other girl, who's got some type of shiny gold good luck charm that protects her from everything, shoots the old guy in the head and the zombies turn away from his wife and daughter and begin to eat his brains.

When Kev stops the movie to go pee I'm alone in the room. It's so quiet and I've still got flesh-eating zombies on my mind when a sound on the window pane makes me almost jump a mile. I go check out the window. But it's not zombies, its just some old tree branches scratching the screen.

I hear the toilet flush and Kev comes back in the room. "What do ya think Chris, scary huh?"

I tell him that I have to admit it's a lot scarier than the other zombie movie we saw.

We settle back to watch the rest of it and Kev says to just keep watching, the creepiest part is coming up soon. When I see a zombie chomping on some person's leg, I can't help but think about Cecelia, that poor little kid who had human teeth marks all over her body. Is it possible there might be zombies on Dansbury Plot? Nah, I think. It had to be an animal no matter what anybody said. It had to be. I mean, zombies?! In Bridge Crossing?

After the movie me and Kev talk about our favorite parts and the idea of real zombies existing. Neither one of us talks about what's really on our minds. That little girl Cecelia. Finally, though, because he sometimes says things without really thinking, Kev says that he thinks zombies chewed on Cecelia and that made her crazy.

"It's the fear, she went crazy with fear and stuff. If somethin' dead chewed on me, I'd end up in the nut house too!"

I think about that for a long while. We sit talking until my Grand-Dad comes upstairs. Kev tells him about the movie and my Grand-Dad surprises me by saying, "Oh that movie is a good study of human character. Who would save only themselves, who would try to be a hero and save others, who would sacrifice someone they loved just so they *could* save themselves.

Humanity is strange. No one person acts the same in terrible situations. It brings out the best and, unfortunately, the worst in humankind."

"But Mr. Hopper, the movie is all about real, alive people getting chewed on by zombies."

"Kevin, as I said this movie's plot is a wonderful study of human character but I really don't believe in zombies. Very sick, severely disturbed people capable of unbelievable cruelty, that I do believe exists. But not zombies."

Kev looks so disappointed that my Grand-Dad smiles at him and ruffles his hair. "But then again, Kevin, I could be wrong. It's only my opinion. Anthropologists, those scientists who study all aspects of humans in past and present societies, are finding new members of humanoid groups all the time. Maybe they'll find that zombies may have really existed, who knows?" He looks at his watch. "I know it's after 12:00 but I have an urge to have one of those double chocolate Klondike bars that are just sitting in the freezer and calling my name. You boys want to join me?"

"Hell, yeah!" yells Kev before he realizes what he just said. "Sorry Mr. H I meant—"

"That's okay Kevin. Hell yeah seems a very appropriate response to being asked to eat ice cream after Midnight. So, hell yeah, let's go get those Klondike bars!"

Me and Kev run down the stairs yelling, "Hell yeah!" at the top of our lungs with my Grand-Dad laughing as he follows us down.

He is the absolute best grandfather in the whole world!

chapter

18

It's been a week since we heard that Cecelia story down at Old Man Hobart's and most days we're not really hardly thinking about that story. Not a whole lot anyway. We're just enjoying the summer. I mean we talked about it but kinda put it in the back of our minds. We're just busy doing summer stuff like swimming and bike riding.

Today me and Kev are walking back to the house from a great day at the pool. Billy Sarlewski was there but so was Kev's brother Jeremy with a couple of his buddies. Billy knew enough not to mess with us when Kev's brother was around. So Billy stayed down at the shallow end of the pool near his sister Ellen and her girlfriend who were reading teen magazines and making sure they got even tans by turning themselves over every fifteen minutes. Seriously, they had a timer and everything. Wacko.

Me and Kev swam around, played a couple of games on the rusty old pinball machine near the food court, and stuffed ourselves with cheeseburgers and fries from the refreshment stand. All in all, a perfect day for a kid.

So we're walking back to my grandparents' house when we notice flyers taped to trees and telephone poles. There're like hundreds of them. Kev drops his gym bag and grabs one of the flyers. His eyes grow huge as he reads.

"Holy crap, Chris! Look at this!"

I drop my bag next to Kev's and lean over his shoulder to read it.

Townspeople of Bridge Crossing:

Would YOU like lower property taxes? Would YOU like to see the value of your property up-graded? Are YOU wondering how this can this be accomplished? Here's how:

Revenue from a proposed new shopping mini-mall in Bridge Crossing will put money in the town's coffers and at the same time help to lower your taxes while enhancing your own property. Many towns in our state have successfully done this and we need to do it too. Your investment in this mini-mall is a necessary step toward a prosperous future.

We are living the way we did a century ago and the Township of Bridge Crossing needs your help to come into the modern age. A meeting will be held on the town Little League fields on Saturday, July 4, at 6:30 PM to address how all the above can be accomplished.

Refreshments served courtesy of Mrs. S's Simply Sensational Cookies.

Free beer courtesy of Mark Colbert and the Tuckman Real Estate Agency.

"Wow, Chris, this flyer has got to be from Mr. Sarlewski and that real estate guy. That meeting is like in," Kev counts on his fingers, "six days! He's doin' it on the Fourth of July when the whole town is out celebratin' and stuff! The streets are all closed off and there're tents with all that food and those games. And that hotdog eatin' contest! Brad said he was gonna enter it. Sarlewski has a lot of nerve havin' his stupid meetin' on the Fourth!"

I re-read the flyer. "Yeah, that lousy Mr. Sarlewski. I guess he thinks that Mrs. Sarlewski's cookies will make a lot of people come to the meeting. And the beer too. People will come just for the beer. That's why he underlined that part about the refreshments. What a cheap trick to get people to come and hear his crap."

"That creepy creep. Havin' a meetin' on the ball fields right across from The Plot 'cause he wants to build stores and stuff on The Plot. On *The Plot!* Old Man Hobart is gonna have a cow when he hears about this. He's goin' nutsy-cuckoo over it already."

Kev looks at the flyer again before folding it up and putting it in his pocket. "Yeah, it is a cheap trick. But, you know somethin' though, Chris? I mean I know we both hate Billy and stuff but you gotta admit that his mom really *does* make sensational cookies. I mean, like those chocolate macadamia nut ones you like and those peanut butter almond cookies." Kev sighs and says, "Oh man, I wish I had two of those peanut butter almond ones right now! I'm sorry about sayin' that—but, Chris? She does make the best cookies in the whole universe. Boy!"

I nod my head. I have to agree with Kev. They are really sensational all right. Mrs. Sarlewski sure knows how to bake cookies. But, like I said, after what Billy did to me at The Plot, I promised myself, and swore to all my friends, that I would never eat another one of *Mrs. S's Simply Sensational Cookies* again.

I sigh.

Sometimes I make really dumb promises.

We pick up our bags and start heading to the house. On the way, we make a deal—we'll grab all the flyers we see on the way and stuff them inside our bags. The less people who see the flyers and don't know about Sarlewski's meeting, the better.

Building stuff on The Plot.

Holy crap!

Old Man Hobart *is* gonna have a cow over this!

* * *

Nobody's home when we get back to the house, just Kirby and of course Louie-Louie. My Grand-Dad left a note telling us he went back to the *The Willin' Cate* 'cause something he ordered just got delivered. He said he'd be home around 6:00 PM and that he's bringing us dinner from this Cuban place that he likes. I hope he brings us empanadas. Me and Kev are totally nuts for empanadas, especially the beef and potato ones.

Kev tells me he has to take a pee. I tell him thanks for sharing the news flash. I'm being sarcastic but Kev just says, "You're welcome." Jeez!

"I'm gonna go check on Louie-Louie too and let him know I'm here. He gets lonely, you know. I just have to let him know I'm here so's he doesn't feel alone."

I guess rats can get lonely when nobody's home so I nod and tell him to leave the bedroom door open so Louie-Louie can hear us and feel like he's got company and I'll close the pet gate to the kitchen so good ol' Kirbs can't go upstairs.

I take Kirby out the back door and into the yard where he immediately tramples my Grand-Mom's hyacinths. I call him back to me but he's busy sniffing around and having a good old time peeing on the rose bushes. I feel a couple of raindrops and I look up at the sky.

It's getting cloudy—really big dark clouds that make it almost look like it's night time.

"Kirbs! C'mon, boy. Hurry up. C'mon, Kirby!"

There's a hot wind kicking up too. Probably going to get one of those summer storms tonight. It's still June and we're only out of school for one whole week so it's kinda funny that we're having all these storms *now* so early in the summer. I mean we *always* have thunderstorms but they usually don't begin until the *middle* of summer and there's always rain with the storms. This year they're starting really early but without any rain at all.

"Kirby!"

Where did he go?

"Kirby, Kirby, c'mon boy. Let's go."

I can't see him even though the yard isn't all that big. He probably went behind the shed where my Grand-Dad keeps the lawn mower and other stuff. Probably digging in the dirt back there and making a mess. I hear the sound of thunder and it sounds pretty close. The rain could start at any second now.

I should go get Kirby. I mean, I *should* get him before he gets his paws all caked with dirt from digging and stuff. I can't bring him back into the house like that. I *have* to go get him.

But for some reason I don't *want* to go back there. It's so dark back there—darker even than where I'm standing on the deck. The thunder sounds even closer now. A streak of lightning shows suddenly in one of the dark clouds and I know I have to get Kirby inside before it really starts to pour and he gets wet and muddy—but I can't seem to move. Crap! I gotta go get Kirby!

"Kirby, Kirby! C'mon, *c'mon!*"

There seem to be shadows moving by the edge of the shed, shadows caused by the darkening clouds which hang really low. The back yard I love, the place where I've played catch with Kev and my Grand-Dad and Frisbee with Kirby, the yard where I've had the best barbecues ever, now is a place that has me scared crazy.

"Kirby! Kirby come back here now!"

I force myself to move toward where Kirby went behind the shed. My legs feel like they're heavy weights. I finally make it to the front of the shed door. From behind the shed I see dark shadows and I hear Kirby give a low growl. I want to go get him but when I look at those shadows—I swear there's something moving in those shadows!

"Kirbs? Come here Kirbs, let's go inside. C'mon Kirby, *please* come to me!"

The thunder suddenly cracks overhead at the same time that lightning splits the clouds. The palm of my pitching hand itches like crazy. It's still kinda raw. My heart almost stops and I let out a loud scream when I feel something grab my shoulder. Something's got me, something's gonna eat my pitching hand! I can't breathe!

"Chris? Hey, Chris, didn't you hear the phone ring? Jeez! I had to run all the way downstairs to answer it. You guys should get one upstairs like we have at my house."

I turn slowly—very slowly—around. Kev is standing behind me, holding the phone receiver in his hand. "Anyhow, it's your Grand-Dad. He wants to know if we want potato chips or fries with the empanadas."

I'm so relieved to see Kev. My legs give way and I stumble a little. Jeez! I feel like I'm gonna puke. Bending over I actually do spit up hot liquid from my gut.

"Chris? Fries or chips? C'mon, I'm starvin'!"

I take a deep breath and tell him whatever he wants is okay with me.

"Yeah? All right!"

Kev tell my Grand-Dad that we'll have both fries and chips and to make them the jumbo size. I start to laugh at the thought that all's right with the world for Kev as long as food is around. I laugh so hard that I almost begin to cry and end up hiccupping like crazy.

"It looks like it's gonna pour any second now, Chris. It's so dark that I put a light on for Louie-Louie. Hey! Where's Kirby?"

I point to behind the shed and, before I can stop him, Kev goes back there to get him. I hold my breath in case I hear a scream coming from Kev but within a couple of seconds, Kirby comes running up to where I am and begins to lick my face just as the clouds get so thick they make the day turn into the dead of night. Kev hurries after him.

"Jeez, Chris. Let's go inside. It's gonna rain like hell! These are my brand-new Batman sneakers. I just got them. My mom will kill me if they get ruined!"

I look at the images of Batman and the words 'pow!' and 'bam!' on Kev's sneakers and nod. They must've cost a lot so I can see Mrs. Lingle going nutsy if Kev ruins them. But I've got more to worry about than his sneakers.

Inside the kitchen, I stand with Kirby and look back at the shed. The darkness makes it hard to see anything. But I know there was something in those shadows—I just know it. Kirbs knows it too. His fur is standing up again and he's just staring outside.

"What a day, huh Chris?" says Kev opening up two bottles of soda. "The flyers, a thunder and lightnin' storm without any rain. Wow! Wacko unreal!"

Boy, he might totally screw up most words but Kev is right on target with the words he just said.

Wacko unreal is right.

chapter

19

There's something about food when you're a kid that sorta makes things all right, even when you've been scared enough to almost pee your pants. The empanadas, hot fries, and chips made me feel a lot better. That warm feeling that food gives you, boy! Yeah, food really helps a lot.

But I guess that food can't solve everything because when my Grand-Dad asked me to take Kirby outside to do his business, I put a leash on him and took him out the front door instead of just letting him loose out into the backyard like I always do. I don't want to go out in the back with him just yet. Not yet.

I look up at the sky. Not one cloud now, just that hot wind again and that funny smell. God, I wish it would pour, just rain and rain to get rid of this heat. This hot wind is spooky.

After dinner Kev convinces me to ride our bikes over to Sal Minella's house. There's a sinkhole in his backyard that just appeared overnight. Sal says it's like having the Grand Canyon in your backyard. He called and told us to come as soon as we can 'cause some engineers are going to check it out tomorrow afternoon. They're going to see if the foundation of the Minella house is solid and not in any danger of sliding into the hole. His mother says maybe the hole can be filled in with cement. Sal's whole family is going to stay at his aunt and uncle's house until his parents find out from those engineers if it's okay and safe to live in their own house. He also added that Billy Sarlewski came over earlier and spit into the hole.

Kev said that we'd be nuts to miss seeing the hole. "I mean a big hole right in your own backyard?! Sal's so lucky. And you know that creep Sarlewski will brag about seein' it. We can't let him one up us. We *gotta* go see it."

I kinda didn't want to leave the house after what I thought I saw during the thunderstorm with those shadows moving and everything. Then, too, getting to Sal's house is going to be a problem especially if Kev wants to get there really fast. The shortest route goes past The Plot.

But Kev kept bugging me about how we shouldn't miss going to see the 'ginormous' hole in the Minella's back yard. "C'mon, Chris! It'll be great. We can take pictures of it—I brought my camera with me, mostly so's I can take pictures of Louie-Louie on vacation here. I mean it is a vacation for him. He really never goes anywhere. Your grandparents' house is a vacation spot for him."

I roll my eyes when he says that but I don't say anything. I have to remember that Kev and Louie-Louie have a bond like Jonesey said. Kev saved his life.

"And we can take turns yellin' down the hole to see if an echo comes back. That echo thing is really cool. I saw some guys do that on some docu-somethin' about the Grand Canyon. C'mon Chris! Please? *Pul-eeze?*"

"Okay. I'll ride over with you."

"Boy, you are the best, best, *bestest* friend ever! I'll be right down I gotta change Louie-Louie's straw. He likes it clean."

I called Sal and told him we'd be over around seven. I mean it isn't every day you get to see a giant hole in a friend's backyard.

While Kev changes Louie-Louie's straw bedding I go outside on the deck and look around. I'm still scared, a little anyway, but I make myself do it. The sun is out so it's not dark anymore. Right now, there's a cooler breeze blowing too instead of that hot wind from before when I took Kirby out into the front yard. The backyard doesn't seem so scary with the sun shining and I even make myself walk behind the shed to check it out.

All I see back there are a couple of flowerpots and some bags of mulch piled high under a black tarp. I jump a little when a breeze makes the loose ends of the tarp blow toward me. Maybe that's what I thought were shadows, maybe it was just the dark plastic of the tarp blowing in that wind, maybe the dark sky and the thunder and lightning made me imagine things.

Maybe.

I don't know.

Maybe.

There are two ways to get to Sal's house. The long way, which takes about forty minutes and goes through the center of Bridge Crossing—and the short way. If we take the short way, we can get there in fifteen minutes but—we have to pass The Plot. Sal lives across two streets away from The Plot. The Plot separates his house from the ball field. The streets are wide and everything so he's not exactly close to it but *I* wouldn't want to live there.

With the thunderstorm scaring the hell out of me today and the lightning storm that we saw over The Plot a few days ago, I really want to stay as far away from Dansbury Plot as I can. Even just the thought of *passing* it makes me feel a little creepy.

I think Kev figures that I don't want to pass near The Plot. I didn't tell him anything about this afternoon's storm and the shadows and all but for some reason I think he kinda suspects something happened.

My Grand-Dad went out to pick up dessert and left me and Kev still chowing down on the empanadas. Before he left, he looked at us and said that me and Kev should enter an empanada eating contest.

"You two boys love them so much I am positive you'd both win first place in a tie!"

I'm slowly chewing on a beef and potato empanada when all of a sudden, Kev nudges me hard and asks me why I'm not answering his question about Batman's butler.

"Chris! I asked you three times already about Bruce Wayne's butler-guy Alfred."

"Huh?" I turn to him and try to focus on what he's saying.

"Do you think Alfred's real name *really is* Alfred Thaddeus Crane Pennyworth? I mean in the *movies* that's his name but I never saw that in the *comic books* and I have almost all of them. So, is that long name his *real* name or is it just Alfred? What do you think Chris?"

I concentrate on his question. I like Batman but I never thought too much about Alfred his butler. He was just there when Bruce Wayne needed him. But I guess Alfred had to have a last name like everyone else.

"I don't think you can just name a kid Alfred with no last name. I think it's a law or something that a kid has to have a first and last name. Unless maybe you're an orphan but even then you couldn't just have a first name. So, yeah, I guess he would have that long name."

"Okay, but why isn't it in the comic books? Why just call him Alfred in the comic books? Did the movie make up a name? That's not really fair though, right? And anyway, why would they—"

"I don't know, Kev. I mean I really don't know. Why is that so important anyway? Who cares?"

Kev stops talking for a minute and looks at me. He knows that I know how important the whole Batman story is to him. Then he asks me if I'm okay. I tell him yeah, I'm okay. It's just the whole thing with The Plot—Mr. Sarlewski trying to get people to agree to build stuff on it, the lightning over The Plot—everything.

"All that stuff's been botherin' me too, Chris. Dansbury Plot. Boy, that place gives me nightmares sometimes. I don't think there's another place in the whole state that's as spooky as The Plot." He slurps his iced tea. "So, ya know what I think? I think that we'll take the long way to Sal's. I don't want to pass too near The Plot. I know we'll probably get back here before dark but still—nope, no way are we goin' near The Plot. Anyway, let's finish this food. I love empanadas!"

I think about what he just said. "Hey, Kev? How'd you know I didn't want to pass The Plot today?"

"Me? I can tell things about another guy. I'm psycho."

I laugh like crazy. Kev's word confusion can be hilarious sometimes. "You mean *psychic,* Kev. Psycho would mean you're nuts."

"Oh, yeah." He thinks about it for a second and then says, "Well, maybe I'm both!"

Both of us are laughing so hard we're practically falling off our chairs. I hear the front screen door open.

"Who's up for apple pie?" My Grand-Dad walks in holding a large box from Aromi di Napoli pastry shop.

"Boy, Mr. Hopper! How did you know apple pie is my favorite of all time?!" asks Kev.

"I don't know Kevin. Something made me think that you'd like it. Perhaps I'm psychic."

Me and Kev look at each other amazed and then we fall on the floor laughing like crazy.

chapter

20

My Grand-Dad said that he's seen sinkholes before. He says they're not all that common around here but he knows of two others that appeared about twenty years ago on the edge of the Township of Bridge Crossing. He says he's staying home.

"An old book I ordered last week was just delivered to the book shop today and I want to begin reading it. It's a small book so I may be able to finish it tonight. I'll be in the library room," he said.

He tells us to be careful and only look at the hole from the safety of the street. "Don't get close to it. Promise me that, both of you. *Do not* go near that sinkhole."

After me and Kev quickly promise we'll only look at it from the street, he tells us to make sure we get back before sunset. "I don't want you boys riding your bikes in the dark."

"Why not Grand-Dad? I've ridden my bike just after sundown. I mean sometimes the sun goes down while I'm still on my way home so I *have* to ride it in the dark. I've got a light on my bike. There's practically no traffic in this town anyway."

My Grand-Dad pauses before answering, almost as if he's thinking of a reason for us not to ride after dark.

"It is true that there's not a lot of traffic in this town but still you never know what teen with a brand-new license might just go speeding through Bridge Crossing."

I look at Kev and he nods solemnly. One of his brother's friends was stopped for speeding over by Old Man Hobart's store. It was dark and he was showing off for his friends but he almost mowed down one of the old guys who hang out at Hobart's. The cop who gave him the ticket told him next time he'd lose his license. Kev's brother Jeremy will get his license next month. Mr. Lingle told him that if he ever drives carelessly and takes any 'God- damn fool chances', he'd take his license away and make sure Jeremy didn't get it back until he was *forty years old*. I really believe that Mr. Lingle would do that too. I guess so did Jeremy because he promised he'd be a careful driver and not take any 'fool chances'. He left out the 'God damn' part because his mother was standing right there.

"I am asking you boys to do two things—stay a distance from that sinkhole and get back here before the sun goes down," repeats my Grand-Dad. "Understood?"

I don't really believe he wants us back before sundown because of the danger of some teen kid racing a car down the streets of Bridge Crossing. I don't know why but I think it's some other reason he wants us home before dark; I just do. I want to ask him, but Kev's in a hurry to get going and so we promise we'll do both and then run to get our bikes.

The ride over to see the hole in the backyard of our friend Sal Minella, aka Salmonella, is nice and easy. Just two kids riding their bikes on a lazy early summer evening. Hours of daylight left yet, heck we may even get a chance to play a quick game of catch with Sal.

There's a soft breeze blowing and the sky is clear now with no clouds anywhere. We don't talk much as we ride our bikes except to challenge each other to jump over the traffic bumps they have in the streets that are supposed to slow down cars and stuff. That's a load of crap because Kev told me that his brother's friends like to pop wheelies with their dirt bikes coming down certain 'bump' streets. Cars zoom over them too just for the fun of getting that jolt when they go over the raised tar that stretches across the middle of the street. Slow down? No way. Me and Kev jump them easily.

Summer, riding bikes with your best friend, and baseball. Nothing better.

There're a few neighbors standing in the street in front of Sal's house drinking beer and talking when we get there. It's kinda like a party or something. I mean, how often do you get to see a giant hole in someone's backyard?

People are talking about why the sinkhole just suddenly appeared overnight, what could possibly cause something like that to happen, and how the Minellas are real lucky that their backyard is so big and that their house is closer to the sidewalk. I guess that that distance kept the house safe from falling into the hole.

Sal comes over to us and tells us to park our bikes over by the front steps. After we do that we all go stand on the sidewalk. Mrs. Minella says a quick hello to us and then yells at Sal to make sure we stay in the front of the house.

"You boys stay here. I don't want anybody falling into that God-damn hole. You understand me Sal? I can't wait until it's filled in with cement."

What with having heard Mr. Lingle and the old guys down at Hobart's say certain choice words quite few times—their favorites being 'shit', the 'F' word and 'Godammit'—and now hearing Mrs. Minella say God-damn, I've decided that some adults seem to curse a lot when they want to make people understand something is important. It doesn't bother me. Like I said, me and Kev can curse pretty good too.

From what we can see of the yard, the hole *really is* ginormous! I guess I didn't know what to expect when Sal called to tell us to come over and see the hole in his backyard but I have to admit that this hole is big! Big enough for an in-ground swimming pool. Even from the street it looks deep. Boy, is Sal lucky!

Sal's all proud and stuff like he dug up the dirt and made the hole all by himself. He tells us he thinks there's a lot of junk down there—roots from old trees and lots of other junk. Could be treasure or something down there, he says, and, if there is, then he'd be rich.

"Treasure? Like gold or something right?" Kev's all excited and kinda jumping up and down. "Maybe like someone robbed gold and diamonds and stuff from a jewelry store a long, long time ago and maybe hid all the loot in the ground before there was anything built here. The ground covered the jewelry up but it's still there! But after a lotta years the guy could never come and get the treasure because your house was being built here and he couldn't ask you guys if he could dig the treasure up because he didn't want the police to know he was a thief!"

I shake my head. Kev's got the greatest imagination in the world, but like I said I think he watches *way* too much TV.

I look around and the grown-ups are all still drinking beer and talking. No one is paying any attention to us kids. Sal says not to mind what his mother said. He and his cousin got really close to the hole and nothing happened. "She's gabbing with her friends and she's not even gonna notice we're gone, trust me. We'll be back before she even knows that we're not here."

And then, even though we promised my Grand-Dad and told him we would only look at the sinkhole from a distance, me and Kev sneak into the backyard with Sal. We want to get as close to the hole as we possibly can without falling in.

I look down the hole for a few minutes and squint really hard trying to see anything that looks like treasure.

"*I* don't see anything that looks like treasure down there, just a lot of dirt and some stones and big rocks and all." I turn to Kev and Sal. "If there's anything there it's gotta be buried really deep."

Sal goes into his house to get his father's big work flashlight. When he comes out we shine the light down into the hole, going over the sides first and then smack down to the bottom. We do this for about fifteen minutes, taking turns holding the flashlight while the others tell whoever's holding it where to shine it. For a long time we don't see anything. Kev's got the flashlight and I'm looking really carefully as he shines it slowly over the sides and then the bottom of the hole. Nothing.

I take one more good look. This time I'm inching on my belly toward the ginormous hole while Sal holds my ankles. I ask Kev to give me the flashlight. As I reach over to take it from him I lean too far to my left and the loose dirt at the top of the hole shifts under my weight and I slide forward. Sal can't hold me and I do what Sal's mother warned him not to let us do—I fall forward right into the God-damn hole!

"Holy shit!" I hear Kev curse. He lays flat on his belly and reaches out his hands to me. But I'm already falling and I'm too far to reach them. My hands grab like crazy at some tree roots but they're too thin to hold my weight. Loose dirt falls in my face and I spit it out of my mouth. I dig in the side of the hole hard with my sneakers but they slide through the soft dirt scattering chunks of it off the sides. It's like being at the top of the big drop on a roller coaster—I can't stop going straight to the bottom.

Halfway down I get lucky. My left foot gets caught on something hidden by all the dirt, something that feels thick and solid like a big rock or thick tree root, and my body stops freefalling. I dig my hands into the dirt where I find more solid roots. I'm stuck but at least I'm not falling anymore. I look down and almost pass out. The bottom of this hole is a long way down

Kev's screaming my name and I see the flashlight shining on me. Sal must've gone to get his parents and the other people who were drinking beer in the front of his house because I hear adult voices calling to me, telling me to hang on, someone's getting a rope, don't move, whatever you do, don't move. Boy, they don't have to tell me twice to stay still. I'm not moving. I'm even afraid to take a deep breath. Please keep my foot wedged in here. Please don't let it get loose. I don't want to fall any farther down the hole.

"Hang on, son," yells someone. "We're coming. Just hang on."

Someone says to call the fire department. Another person says we don't have time, we have to act fast. "He could fall all the way to the bottom by the time the firemen get here. I'm getting a rope. We'll tie it to the back bumper of my truck."

I concentrate on staying as still as possible. My foot feels numb. Please,

please don't let the rock move. Please let me hold on really tight. I look at my right hand buried in the side of the dirt.

And then I see it.

Right next to where my right hand is dug deep into the dirt wall, holding on to a thick root like crazy.

Something shiny caught right in the middle of the glare from the flashlight.

I stare at it until my eyes blur. Maybe it's a good luck charm or something like that girl had in that zombie movie *Night of the Living Dead*. Like a sign telling me everything is gonna be okay.

I hope so.

chapter

21

Sal's father comes down on a rope to where I am. He's a big man who climbs telephone poles for a living. The rope slides down slowly, so slowly. There's a loop around his chest and under his armpits as he dangles just next to my right shoulder. In his hands is another rope with a smaller loop. He reaches out to grab me and some of the dirt gets loose and falls toward the bottom. He reaches out again but I can't seem to move.

I'm afraid to move. I'm frozen, just like I was last summer when I was going up the ladder to the high diving board. It's like my body is part of the dirt and I can't move away from it at all.

"Can you let go of the side of the wall, son? I got to loop this over your head and under your arms so the men at the top can haul you up with me."

Very, very slowly I slide my right hand out from the dirt where I've been hanging on for my life. Now comes the scary part—pulling my left hand out of the dirt wall so I'm not holding on to anything.

"C'mon, Chris! You can do it!" Kev is screaming from somewhere in Sal's yard. "You're braver than anybody I know, braver even than Batman! C'mon Chris! Make believe you've got the bat-rope."

I pull my left hand out of the dirt. Mr. Minella quickly places the loop around my chest and tries to pull me closer to him so the guys at the top can begin to pull us up. I feel a tug but I don't move. My foot is stuck by that rock.

"Okay, son. Looks like your foot might be caught in a tangle of roots. I've got hold of you so don't worry, you won't fall. Can you try to get your foot free? Wiggle it. See if it will come loose."

I try but whatever my foot is stuck on is something that won't let go. Mr. Minella sighs and says okay, then suddenly kicks my foot hard. A shower of dirt and small stones falls down the sides of the hole and my foot is free. I'm dangling on the rope around my chest over what looks like a bottomless pit. I feel like I'm going to pee my pants. I'm just swinging there with that big drop under me.

"Okay! Start up the truck and move forward real slow," yells Mr. Minella grabbing me and holding me real tight. "Pull us up!"

The rope begins to slide upward slowly and just as they're starting to pull us up, I see that shining stone that's still stuck in the wall of dirt. For some reason I grab that shiny something and stuff it into my pocket.

At the top of the hole, I'm grabbed quickly and moved away from where I fell. I'm practically dragged into the front yard. Mrs. Minella is crying and hugging me and yelling at Sal all at the same time.

Kev grabs me too almost knocking Sal's mother to the ground.

"I knew it! I knew that you were braver then Batman. I told ya! You're stronger than any zombie too. Like you pulled your hands right out of that old dirt! Really zombie-strong!"

Everyone is asking me if I'm okay and I'm nodding yes and just feeling embarrassed about what happened. Sal's dad, finally standing on solid ground again and covered in soft dirt, walks over to me and says that maybe I'd like some ice cream or something. It's like I'm a celebrity or I became someone famous just for being dumb enough to fall into a hole in the ground. I keep my head down and just mumble answers to questions.

Sal's mother makes us go sit on the curb across the street—she practically screams at Sal that she doesn't want us anywhere near the backyard again—and brings us each a chocolate almond bar.

I hear the rumble of thunder and see lightning flash in the distance. The hot wind is back. The chocolate ice cream melts in my hand dripping onto the ground.

It makes me think of blood dripping onto The Plot.

* * *

The sun is just starting to set when me and Kev start pedaling for home. I'm feeling sick from sipping some beer that Sal snuck over to me and Kev. He said that's what his dad does whenever he's had a hard day—drink a couple of beers. He said falling into a hole kinda qualifies as a bad day. I sipped it but I didn't really like it. I don't understand why anyone wants to drink beer. It just made me dizzy. Kev said the same thing.

We peddle fast and make it back to my grandparents' house just before dark. That shiny thing is in the pocket of my shorts. I'm going to show it to my Grand-Dad. Maybe it is gold or something. If it is I'll guess I'll have to give it back to Sal but, until I find out for sure, I'm keeping it.

"Mrs. Minella called."

My Grand-Dad is sitting on the front steps with Kirby, waiting for us. He looks tired and worried. Before we left Sal's house, me and Kev swore to each other that we wouldn't tell my Grand-Dad anything about me falling in the hole. I guess we hadn't counted on Sal's mother calling and telling him everything that happened. Mrs. Minella waited until me and Kev had left before she called because she probably wanted to make sure I had no broken bones or anything so she could truthfully tell my Grand-Dad that I was okay and on my way home.

He doesn't say anything else, just waits until we put our bikes down next to the house. Then he asks us to sit down next to him. I bury my face in Kirby's soft fur. Good ol' Kirbs. Must be great to be a dog and not have to worry about doing something stupid.

"Mrs. Minella called here and told me what happened."

I lower my head and snuggle deeper into Kirby's fur.

"So, I want to tell you that I'm not angry that you didn't listen to me and heed my warning. I'm not upset, just deeply concerned and disappointed that you broke your promise about something that could have turned out to have had a much more serious outcome than it did. I'm relieved and thankful that nothing more serious happened. That being said, my first and only question Chris is this—how are you? You feel all right?"

"Yes, sir. I'm okay. A little scraped up but I'm okay. I leaned over the hole too far and the dirt was too soft to hold me. I know you said that we should just look at it from the street but we really wanted to see it closer and Sal said it was okay. That *he* went to look at it with his cousin and they got close to it and nothing happened. Sal even said that Billy Sarlewski spit in it so he had to get close to it to do that, right? I didn't think I'd fall in, honest Grand-Dad. It was kinda a stupid accident."

He pats my back. "I should have gone with you. I blame myself for this. I'm just so grateful that you're all right." He sighs deeply. "Well, we all make mistakes, stupid or not, when we're young. Sometimes when we're old too. It's a way of showing us what we shouldn't do I guess. The main thing is that you're not injured." He messes up my hair. "Let's just resolve to be more careful in the future, Okay?"

"What's re—?"

"It means to make sure, Kevin. To make a decision to do something. In this case, to be careful, to think carefully before taking action."

"Oh, yeah, I get it Mr. Hopper. Like when Batman makes decisions about what to do to catch the bad guys, right? Like should he use the Batmobile or the Bat-copter. He has to resolve to use the right one. Stuff like that."

My Grand-Dad smiles. "That's right Kevin Lingle. Just like Batman. Think first, then act." He gets up and so does Kirby. "Let's forget about what happened, Chris, and chalk it up to a lesson well-learned. We'll all just relax and watch our favorite baseball team beat those Red Sox."

We go inside and get comfortable so we can watch a Yankees game. The game goes into extra innings but the Yanks win three to two over their rivals.

Guess their closing pitcher resolved to throw a great game.

* * *

It's just after Midnight when I get up to go pee. Kev is kinda talk-snoring in his sleep, completely out of it. Even asleep he's talking. I can't help but feel a little bit jealous—Kev's life is so uncomplicated. He can bite a kid in the stomach to save his best friend from being drowned, hear about horrible things that happened in the past, and still just sleep like a baby. Not much really bothers him. His whole world revolves around Batman comics, scary zombie movies, and Louie-Louie.

I don't want to wake him so I walk quietly past his bed on my way to the bathroom. From the window over the big tub, I can see the deck. My Grand-Dad is sitting outside with Kirby. Maybe Kirby had to pee too.

After I'm done, I turn to go back to bed when the sound of a familiar voice makes me look out the window again. Standing in the yard is Jonesey. Jonesey? What's he doing here after Midnight?

chapter

22

It's really quiet tonight so their voices carry up to where I am. I like to listen to adults talk—a lot of times they've got interesting things to say. Plus, I'm nosy. I want to know why Jonesey is in the backyard this late, so I lean my chin on the windowsill to listen to them talk.

I hear my Grand-Dad say in a surprised voice, "Well Jonesey, what are you doing out so late? Can't sleep? Me either. Even a nice hot shower didn't help me get to sleep. The book I've been reading is on my mind. Left it in that little room my wife calls a library and decided to come out here to get some night air." He sighs deeply. "Come here and sit with Kirby and me awhile. Good company for both of us."

Jonesey sits on a deck chair across from my Grand-Dad. I hear Jonesey say that he hasn't been sleeping 'real good' ever since we were at Hobart's talking about that little girl Cecelia. He's got something on his mind, he says, and it's bothering him a lot.

"Listen, Professor Hopper, there's something I have to tell you. I just *know* there is a connection between Dansbury Plot and what happened to Cecelia. And Cecelia's isn't the only story that concerns that empty lot. Years ago, people were known to vanish outright near that accursed place. They were mostly vagrants, like railyard hoboes. They weren't from around here and they didn't know enough to avoid The Plot. But if they weren't seen after

106

a time, the townsfolk just thought they'd moved on, like hoboes do. You know, catching one train after another, going from town to town.

"My wife Elizabeth knew about certain stories that were told about The Plot and she did a lot of research on it. She was fascinated by the local legends but she couldn't find any books written specifically about Dansbury Plot. Not a one."

He pauses and looks out into the dark night. "But I know what the secret of The Plot really is, yes I do. It's the dead come back, Professor. That temporary prisoner-of-war camp some say the Confederates had here, the one nobody really knows about? It's them, the poor souls who died there, died of starvation. They're coming for human food, human flesh to eat. They turned cannibal rotting in that prisoner-of-war camp with no food. They turned on the dead and the dying and ate their flesh. Hobart thinks he knows it all but he doesn't. All he knows is that terrible things happened there during the Civil War and that there's going to be a price to pay. He knows it is haunted but he doesn't know by what. I do, oh God, I believe I do!" His voice breaks.

"It's okay, Jonesey. It might help if you talk about what you know. Go on."

"Hobart left the room after Old Pete told us about Cecelia. It was raining and Hobart had to shut the windows downstairs. We both thought Pete was asleep. I just sat there thinking about the story and that's when Pete started mumbling again. I went up close to him and he told me about the dead flesh eaters from The Plot. Said it was in some book his Great-Grand-Daddy wrote or something.

"He talked about a prisoner-of-war-camp for Yankee soldiers. Something about a cruel Confederate commander who let them starve so that they began eating their dead and dying fellow soldiers. Said the dead with their Hungry Teeth were coming back. I thought maybe he was hallucinating. Maybe he *was* just a crazy old man like people thought. But, Professor Hopper? I knew, knew in my heart that it was true. I never told anyone, not even Hobart, about what his Uncle Pete told me. Then I blocked it out because it was so horrible, too horrible to be true. I was just a kid and my own life was hell as it was. I couldn't, *didn't*, want to believe any of it.

"It wasn't until years later, after I met Elizabeth, that I even thought about it. She liked old legends and ghost stories, you know, like *The Legend of Sleepy Hollow*. I told her what I thought was an old legend. At first, it was just bits and pieces of the Cecelia story. I didn't even remember that it was Pete who had told me. I had blocked it out good and proper about Old Pete telling me.

"But as Elizabeth began asking questions, the whole scary night Pete told us the story came back to me. I told her everything I remembered about the doctor and that university professor and what he said about that poor little girl. Then I told her what Uncle Pete said to me about starving prisoners and the teeth of the dead. Elizabeth was fascinated by it. She tried to find that book the professor wrote but she never did find it. She did find some newspaper articles though, real old ones that you find on those files in libraries, and those she read. There was nothing about what happened to Cecelia. The articles were about people who went missing over the years, strange lightning over The Plot, and sounds of moaning that seemed to carry on the wind in that area.

"Elizabeth and I, we kind of thought it was an interesting story about little Cecelia and the dead coming back. I wasn't so scared about that night after I told Elizabeth. She said sharing something that scares you helps take away some of the fear. My sweet Beth."

His voice is so sad when he says 'Beth'. I guess he will never not miss his wife. I feel really bad for Jonesey and I hate myself because I used to think of him as a derelict kind of guy but he's really just a sad old man like my Grand-Dad says. And he's a poet too, so that's something.

"Hey."

That whispered word and a hand on my shoulder almost makes me jump a mile. Kev is standing behind me. He begins to say something more but I stop him by putting two fingers over my mouth and turning my head to the left. It's a secret signal we use to tell each other somebody might be listening in on what we're saying. It works great at school and around nosy Billy Sarlewski.

I point out the window. We both lean our chins on the sill. Kev turns to me and mouths "Jonesey?!" I nod yes. Jonesey is talking again and we both look out the window.

"Professor, I can feel like something bad is going to happen and soon. The night lightning hit Dansbury Plot? I just got a feeling, a strange feeling in my gut. Whatever horrible thing is going to happen, is coming soon." He looks out toward the darkness of the night. "Real soon."

My Grand-Dad gets up from his lounge chair and asks Jonesey if he'd like a whiskey.

"I surely would Professor. I don't drink that much anymore. Well, not since I moved into Hobart's back room, just a beer now and then and maybe a shot of bourbon with Hobart, but I think I really would like a good dose of whiskey right now."

The back screen door opens and closes with a soft swoosh as my Grand-Dad enters the kitchen. In a few seconds we hear the same swoosh and my Grand-Dad is standing there with a bottle and two glasses. He pours the whiskey into the glasses and hands one to Jonesey.

"Here, Jonesey. Take a good drink before I tell you what I just learned about The Plot from that book I mentioned. The one that's making it hard for me to sleep."

chapter

23

"When Hobart said that terrible things happened on Dansbury Plot he was telling the truth but I don't think he knew how terrible it really was. It was a place of unimaginable horrors, a veritable living hell. It's been one-hundred-twenty-five years this July that the camp was liberated and closed by the Union army. What those men saw when they came to free their fellow soldiers who were prisoners in the camp was the cruel viciousness of what human beings can do to their own kind."

"That book you mentioned. The one that's on your mind. Is that the one you gave to Hobart?"

My Grand-Dad shakes his head no. "The book I gave to Hobart is about the Andersonville Civil War prison camp and what happened to Union soldier prisoners there was bad enough. No, the book I'm talking about is the book written by that ancestor of Hobart's, his Uncle Pete's great-grandfather. I came upon it by sheer accident."

"That book by the university fella who examined little Cecelia? The one who traveled around the world?"

"It is indeed. It was privately published by Hobart's ancestor, what we call self-published today. The author's pen name was misspelled. Instead of the correct spelling of Bathclift, the printer spelled it Balif. That was a common error with people who used private presses back then. Sometimes the printers spelled the name the way they thought it should be spelled. Even the great William Shakespeare saw multiple spellings or misspellings of his name."

My Grand-Dad looks up at the stars and sighs so deeply that the sound puts a cold fear into my chest.

"But that book—what that author wrote about Dansbury Plot and the area that eventually became the Township of Bridge Crossing. He obviously did intense research. It's a small tome to be sure, but frighteningly large in details. The book tells the true, and unbelievably cruel, story of what actually occurred on Dansbury Plot, a small but notorious Confederate military prison during the Civil War. First, let me give you a little history about our state.

"Delaware was a border state during the Civil War meaning that it bordered the Union as well as the Confederacy. Our fair state was also, unfortunately, a slave state during the Civil War although it remained loyal to the Union and it voted against secession. It had been the first state to embrace the Union by ratifying the Constitution. It never left the Union. Be that as it may, the Confederacy did have its presence here. It's a complicated legal issue but it seems that the Southern armies could, and did, have some troops quartered here temporarily.

"The Plot was only supposed to be a wayfaring station, a stopping place on the way to a main prisoner-of-war camp farther south. There were two small abandoned buildings off to the west of Dansbury Plot. One was where the Confederate staff was temporarily quartered. The other building was supposed to hold prisoners. Because of its small size and cramped quarters, it was never meant to be a permanent camp

"However, when the southern prisons had no more room and the war was turning against them, they had no choice but to leave the prisoners at the small station here. It didn't even have an official name at first, just referred to as the 'Station at the Bridge Crossing'. Later it was called Camp Death by the Union army who arrived and saw the remains of the horror there.

"The small building at the station couldn't hold all the prisoners that were taken there and the inexperienced commander-in-charge feared that his Yankees prisoners might escape and run back up north to their old regiments. He asked for help.

"Central command sent a captain up north—by all accounts a cruel man, a former prison warden in Georgia known for his penchant for strict discipline—to handle the situation about the inadequate space. He commandeered the land known as Dansbury Plot from the original owner, and made it one of the worst prisons of the Civil War. For cells to hold those poor prisoners, he created 'hot-holes', a place of punishment he'd used at the

Georgia prison for what he termed were 'for men who don't follow my rules'.

"These hot-holes were nothing more than an underground area, eight feet down, twelve feet wide and fifteen feet long, dug deep under Dansbury Plot with only small grated windows above that looked on the prisoners down below and a few buckets for human waste. The buckets were rarely emptied so the prisoners lived in their own filth.

"Small rations of food were dropped by cloth bundles into the cells once a day, never enough for even one man, let alone the twenty to thirty men who were sequestered there. So the starving men got—creative. They saw the dead and the dying as more than just their fellow recruits, they saw them as a food source. In order to survive, they resorted to cannibalism."

Kev grabs my arm and I know what he's thinking. People eating people. Zombies.

"Cannibalism. So Old Pete was telling the truth. My God, professor, my God," says Jonesey shaking his head.

"Yes, Jonesey. My God indeed." They stop talking and sip their whiskies.

Jonesey and my Grand-Dad talk until almost one-thirty and then Jonesey gets up to leave asking my Grand-Dad to drop by Hobart's store within the next day or two. "We need to talk to Hobart about that book professor."

I hear my Grand-Dad come into the house and go into the small room my Grand-Mom calls the library. I know that next he'll check on me and Kev before going to sleep. He always does that because he knows that I have bad dreams sometimes. I grab Kev and mouth, "C'mon" and we walk as quietly as possible back to my room, jump in our beds, and pretend to be asleep.

Just as I thought my Grand-Dad looks into my bedroom to see that the overhead fan is still on so it's not too warm for sleeping and that all's okay with me and Kev. Kev pretend snores and I hear my Grand-Dad say softly, "Ah, the sweet, untroubled sleep of youth," before moving down the hall to his own bedroom.

After I hear the door to his room close, I watch the numbers on the digital clock radio and wait about five minutes before getting out of bed and tapping Kev on the shoulder. He follows me out of the bedroom and down the stairs to the library.

It's a crowded room because my Grand-Mom has books packed tightly onto book shelves and piled high on a desk. She's a collector of a lot of really old books and first editions. Some of them she brings to *The Willin' Cate Book Store* to sell. Most of the time I love being in here because I like the way the books smell and I kinda like to browse through books that're old and all. But right now I'm interested in finding only one book and reading about that prisoner-of-war camp my Grand-Dad and Jonesey were talking about.

I look around for the book, glancing at the authors' names. Balif, my Grand-Dad said the name was Balif. Where's the book with that author's name? I'm doing my search by the small amount of light coming in from the window. I don't want to turn on the lamps in case my Grand-Dad comes back down for some reason.

My Grand-Dad said it was a small book. I know that when he's reading he likes to sit in the chair by the fireplace. A lot of times he'll leave the book on the chair so it doesn't get mixed back in with all the other books that are taken to the bookstore to sell. But—there's no book on the chair now so where did he put it?

Kev stubs his toe and before he can curse or make a loud sound, I cover his mouth with my hand. "Shhh!" I whisper. "Help me find that book. It's small, so look for a small book."

"Maybe your Grand-Dad hid it," whispers Kev sitting in the chair and rubbing his toes.

Maybe but where would he hide it? I look around. Maybe the desk? I scan the authors' names on the books piled there and don't find it.

"What about the drawer? You said it was a small book. Maybe he put it away 'cause it was so horrible and he didn't want to even see it," says Kev quietly.

I don't know why I didn't think of that. I try the drawer but it's locked. My grandparents lock it 'cause sometimes they keep checks from customers in there. But I know where the key is—it's always in an old tin box in the bottom right hand corner of the smallest bookcase.

I get the key, open the drawer, and find pens, papers, and, hidden underneath a folder is the book with a *Willin' Cate* bookmark inside it. It's small, with thick fabric used for the front and back covers, and it's as old as anything. When I look at the title I know it's the book I'm looking for. Printed into the book's front cover is—

The Terrible True Story of the Civil War Death Camp at Bridge Crossing by J.P. Balif.

chapter

24

'$\mathcal{P}$rison camps on both sides, Union as well as Confederate, fueled many facts setting forth the atrocities that resulted from mass starvation and famine, abundant infectious diseases, the cold; all of which ultimately resulted in cases of deaths involving hundreds of prisoners daily. The shortage of food as well as lack of hygiene and the gross maltreatment of the prisoners, contributed greatly to these deaths.'

Because my grandparents own a bookstore, I learned a lot of literary terms. Some books have what's called a prologue that sets the reader up for what's going to happen and that's what this little book has. I don't bother telling this to Kev because he wouldn't be interested. He just wants to get to what he calls the 'scary parts'.

We're sitting in the basement where we can read without waking my Grand-Dad. Kev's holding a can of ice tea he took from the 'fridge. There's a light over the laundry area and me and Kev sit on the floor to read the story of Dansbury Plot. Instead of chapters, the book is divided into sections with titles.

"Read it out loud Chris. You're a better reader than me and there might be some words I won't know and then you can explain them." Kev leans back against the wall and waits.

"Okay. I'll explain any words you don't know." I turn the page. "This section is called *The Confederate Prisoner-of-War Camp on a Plot of Land Known as*

114

Dansbury." I clear my throat and begin to read.

The captain at the Bridge Crossing way station starved and tortured the Yankee prisoners on a plot of land called Dansbury. Sometimes—'

I stop reading out loud 'cause the next sentence would really make Kev sick. It kinda makes me sick when I see it. I just can't read this part to Kev.

'Sometimes the captain would hold what he called a "rat throw", where he'd toss a live rat into the crowded hole and watch the prisoners scramble for the chance to catch it and eat it.'

"Why'd you stop, Chris?"

"Um, no reason. Just that my throat is, um, kinda dry is all." I cough hard a few times and he hands me the ice tea. I make a big show of gulping it before I hand it back.

"Keep reading. Sometimes what?"

Kev leans closer to me. I look down the page to the next paragraph pretending I lost my place.

"Yeah, right. Okay. Sometimes they were really starved and all. Listen to this part Kev!"

'So starved and desperate were the men in the cells called 'hot-holes' that they would rub together the flint found in the chalky stones in the ground to start a small fire. Over this fire they would roast the arm or foot of their own dead. It is also believed that there were times they broke off a foot or hand to eat when a prisoner was still alive but unconscious and at death's door. It was relatively easy to break the bones of a hand or foot since the dying man was so emaciated—

"That means like really, really skinny," I stop to explain the word to Kev.

'So emaciated and sickly that their bones broke quickly. The prisoners then tore the flesh and tendons apart with their teeth and with the aid of sharp rocks found in the holes. A guard who was captured by the Yankees gave a detailed account of how the captain tortured one prisoner he felt was 'non-compliant with his rules'. After starving the man for ten days straight, allowing only two sips of water in the morning and two at night, the sadistic captain roasted the hand of the poor man's dead brother and fed it to the starving soldier.

"What'd I tell you, Chris? Zombies! They do exist. Wow, zombies in Bridge Crossing!"

"They weren't zombies, Kev."

"Of course they were zombies! They ate human flesh like in that movie we watched!"

I shake my head. "No, no they weren't. It's not the same thing. I mean, yeah, they ate people but the people they ate were already dead or kinda dead anyway, almost dead. Zombies eat live people. And anyway, zombies are mindless dead guys that somehow get revived by some type of voodoo or spell. The guys in that prison weren't zombies, no way. They were living people who still had a mind but just went nuts because they were starving."

"No, they *were* zombies. I know it. And anyway what does

non-compy-something mean anyway."

"Non-compliant. It means the prisoner didn't follow the captain's rules. Jeez, Kev! How did you ever pass vocabulary tests in English class this year?"

"I cheated."

I stare at him surprised that he would even tell his best friend what he did. You can get suspended for cheating.

"Seriously? Cheated on tests? How'd you get away with that?"

"Easy. I always sat between the Benjamin twins, remember? Those girls are smart as hell and they never covered their test papers. They actually kinda *showed* me the answers. I think they like me. So yeah, it was easy."

I groan and roll my eyes.

"So about those zombies. Let's read some more."

"They weren't zombies, Kev! Believe me," I say turning the page as he leans over my shoulder.

It is unfortunate that some men who have power over others choose to use that power in cruel ways. Thus it was with some of the administrators of the prisoner-of-war camps during the Civil War. However, no camp commander was as viciously cruel as the man who controlled the lives of the prisoners at the Dansbury camp. The man who was called Captain Death, one Captain Albin F. Sarlewski of the Confederate Army.

I grip the book tightly and try to reread the name to make sure I got it right but Kev rips it from my hands and stares at the page.

"Chris! Look!" Kev practically shouts. "It says Sarlewski. The captain's name was Sarlewski!" He turns to me, his eyes wide and says loudly, "Sarlewski. As in Billy *Sarlewski!* You think they're related or somethin'?"

I grab the book back and give Kev a scare stare. "Shhh! I don't want my Grand-Dad to hear us. And yeah, that captain is probably some great-great-something-or-other relative to Billy, but please don't shout."

"But we're in the basement for crissakes," whispers Kev. "He can't hear us from all the way up on the second floor!"

"I know," I whisper back. "but what if he comes downstairs to the kitchen to get something to drink or what if he can't sleep and decides to go out on the deck again. He can hear us then. Just keep it down, okay?"

Kev shakes his head okay. For a long time we just sit there staring at the name Albin F. Sarlewski in the book. Sarlewski. I don't know about Kev but I know what I'm thinking as I stare at that name. They must be related all right.

Mean and cruel. Evil probably runs in that family.

chapter

25

When Union troops liberated the camp and attempted to rescue soldiers from the underground cells, they found bones and teeth and only one survivor. He himself, was nothing but skin and bones. Legend has it that the dying soldier gave the men who found him a strange warning.

"One-hundred-twenty-five of the finest men God put on this earth died here on this plot of land, died horribly, suffering every day, being made to commit an unthinkable act of savagery on their fellow prisoners simply in order to survive. But we will have our revenge against those who tortured our bodies and our souls. We will wait one year for every one man. In one-hundred-twenty-five years, upon the celebration of Independence Day we will wait to be awakened. Until that time, beware all, the Hungry Teeth of the Dead of Dansbury Plot."

Some of the rescuing soldiers thought that poor creature before them, a creature who was more skeleton than human being, was hallucinating from starvation, but most believed what he said. He was taken to a field hospital where he died a week later, repeating his warning of revenge 'til he breathed his last breath.

The remains in the 'hot-holes' were covered over with massive amounts of dirt and it became a common grave for those poor souls who had perished there.

After the Civil war ended, the Dansbury family, who had owned that land since the 1700s, wanted nothing to do with what the matriarch of the family, one Idelle Bethune Dansbury called, "A cursed and soiled plot of land made uninhabitable by the inhumanity of man to his fellow man."

TEETH: THE HAUNTING OF DANSBURY PLOT

Idelle Bethune Dansbury was correct when she called the land 'soiled and cursed'. Dating from 1866, there have been stories of strange occurrences that have happened on or near the cursed land. Strange lightning storms, people gone missing and never found again, eerie sounds of moaning carried on the wind, a plot of land so barren that nothing would grow on it. There is also a personal story which I humbly take the privilege of relaying.

A child, whose name and identity I am sworn to never betray, went missing during a holiday berry-picking jaunt. Weeks later she surprisingly made her way home where her mother found her in the backyard, her torso covered in bite marks. At the request of a physician friend of mine I, myself, examined this child, now a terrified mute. It was, and still is, my firm belief that the bite marks were made by human teeth and those who bit the child were not alive as science defines living. I believe that the child was looking for berries and was scratched by the sharp brambles near the berry patch. The child obviously bled onto the Dansbury Plot and the hungry dead smelled the blood, then surfaced to try to eat the poor mite. By the grace of God, the child somehow managed to escape a horrible death and return to her family. By all that is holy, I swear that, after my examination of that poor child, this is what I am convinced to be true.

I close the book and sit with my back against the wall. This isn't just some story like Hobart told us. It's what people on the news call an 'eyewitness report'. This guy Balif? He's actually writing about Cecelia, that little girl who went crazy after being bitten by what that old doctor said were human dead teeth! Balif knows all about it because he was the professor the doctor asked to come and examine Cecelia's body.

I feel sick and my stomach hurts. I look at Kev and his face is all screwed up and scared looking. We just sit there, the book between us, and don't even say anything to each other. I can't talk and for once in his life, Kev is quiet.

I remember what my Grand-Dad said about horror stories, the ones that are fiction and the ones that are real. A writer can make up stories with monsters like Frankenstein or Dracula and stuff but it's only some writer's imagination. We get scared but we still know the stories aren't true. But this book about The Plot is real—these things *really, really* happened—and that makes it a whole lot scarier than any book about made-up monsters, even ones about zombies.

* * *

Kev plays lookout in the hallway while I go into the library to return the book. To make sure that no old steps creak, we sneak up the basement stairs slowly, stopping on every step and holding ourselves completely still like statues, listening for my Grand-Dad. My whole body feels tight and ache-y from doing that. Being sneaky isn't something I'm really used to doing. Most of the time I have no reason to be that way. Kev on the other hand has sneaky down to a type of wacky science. He actually likes it.

One time, while his brother Jeremy was taking a shower, he stole a key from his wallet and opened up a box where his brother keeps special stuff he doesn't want anyone knowing he has. Kev said he found a couple pictures of naked women ripped from some magazine, a penknife, a mushy letter a girl wrote to Jeremy, and a small gold ring with Jeremy's girlfriend's initials on it. He put everything back in the box, locked it, and put the key back in Jeremy's wallet before his brother was halfway through his shower.

Another sneaky thing he did was read a note a teacher had asked him to bring to the office for her. On the way to the office he went into an empty custodian's closet, shut the door, and opened the envelope which the teacher didn't seal closed! That's how I found out that Billy Sarlewski was in a whole bunch of trouble for pushing a first grade boy off a swing at recess. The poor kid fell really hard on the ground. Then, when he tried to stand up, Billy shoved the swing at him hitting him in the head. The first grade kid had to get stitches on his forehead. Kev told me every word that was in that note including how the teacher described Billy as "a bully" and "totally uncaring about hurting others".

Kev didn't get caught that time either. He's really good at sneaky all right.

* * *

I'm putting the book back in the drawer when I see the light on the stairwell come on and hear Kirby's muffled bark and my Grand-Dad's surprised voice. "Kevin!"

I freeze and hold my breath.

"You scared me half to death! I was coming down to see if I shut off the lights outside. I didn't expect anyone to be down here in the middle of the night. Are you okay?"

"Ummm, yeah?"

Oh man, Kev, c'mon. Think of something to say quick!

"Yeah, yeah, I'm okay, ummm, I was just, uh, just gettin' a drink of water. You know, all that nice cold water you got in the 'fridge? So, ummm, I'm okay, it's just that, uh, my throat's, um…, kinda dry."

I almost laugh 'cause he's using exactly the excuse I used before when I stopped reading 'cause I didn't want Kev to know about that rat throw thing. As great as Kev is at sneaky, he's lousy at thinking up a good lie in a split second. A lousy lie and my Grand-Dad knows it. I breathe out very slowly. But I know my Grand-Dad—he's probably more concerned about Kev than annoyed. He probably thinks Kev's worried about something like his brother Jeremy being on the ball field right across from The Plot or maybe me falling into that sinkhole.

"Kevin? Is something on your mind? Do you want to talk about something with me? Is it about what happened to Christopher in the Minella's yard tonight? Any particular thing you're concerned or worried about, or even only thinking about, just tell me."

Oh, boy, if he only knew!

"Uh, I am, yeah, I am thinkin' about, about—".

Kev's trying to hit on something that he can talk about with my grandfather.

"Yes, Kevin? Just tell me," says my Grand-Dad in his kind and concerned voice, the same voice that has helped me through a lot of stuff with Billy Sarlewski.

"About, about—Louie-Louie. I mean we have a connection 'cause I saved his life. I woke up thinkin' that I don't want anythin' to happen to him. He's a really great pet."

"That's what's gotten you up in the middle of the night Kevin? Really?"

"Yes, sir, really. I'm really kinda—like you said—concerned about something happenin' to Louie-Louie. The lightnin' and the storms. I think Louie-Louie is scared and I'm worried. I don't want him to have a heart attack or anythin'."

My Grand-Dad sighs so deeply I can hear it. He's tired but he'll still make sure that he listens to Kev's concerns about Louie-Louie.

"Well, all right Kevin, I don't want you worrying over this. We both need to get some sleep and I can see that you won't be able to sleep until you've told me your concerns. So why don't we go into the kitchen and get a couple glasses of cold water and we'll sit and talk about Louie."

"*Louie-Louie* Mr. Hopper, sir. He's got a double first name. It's from some song way back, like a hundred years ago. My dad sometimes sings it."

"Right, of course, I meant Louie-Louie. Everyone deserves to have their name pronounced properly. Louie-Louie. Let's sit and talk about your concern a bit."

When I hear them go into the kitchen, I lock the drawer and put the key back where it's supposed to be. Then, with my ear pressed against the library door, I listen to their voices for a while. As soon as I think Kev's got my Grand-Dad's full attention, I slowly open and close the door as quietly as I can and sneak upstairs to my room.

With everything that's going around in my head, there's no way I'm going to be able to fall asleep.

chapter

26

"Chris, hey, Chris! Wake up!"

Even though I thought I wouldn't sleep, I guess I must have just zonked out from exhaustion because Kev is shaking me to wake up. It's a good thing too because I was dreaming about dead people falling down in the hole in Sal Minella's backyard. Then, for some reason, the dead guys were down at Old Man Hobart's store eating doughnuts. It was horrible.

"Wha-?"

"Chris, open your eyes. Wake up!"

"What—what time is it?" I open my eyes and try hard to focus.

It's still dark but there's a small sliver of pale light from the streetlamps peeking under the window shade. I shake my head to try to get rid of the nightmare.

"It's about a quarter after five. Me and your Grand-Dad just finished talkin'. He's really cool and he likes Louie-Louie even if he called him by just one Louie."

"What?! You're not making sense Kev."

"He called him by just one Louie!"

I'm still not completely awake so I say, "Who's One Louie?"

"There *is* no *One* Louie. I'm talking about Louie-Louie, my rat! Mr.

121

Hopper called him by one Louie and I told him it's *two* Louies—Louie-Louie! Jeez! Wake up Chris."

As if to let us know he's in the room, Louie-Louie starts running on that crazy wheel in his cage. My jaw hurts where I must've been biting down hard on my retainer while I was dreaming. I sit up against the pillows and take it out of my mouth.

"Chris?"

"Okay, okay. I got it. Louie-Louie, okay. What else did you talk about?" I'm awake now and look right at Kev. "Do you think he knew we had the book?"

Kev shakes his head no. "I doubt it. He just thought I was worried about Louie-Louie and you know what, Chris? I *am* worried about him, how all the stuff that's kinda goin' on in Bridge Crossing could make him sick. We got a connection and I think he gets just as scared as me when things aren't right. He can sense that I'm scared you know." He shakes his head again. "Nothin's right." He stands by Louie-Louie's cage and puts his finger inside the bars to pet the rat's head.

I get up and walk to the window. I don't say anything for a few minutes, just lift the shade and look out at the empty street. Gathering my thoughts is what my Grand-Dad calls it. It's when someone is thinking and not saying anything—they're gathering their thoughts before they speak so they have everything right. I'm gathering a lot of thoughts right now.

Finally, I turn around and face my best friend. "Kev, listen to me. You're right. Nothing is right and everything is wrong in Bridge Crossing. And maybe Louie-Louie feels it too. I know Kirby is acting funny like he's just waiting for something bad to happen.

"I know, I just *know*, it all has to do with The Plot. The lightning storms, the hot wind and thunder but no rain the other day, the sound I heard when I cut my hand and bled onto The Plot. That story about that little girl Cecelia —it's all connected. And I think it's going to get worse. Remember in that book how the guy who wrote it said that some freed prisoner told the soldiers that the dead would get revenge for every man who died there on The Plot? He said the dead would wait one year for every one man who died. One-hundred-twenty-five men died there. That was in 1865."

"Yeah, so? I don't know what you're gettin' at."

"What year is it now, Kev?"

"C'mon, Chris, you know it's 1990."

"And how many years is it from 1865?"

Kev sucks at vocabulary but he's a damn sure-shot whiz at math. He looks at me with wide eyes and whispers, "One-hundred-twenty-five years."

"That's how many years that prisoner said. He said that the hungry dead would return in one-hundred-twenty-five years on Independence Day. My

Grand-Dad once told me that that's what they called the Fourth of July like a hundred years ago. The Hungry Teeth are just waiting for something to wake them up again on that day!"

"Yeah, you're right. Holy crap, July fourth is coming up real soon!! And Chris? He also said somethin' else about the hungry dead. Remember readin' that part?"

It's a hot night but a shiver runs through my whole body. I nod my head. "That dying prisoner said, *Until that time, beware all, the Hungry Teeth of the Dead of Dansbury Plot.*'"

I look at Kev. "And the first letters of those words, Hungry Teeth, were in capitals, so that means they're important, like they're the name of a group or something. A group of hungry dead people."

The Hungry Teeth of the Dead. Those hoboes and others Jonesey said went missing over all these years. And one who survived and went bonkers crazy. Little Cecelia.

All victims of the Hungry Teeth of people who were starved to death.

chapter

27

When my Grand-Dad hands Kev his plate of pancakes the next morning, he asks him if he's okay. "No worries young man? All good?"

"Yes sir, sir. All's good. Thanks for talkin' to me about Louie-Louie."

My Grand-Dad smiles and pours himself another cup of coffee. That's another drink that I don't understand grown-ups liking. Maybe I'll change my mind when I'm older but I don't think so. I want stuff that tastes good. Beer or coffee? Yuck!

I don't think me or Kev slept much, maybe just kinda dozed a little for about thirty minutes. I had a lot of thoughts gathering in my head, that's for sure. Just after the sun started shining through the shade in my bedroom, I began thinking that maybe I should tell my Grand-Dad that me and Kev read those parts in the book he hid in the library. We shouldn't have read it without his permission because he hid it for a reason. I should tell him, I really should, but—

Who am I kidding? I only want to tell him because what I want *him* to tell *me* is that the book is all the author's imagination, that it wasn't really true. That the author maybe heard a story about that prisoner-of-war camp and took what my Grand-Mom calls 'poetic license' with that sad true story turning it into scary fiction. I so badly want to hear him say that the almost dead prisoner was just out of his mind with weakness and being hungry, none of what he said about the dead returning after one-hundred-twenty-five years will actually happen. I want him to say that, but I know it's just wishful hoping on my part because I know in my heart that the book is based on facts about what really happened.

I pour like a gallon of syrup on my pancakes and mush them around and think about what's happening in my town. Dansbury Plot, The Plot. I think about it and know that I've always been afraid of it but I just never really thought anything would happen there that would affect the whole town. It was just there, just a part of life in Bridge Crossing for kids and grown-ups. Kids were all extra careful to avoid it, told dumb kid stories about it, and just went about doing our own thing. But now, it's like The Plot is somehow coming alive, making *absolutely sure* we know it's there, and somehow giving us a warning that we'd better watch out. The Hungry Dead. Hungry Teeth.

"When you boys are finished with breakfast, go upstairs and bring down your laundry. I've been a little lax lately about washing our clothes so I want to at least get one load started in the washer before I drive us to the pool."

He turns to put his dish in the dishwasher. "I want to do some laps and then just relax in a lounger for a couple of hours. Maybe have some of those cheese-y fries with that side of brown gravy you two like so much."

"You stayin' with us at the pool Mr. H?"

"Yes, Kevin. I think I'm in need of a bit of pool time today. I believe it'll be good for this aging, but young thinking man, to get some relaxing time in at our town pool."

He looks tired and I know what's on his mind. I want to talk to him about that book but maybe it'll be better to talk to him later after he's had some time at the pool.

He sips his coffee and winks and smiles at me and Kev. "Now finish your breakfast boys and go upstairs and get the clothes you want washed. I want to get to the pool early."

* * *

Upstairs I grab all the clothes I stuffed in the hamper in the bathroom and put them in a laundry basket. Kev gets his dirty stuff which he balled up in a plastic bag next to Louie-Louie's cage. I told him he could put it in the hamper but he said the clothes have his smell on them.

"So when I'm *not* here Louie-Louie will have my smell and still think that I *am* here and he won't feel lonely. When I'm in school, I put a sweaty undershirt right by his cage so he won't get lonely."

Boy, Kev has some strange explanations for the things that he does. I stopped trying to figure out how he thinks a long time ago. I shake my head and just tell Kev to make sure he empties his pockets before putting his clothes in the basket. We don't want candy bars melting all over the clothes or anything.

I clean out the pockets of my clothes and dump used tissues, a napkin from the Dairy Barn, and some bubble gum into the trash can in the bathroom. Then I grab the shorts I wore yesterday. Boy are they filthy with the dirt from that hole in the Minella's back yard. I dig into one pocket and come up with fifty-seven-cents and a hard candy. Then I slide my hand into the other pocket hoping for more change. My hand closes on something that feels like a stone and then I remember. It's that piece of maybe gold I found when I was down in the hole. I can't believe I forgot about it. I wanted to show my Grand-Dad and ask him if maybe I can keep it. He'll probably say that I should give it back but the way I figure it, Sal will never know I have it and, anyway, it's not like it's a *big* chunk of gold.

"Kev? I want to show you something."

Kev brings his dirty clothes over to where I am and dumps them into the laundry basket. I hold the gold thing in the palm of my hand and show it to him.

"Holy crap! A gold nugget! You got a gold nugget! Where'd you find that?! Omigod, you're gonna be rich!"

I tell him the whole story about how it was stuck in the side wall of dirt and was kinda shining. "I grabbed it because I thought it was a lucky stone. I don't even know if it's really gold."

Kev starts nodding his head. "Oh, it's gold all right. It looks like that ring Jeremy was gonna give to his girlfriend, I forget which girl that was. Remember I told how I looked in his lock box when he was taking a shower one time and found his secret stuff?" I nod yes. "Also it looks like one of my mom's special earrings, the expensive kind she got for her birthday and only wears when my dad takes her out to dinner. Yeah, this is real gold."

I look at the small shiny stone. Kev asks me what I'm going to do with it and I make a decision right then. "I'm going to show it to my Grand-Dad."

"Show me what, Chris?"

We both turn and see my Grand-Dad standing outside my bathroom door holding two baskets of clothes.

chapter

28

"Well, Chris, Kevin is right. It *is* real gold. But it's not a nugget of gold. It appears to be a gold tooth."

We're standing in the bathroom by my bedroom. After rubbing the dirt off of the gold nugget with a tissue, my Grand-Dad examines it in the light and tells me my piece of gold is actually a tooth!

"A tooth? Who has a gold tooth? I mean this was in Sal's backyard. Nobody in his family has a gold tooth, right Kev?"

Kev thinks for a minute and then shakes his head no. "No, no way. I never saw anyone in Sal's family with a gold tooth. I'd remember somethin' like that."

"Oh, I doubt that this is from the mouth of anyone in the Minella family. It looks old and worn. It may have been in the ground a long time."

"Wow, a gold tooth, just like a pirate!" says Kev kind of awestruck. "You found a pirate's tooth Chris! Old as anything. Wow!"

My Grand-Dad shakes his head and continues examining the tooth under the bathroom lights. "I hardly think this is a pirate's tooth, but it is very old. Whoever had this tooth in their mouth is long gone. It's a very interesting subject you know, using gold fillings for decayed teeth. Gold was first used in dental fillings to cover cavities dating back to the 1500s and that is recorded in the first printed book on dentistry. If you don't mind Chris, I'd like to have Tom Sheraton examine this tooth. He'll be able to give us an approximate date on it."

Dr. Tom Sheraton is the dentist at *Happy Teeth* and everybody likes him. I got my braces and retainer from him. While he's examining kids' teeth he makes bird calls and stuff. He's a pretty cool guy. His hobby is archeology and he likes examining old things from what he calls his 'digs'. He can probably find out a lot about this tooth including its age. I nod okay. I'd like to know how old this tooth is too.

"Um, Grand-Dad?"

"Yes, Chris?"

"I don't have to return the tooth to Sal, do I? It *was* on his property but he doesn't even know I found it. I don't want to give it back. Do I have to?"

"Yeah," chimes in Kev, "Chris found it. You know, like finders-keepers and stuff. And anyways, it's not like it's a big chunk of gold maybe worth a gazillion bucks. It's just a small piece."

"Do I *have* to give it back?" I ask again.

My Grand-Dad sighs and looks at the tooth in his hand. "No, Christopher, you don't have to give it back. At least not at this time. Actually, it's probably best if you don't even let Sal know that you found it. Right now let's keep what you found and where you found it between you, Kevin, and me. All right boys? Can you both promise that and promise to really keep your promise to me this time?"

Me and Kev shake our heads yes and do a solemn pinkie swear. That's really important because a pinkie promise means that if the other guy breaks the promise, his pinkie finger will break. I don't know if that's ever really happened to anyone but that's what I heard kids say. Then, to seal the pinkie promise, we cross our hearts, spit on our hands, and shake.

For us kids, that's a real promise all right.

* * *

After we drop the gold tooth at the *Happy Teeth* dentist's office, we go to the pool and get settled with our chairs and towels. Standing in chest-deep water, I watch my Grand-Dad easily swim laps back and forth, back and forth. He's been a swimmer all his life and was on the swim team in college so I guess swimming is as natural to him as baseball is to me. Probably sports stuff you do as a kid just stays with you forever. I hope so because I love playing baseball.

Across the pool me and Kev see Billy Sarlewski sitting on the edge of the pool splashing his feet like a mad man in the water, getting everyone around him wet. Two girls who are trying to get a tan yell at Billy to stop splashing but he just sticks out his tongue and splashes some more. One girl calls him a jerk and another one yells, "You're a little creep asshole!" They grab their towels and walk away.

I stare hard at Billy trying to picture him in a Confederate army uniform. I know he's a bully and likes being mean to little kids in the lower grades at school 'cause he knows they can't fight back. Like that little first grade kid who Billy pushed off the swing, the little boy who had to get stitches. That's Billy—just plain mean and a bully. I don't understand meanness in people. I just don't know why someone has to be that way.

Around noontime, Kev goes to the food stand and comes walking back with a big tray of chili dogs, cheesy fries, and large gulp cups of lemonade. Billy sees him and gets up from the pool's edge. I know what's coming—Billy's done it before to other kids. He'll deliberately trip Kev so that the snacks end up in the water. I go to get out of the pool to warn Kev but just as I'm lifting myself up out of the water I stop. Then I smile because I see Billy stop dead in his tracks, turn, and walk away fast. Running up behind my buddy Kev is his brother Jeremy.

"Kev, wait up! You left your change on the counter. You got to be more careful with your money little brother, okay? It's a good thing I was there."

"Oh, wow! Okay. Thanks, Jeremy."

Kev lets Jeremy take a couple of French fries and then walks over to a table, motioning me to come over.

"Boy, Kev," I say as soon as I sit down, "you got lucky! Billy was going to bump you into the pool with all this food. It was lucky for you that you forgot your money at the food stand and that Jeremy ran after you to give it back."

Kev stares at me and then starts laughing so hard he squirts lemonade through his nose. "It *wasn't* luck," he says taking a deep breath from laughing. "I had a great plan in place. I *asked* Jeremy to follow right behind me and told him what I wanted him to say. He was all for it. Jeremy said that if Billy came anywhere near me, he'd knock him flat on his ass! He knows what a little shit he is."

I grab a lemonade and a plate of cheesy fries and smile and gobble French fries as I listen to Kev describe his 'great plan' and how he and Jeremy agreed on what to do. Kev and his big brother. They're so close and tell each other everything.

Then a thought hits me. The book and that guy called Captain Death, Captain Albin F. Sarlewski of the Confederate Army. "Kev?"

"Yeah?"

"You didn't tell Jeremy about the book did you? You know about that guy with the same last name as Billy?"

"Captain Death?" he shakes his head really hard. "Nope, I didn't say *anything* about him or the book. Why? You think I should tell Jeremy?"

"No!" I shout out, leaning forward and almost spilling my drink. A couple of people turn and look at me curiously. I lower my voice. "No. We can't. Not yet. Not until we talk to my Grand-Dad."

"Yeah, I guess we have to tell him, huh? You think he'll be mad at us for taking the book?"

I think about that for a minute. I've never really seen my Grand-Dad mad. Ever. I don't even know if he gets mad. I shake my head no.

"I don't think he'll be mad— I think that maybe he'll say he's disappointed in us again that we snuck the book out to read it. But we *have* to tell him Kev. This is too much crazy stuff for us to keep to ourselves. That part about the Hungry Teeth dead people. It," I take a deep breath, "it scares me Kev. It really does."

Kev nods, talking with his mouth full of fries. "Yeah, I don't know how the dead can be hungry unless they're zombies and you said that they can't be zombies unless someone put a voodoo spell on them. But these soldiers—maybe they weren't real zombies under a voodoo spell—but they were starved to death and I guess, even though they're dead, their teeth are comin' back. I mean that little girl Cecelia—the Hungry Teeth sure got her and probably a whole lot of other people too. I don't want them to get *us*."

I stare at the half-eaten chili dog in my hand. Human teeth. Biting through food. Biting through flesh. I think about people who probably got bitten to death by the Hungry Teeth in the last one-hundred-twenty-five years. Suddenly I'm not hungry anymore.

I hear a rumble of thunder and one of the old guys, his nose all white with sunblock, tells a lifeguard that she should get everybody out of the pool in case lightning strikes. She tells him we've got a little while yet—the thunder seems far away, she says, probably over The Plot which is blocks away.

"Lightning strikes fast, girlie," says the old guy grabbing his stuff off the lounger. "Me? I'd rather be prepared for lightning than just sit on my butt and wait for it to strike me."

Lightning. Over The Plot.

Fifteen minutes later, I'm watching the lifeguard climb onto her high seat and then blow her whistle signaling everyone to get out of the pool.

"Hey, Chris?"

"Yeah?"

"Let's tell your Grand-Dad today about readin' that book, okay? I think we really have to tell him."

I nod. Better for us to be prepared for lightning—and the Hungry Teeth—than to just sit on our butts and wait.

chapter

29

Before walking to the pool parking lot for the ride home, me and Kev talk a long time and decide that the best time for us to tell my Grand-Dad that we took the book out of a locked drawer and read some of it without his permission is right after dinner.

"You don't ever want to tell grown-ups that you did somethin' you weren't supposed to do before you eat. No man, no way." Kev shakes his head. "Doin' that is a disaster. We gotta eat somethin' good before we tell him what we did. We're gonna need strength."

I agree and we throw our stuff into the tailgate of the car before getting in.

On the drive back from the pool, we stop at Dr. Tom Sheraton's dental office. He told my Grand-Dad that he'd have the information on how old the tooth might be and to come pick it up any time today. He's got this archeology-type lab in the back of his office so I guess he can work pretty fast in checking stuff out.

My Grand-Dad goes inside while we wait in the car. He comes out ten minutes later and when he's in his seat on the driver's side, he pulls a small, soft white cloth from his pocket and opens it up. Inside is the tooth all cleaned up and shiny with that sparkle of gold glinting from it.

"Well, Chris, that tooth you found is, as I suspected, old. Over a hundred years old in fact. Dr. Sheraton said putting an approximate date on it was relatively easy. It's not a definite date but close enough. He examined the tooth and the gold in it and because of the amount of gold used and the deterioration of the tooth itself, he believes that this tooth is from the mid-eighteen-hundreds. As I said it's an approximation—that means it's an educated guess, Kevin—but still, now we know the possible age of the tooth."

"That's really old! Wow!" says Kev leaning over me to look at the tooth.

"I guess wow is a good way of expressing our thoughts on this, Kevin. A tooth from the mid eighteen-hundreds, hmmm. You know boys, it is entirely possible that this tooth could have belonged to someone from the Civil War era. Now that is interesting."

"How much is it worth, Mr. Hopper? It's real gold and everything so how much do you think it's worth if Chris sold it? At least a half a million bucks, right?"

"Kev! I can't sell it. It's really not even mine!"

My Grand-Dad laughs and tells us the only value this tooth would have would be as a museum piece in a display on how dentistry was practiced in the eighteen-hundreds.

"It was rather remarkable what they could do back then. Dentistry was still a kind of step-child, if you will, of any of the health care people received. Most people opted for false teeth back then because they were cheaper. This tooth was from someone who had the money to have a gold filling put in a decaying tooth. However expensive it may have been to have this done one hundred years ago, there's not enough gold in the tooth that would bring in any real money. No, Kevin, it's not worth very much. With the price of gold today, hmmm—I'd estimate about less than eighty dollars."

Kev looks disappointed and so am I, but then I think about it; the tooth isn't really mine 'cause I just found it on someone else's property so the money wouldn't be mine either. That's that.

"How did the tooth end up in the ground Grand-Dad?"

"Oh, it could have happened in a number of ways. Perhaps it fell out naturally from decay or a disease of the gums, or even the natural aging process. Or it was knocked out in a fist fight. There may have been a dentist's office in the area and the tooth may have been extracted—that means pulled out Kevin—and then simply discarded by the dentist who figured the small amount of gold in it wasn't worth reusing. The laws on disposing of medical waste weren't on the books a hundred years ago and a lot of the waste was simply buried in empty lots or even in the back yard of the office of a doctor or dentist. Sometimes the waste material was hauled away and burned on the outskirts of a town away from houses. No one realized how unsanitary those practices were back then. The past is filled with interesting so-called health practices. Some highly unsanitary ones to be sure, but nonetheless interesting."

He wraps up the tooth in that soft cloth and hands it to me telling me to put it in a drawer in my bedroom.

"Well, let's get home then. I'm going to order take-out from AJ Shen for dinner. Tomorrow night we'd better start eating what your grandmother left in the freezer for us, but tonight I feel like having some excellent Chinese food. Anyway, you boys get settled at the house and then decide what you want me to order for us all. I'll call it in around six." He pauses. "After we eat, I need to finish reading something—it won't take me long—and then maybe we can play one of those board games I've got in the library."

Me and Kev look at each and I know he's thinking the same thing I'm thinking—my Grand-Dad's going to finish reading that horrible book.

* * *

Me and Kev are outside playing catch while my Grand-Dad cleans up before going into the library. We offered to help but he said it's just paper plates and containers so he doesn't need our help. He tells us he'll bring out some iced tea for us when he's finished. I'm not sure but I think my Grand-Dad suspects something is up because of the way Kev's acting, like being really helpful and more polite than ever. He probably thinks that Kev's worried about Louie-Louie again or maybe it's something to do with Billy Sarlewski at the pool. I doubt if he suspects it's about the book.

After he cleans up and brings us our iced tea, he goes into the library. An hour later, when he comes outside to let Kirby do his business, I sigh deeply and nod at Kev. He looks at me and quietly says "Okay. Now or never, I guess."

I take a deep breath, walk over to where my Grand-Dad is standing with Kirby, and say, "Ummm, Grand-Dad? Me and Kev have something really important to tell you."

chapter

30

The three of us sit on the deck. We just finished telling my Grand-Dad about stealing the book from the locked drawer in the library room. Kev was totally against using the word 'steal' because, as he said, "If you steal somethin' it means that you're keepin' it for yourself and not givin' it back. We didn't steal it Chris! We put it back, right? So we didn't really *steal* it, okay? We just kinda borrowed it."

I shake my head no and tell him that stealing is *exactly* what we did because we took it without permission and we took it even after we knew that it had been locked away just so we couldn't get it.

"We took the key and opened a private drawer to get it, so stealing *is* what we did."

It took us an hour to tell my Grand-Dad everything—the parts of the book we read, that captain named Sarlewski, eavesdropping on him and Jonesey talking about Dansbury Plot without them knowing we were kinda spying on them—even the part about Kev lying about being worried about Louie-Louie and keeping my Grand-Dad talking in the kitchen just so I could sneak up to my bedroom.

After we finished telling him what we did, there's nothing but silence on the deck—even the crickets aren't chirping like they always do in the summer. The book is lying on the deck table next to glasses of iced tea. My

Grand-Dad went and got it and brought it outside after we told him what we did. I don't even want to look at it. Kev's still got his catcher's mitt in his hands and he's holding on to it really tight like it's a life preserver or something. His left leg is kinda shaking up and down and he looks scared. I just sit nibbling on my thumb nail waiting for my Grand-Dad to say something.

He's taking a really long time to say anything at all and me and Kev are practically holding our breaths waiting. Finally, he looks up at the sky, sighs and says, "First I want to tell you boys that I'm not angry."

"You're *not?!*" says Kev sitting up straight and looking at my Grand-Dad with surprise. "Wow, Mr. Hopper, that's really somethin' all right. A lot of parents and grandparents get mad over just about everythin' we do. And this is the second time *in a week* that you said you weren't mad at me and Chris for somethin' we did but shouldn't have done. Boy!"

I have to agree with Kev. I guess it would take a whole lot more to make my Grand-Dad get mad at us.

"I'm not angry but I am disappointed, deeply disappointed, that you used the key to open a locked drawer, and took the book to read when you knew I had hidden it for a reason. It is a book so much more terrifying in its truth than the history book on Andersonville. That book was horrible enough but this one—"

I look at Kev and nod my head. Disappointed, yeah, exactly like what I told Kev he'd say.

"And I am not happy that you listened in on a private conversation between Jonesey and me."

"Gosh Mr. Hopper, how can kids ever know what's goin' on if we don't listen in on grown-ups talkin' about stuff?"

"Oh, Kevin, Kevin, you certainly have a way of making sense of something in your own way! Anyway, all that being said, well—maybe it's a good thing you read parts of this book. Maybe I was wrong to keep it from you because whatever may happen, if anything happens at all, will affect all in Bridge Crossing. I've been trying to find this book for a couple of months now, Chris, after having read a short Civil War story in a literary magazine at the book shop. The author of the story had based it on a book she had once read. I had no idea that the book that inspired the story in the magazine was written by Hobart's ancestor. It was a rare coincidence that the book I was looking for was written by his ancestor. Rare indeed."

"Wait," says Kev, "are you sayin' that somethin' bad *is* gonna happen here, Mr. Hopper? Like somethin' that is comin' from, um from," Kev stops, swallows hard, and says almost in a whisper, "from The Plot?"

"Yes, Kevin, Dansbury Plot is part of what's going to affect us. I think we need to be prepared for any contingency—that means any possibility—of unexplained events happening here in Bridge Crossing. I'm a man who doesn't really believe in the supernatural but maybe, just maybe, there's more to that belief that others seem to have than I know. Perhaps I'd better explain how this journey towards interest, if not downright belief in the supernatural, began for me.

"As I said, about four months ago I read a fictional story in a literary magazine we received from a small town in Pennsylvania. We get quite a few little-known literary magazines from small towns sent to *The Willin' Cate*. All book stores receive them—the editors of the magazines hope that by having the owners of bookstores display their magazines, their readership might increase from local to national. Personally, I like reading them. Some of their stories are really quite good.

"Since the American Civil War is what I teach, one of the stories in the magazine—a fictional work titled *A Ghost of the Civil War*—particularly intrigued me. It was about a soldier who had supposedly escaped a makeshift prisoner-of-war camp in a town in Delaware during the Civil War. It didn't name our town of Bridge Crossing or Dansbury Plot, but it did mention an empty lot on which the prison-of-war camp was built and the horror of underground prison cells called hot-holes.

"The story went on to tell that the so-called escape of that soldier was actually a lie which guards told to the other prisoners. In truth, the man who was said to have escaped was actually a turncoat spy who had sold classified Union Army secrets to the Confederate captain in charge of the camp in exchange for his freedom. One of the secrets concerned the fact that several other of the prisoners at the camp had been Union army spies and, until their captures, had been able to give Union commanders detailed information about when and where the Confederates would strike and where they were encamped. Their bravery had helped turn the tide of the Civil War in favor of the North. Having this information, the cruel captain of the camp made life even more hellish for those brave men now kept in the underground cells. When the traitor's fellow prisoners found out about what had been done—how they had all been betrayed—they vowed revenge on the man who had betrayed them and thus allowed the sadistic captain to inflict such tortures on them.

"The traitor made his way north, told his lie about his 'brave escape' to the newspapers of the day who proclaimed him a hero, and, according to the story, lived a fairly prosperous life. But, no matter how good his own life had become, he was always haunted by the faces of those he left in the underground cells and by how he abandoned them to horrible deaths by his betrayal. For years he felt compelled to return to that campsite. It was as if some strange, magnetic force was drawing him back.

"After many years he *did* return but when he stood on the abandoned empty lot, something terrible happened. Lightning streaked across the sky over the lot and the sound of thunder was deafening. The ground began to move wildly under his feet. Voices screamed 'Traitor, traitor! Now you will pay the awful price for your betrayal!'

"The ghosts of his dead fellow prisoners, all skeletons with their terrible teeth exposed, arose from the ground and dragged him screaming back to the same cells where they had all died of starvation. He was, the author wrote, devoured by the dead he had betrayed."

Even though it's hot and humid, I feel cold kinda like when you come into a room with the air conditioner on full blast after being outside in the hot sun. I look at Kev. He hasn't interrupted my Grand-Dad even once to ask what some word means or anything. He's just holding tight to his catcher's mitt and staring into space. He looks like he's in a trance.

"After having read that particular story in that magazine—besides being a history prof—I wanted to research what I read. I tracked down the author of the story and called her. The woman was a retired high school teacher in her nineties but mentally sharp as a knife. She told me that her fictional short story was based on some obscure old book she'd read in college.

"She said, *'I don't have the book or remember where I found it. And truthfully, I've read so many over the years that I don't remember the author. I do remember that the title did have something to do with the words 'Civil War and death camp' and the book did speak about the cruelty of some commander at that camp—there were quite a few of those during that war, unfortunately. Think of the horrors at Andersonville in Georgia. After that came to light, it seemed as if camps on both sides were trying to out-do each other with cruel punishments to prisoners.'"*

"Andersonville? That book you got for Mr. Hobart. Hey Grand-Dad," I lean forward, "Andersonville is the name of the place that had the prisoner-of-war camp, right? You know in the book you wouldn't let me read because you said it was too disturbing for young minds?"

"It is Chris. But it seems that Andersonville, as horrible as it was, takes a back seat in horror to the one which stood on Dansbury Plot. Anyway, let me tell you what else this writer told me. She said—

'I guess the book somehow stayed dormant in my brain all these years and became the inspiration for the short story I wrote. That's all I can tell you, Professor Hopper except, well, except that even though the book seemed a bit over the top—there was some outlandish, far-fetched side story about a child having been bitten by the dead—I had the feeling that the author was telling the truth. I don't know why, just a feeling of the young and impressionable girl I was at eighteen, I guess. Perhaps they're only legends or perhaps they are horribly true.'

My Grand-Dad takes a sip of iced tea and closes his eyes for a few long minutes before speaking again. "I asked her if she remembered what became of the book and she told me that she believes it ended up as an item at the estate sale when her parents' house was sold. So I began to call libraries in

Pennsylvania and Delaware to see if they had a book about Civil War death camps and they had some good ones but not what I was looking for at all. Very academic and true history. I had no success with those books. I then wrote to colleges and universities thinking that the book had been an academically published one. But I found nothing.

"Then you and Kev here," he turns and pats Kev's shoulder, "mentioned what one of your friends had told you about a little girl being bitten by God knows what. And finally, talking with Hobart and Jonesey about the child named Cecelia, who actually *had* been terribly bitten by what a doctor at that time said were human teeth—and teeth from humans who were dead— put it all together. I've actually been speaking with Hobart a lot about Dansbury Plot, ever since he ordered the book on Andersonville.

"And then I found the book the writer of that magazine story had read many years ago. The author of the book had published it privately with his own money so it wasn't a book readily available through sources that I knew. Printing was expensive back then so there was only one copy that was printed. I finally found it in an old bookseller's shop in a small town called Cape Charles three weeks ago. The description of the book was spot-on to what the writer of that short story had told me so I had it sent to me.

"When we were at Hobart's store and he mentioned the name his ancestor wrote under I was surprised but didn't let on that I already had the book. I wanted to read it before I let him know I found it. Believe me, I was more than surprised when I found out the book the writer of the short story talked about was the one written by Hobart's ancestor who was the anthropology professor who examined that poor little girl Cecelia.

"I saw that the truth about Dansbury Plot being a war time prison and the legend of ghostly sightings on it had a very similar pattern. Nothing seemed too wildly exaggerated, nothing seemed to be an outright lie. After Jonesey's visit a few nights ago where he talked about people going missing over the years never to be seen again, I began asking myself if supernatural happenings, if things like revenge from the grave—to quote Mr. Hobart—aren't just scary stories to tell around a campfire. I went to the library to do research and was lucky to find an interesting album hidden in the basement archives. That album contained old handwritten stories from around 1866 to 1890 about what were termed 'unexplained apparitions' supposedly terrorizing townsfolk around and near Dansbury Plot."

"What's appa—, what you just said," asks Kev.

"Ghosts. An apparition is a ghost," I say quickly.

"The truth is that I don't know if I believe in ghosts. I'm a little too pragmatic which simply means that I'm very practical and down-to-earth when it comes to belief in the supernatural."

I repeat the word pragmatic. What a great sounding word! I have to add that to my notebook later.

"I don't know if I believe that a type of revenge on the living from the dead is really possible. Everything I've read though—everything that's been happening over by The Plot—it seems that something *is* coming together in a strange and disturbing way to settle a score from a horrible incident that took the lives of one-hundred-twenty-five innocent men. Maybe it's time for me to believe in the unbelievable."

"You just said that you didn't really believe in ghosts and stuff like that Grand-Dad."

"I never *did* believe in all that, you're right, but now—I don't know. What I do know is something strange, something that is unexplainable by rational thinking, is starting to happen and I'd like to be prepared to face it. We all should be prepared to face what is coming our way."

I get it. Just like that old guy at the pool didn't want to wait around for lightning to strike him, my grandfather doesn't want to just sit on his butt and wait for something bad to happen.

"Truthfully, boys, all my life I'd heard stories about The Plot being haunted because it had once been a prison. People talked about legends, ghosts, and strange sounds coming from over there. All desiccated—that word means dry, Kevin—dead earth. Nothing grows there, everyone said. But I never thought there was anything supernatural about that land. To me it was a geological problem—simply a piece of dry land which couldn't absorb and hold water from rainfall. However, even though I didn't believe in the ghost stories told about it, even though I would sometimes laugh at the outlandish stories some people told, I never once walked on that empty lot."

Kev asks him if he saw the flyers put up by Mr. Sarlewski about having a meeting on the Little League ball field to talk about building on Dansbury Plot. He adds that Old Man Hobart is gonna have a cow about that meeting.

"Yes, I saw them and I know Mr. Hobart has seen them as well. As for him 'having a cow' as you so neatly phrase it Kevin, let's just say that he's very angry and concerned by what Sarlewski wants to do. I think we all need to go to that meeting and try to convince people that building on The Plot is a bad idea and no good will come from it."

He sighs deeply. "But I imagine Sarlewski's sale's pitch will be pretty persuasive to anyone who's looking to have their property taxes lowered and maybe make some money from a shop they could own on that land or by investing in the mini-mall."

"Um, Grand-Dad? About the name in the book, that Captain Sarlewswki. Do you think he—"

Before I can finish asking him my question, he says, "Related to the present-day Sarlewski family? Yes, it's a possibility that he is an ancestor of theirs. That name was not a common one around here. Perhaps relatives of that captain with that name moved north after the war and settled in Bridge Crossing."

We don't speak for a while and then my Grand-Dad picks up *The Terrible True Story of the Civil War Death Camp at Bridge Crossing.*

"How far did you get in the book?"

I tell him we only read pages in the beginning of the book and skimmed a few others.

"Then there's one thing that I read in the last chapter this evening that may very well interest you boys. Especially you, Chris. But, it is very, very disturbing."

Kev's squirming like he's got an itch he can't scratch and he scoots to the edge of his chair. "What is it Mr. Hopper? How much more can we be disturbed than we already are by the story in that book? I mean, we're disturbed already, all right. You can tell us."

My Grand-Dad kinda smiles at Kev when he says that 'we're disturbed already' and then tells us.

"The last chapter of the book involves an attempted escape by those poor men suffering in those hot-holes. In their desperation to be free, they decided to tunnel out. The prisoners had devised a plan to dig a tunnel, using only their hands and some rocks, that would go about a mile from the underground cells to what they hoped was freedom. They never made it to freedom. The soft dirt of the tunnel collapsed on them and the men were buried alive." He shakes his head. "I'm sorry boys, that's a terrible thing for your young minds to know.

"Some of the guards went to the captain, pleading with him to let them check if there were any survivors of the tunnel collapse. They thought they could save any one of the prisoners who might still be alive under all that dirt. But the captain refused their pleas. He did not want the men in his command to look for any survivors and said that the prisoners, who he cruelly referred to as' Union army trash', got what they deserved.

"Captain Sarlewski told his men, 'I expressly forbid any man under my command to attempt to look for survivors. Anyone who defies my order will be placed in the prison hot-holes and be accorded the same treatment as those Yankee scum'. Needless to say, no man dared to go against the captain's command."

He turns and looks at me steadily. "Chris, it seems that according to the book's direction of where the tunnel would take the soldiers, it's likely somewhere near the property of your friend, Sal. That gold tooth you found in the Minellas' backyard? It could have been on that tunnel's path. It is entirely possible that it may have belonged to a prisoner who died in that tunnel. I don't know if it did, but the possibility is strong."

"Holy crap, Chris! You got a tooth from one of those Hungry Teeth dead guys!" Kev looks scared like maybe that tooth might start biting us when we're asleep or something.

I remember the thick, soft earth when I fell into the sinkhole in Sal's backyard. The dirt falling on my face, the taste of it in my mouth. The fear of just being in that hole.

And the tooth I found. A gold tooth probably from one of those prisoners who tried to escape from those horrible underground hot-holes. Someone who—I have a hard time saying this to myself—was buried alive! That tooth is in my underwear drawer still wrapped in that soft cloth from the dentist. Like Kev said, holy crap!

"Grand-Dad, what's going to happen now? I mean in that book it said one year for every man who died and then the Hungry Teeth will come back. That's this year, this year!"

"Yeah," says Kev, "and they're comin' back right on July Fourth when all the celebrations and stuff happen—when there's like a gazillion people around. Those Hungry Teeth dead guys are comin' back to eat *all* of us!"

chapter

31

It takes a while to calm Kev down. My Grand-Dad makes him put his head between his knees and tells him to try to breathe normally. But Kev's so hyper that putting his head between his knees only makes him throw up on his new sneakers.

I get paper towels to clean up the mess and my Grand-Dad takes Kev's sneakers into the yard where he hoses them down and puts them on the deck railing to dry.

"My mom's gonna be so mad! Those sneakers cost a helluva lot of money!" Kev hiccups through his words. "I had to *beg* her to get them for me. She's gonna kill me!"

"No, they'll be just fine, Kevin," says my Grand-Dad. "It's very hot tonight and that heated air will dry them out. Once they're completely dry, she'll never know."

"And we're all gonna die! We're gonna be eaten by those dead teeth!"

"Take it easy, Kevin and sip some ice tea."

Kev takes a gulp of the tea and it dribbles out the side of his mouth because he's hiccupping from being hyper again.

"Take small sips. That's good, that's good. Sit here with Chris and me and let's talk about, oh let's see, let's talk about—Batman. All right? Tell me about why you think Batman is the greatest hero ever, better even than my favorite comic book hero Superman."

I've got to hand to my Grand-Dad. He sure knows how to get Kev's mind off of all the horrors of the Hungry Teeth dead people and all that stuff. Batman vs Superman! Boy! Kev's still breathing kinda funny but he wipes his face with a paper towel, takes a deep hiccupping breath, and latches onto Batman vs Superman as if it was the only real and sane thing left in the world. His mind just wants to forget the scary real stuff for a little while, I guess.

"Jeez, Mr. Hopper, don't you know that Superman is only a super hero because he gets his power from our sun? That's why he's so strong and stuff. But if he didn't get that power he'd just be like an ordinary guy. But Batman has skills, he doesn't have any super powers, just real skills. He's kinda real. Realer than Superman anyways." Kev hiccups again and I hand him his ice tea.

So I listen to Kev and my Grand-Dad talk about super-heroes and I almost forget about Dansbury Plot and the Hungry Teeth dead people.

Almost.

* * *

I'm staring at the ceiling. It's hot in my bedroom. Even though the windows are open and the ceiling fan is on, the air seems heavy and thick. Usually Kirby sleeps in my grandparents' room but tonight he followed me and Kev into my room and just made himself at home. That's okay—I feel safer with him here.

Good ol' Kirbs. He's sleeping on my bed and he's being so good about Louie-Louie. He only sniffed Louie-Louie's cage—he didn't whine or bark like he usually does when he's around him— before settling down on the bed. And Louie-Louie didn't seem to mind that sniff either. He just snuggled deeper into the clean straw Kev put in his cage and didn't even do his usual night time wheel spinning.

We're going to see Jonesey tomorrow morning at Old Man Hobart's store, me, Kev, and my Grand-Dad. My Grand-Dad said something about asking Jonesey if he kept any of the articles his wife Elizabeth had read about strange happenings in the Township of Bridge Crossing.

"I'd like to read them myself," he told us, "just to see what people say they saw and heard back then."

He's also gonna bring the book written by Old Man Hobart's ancestor with him. I asked him if he's gonna give it to Hobart and he said he's going to let him have it for a bit but that there's some chapters he wants to read again.

I sigh as I try to get comfortable. I think we're gonna have a busy morning tomorrow.

"Hey, Chris? You asleep?"

I turn toward Kev's voice and lean up on one elbow. "No, I'm not really tired and I don't want to close my eyes. You?"

"Hell no. I'm just lyin' here thinkin' about everythin'. It's only a few days until July Fourth. I'm scared Chris. What's gonna happen to all of us?"

His voice is low but he doesn't sound hyper like he did before when we were outside. He sounds like someone in a movie who's scared and knows something bad could happen and that he needs to make sure he's ready for it and can handle it.

Maybe that's got something to do with what my Grand-Dad said out on the deck, just before we came inside.

* * *

We were just sitting on the deck after Kev had calmed down and made his point about Batman being better than Superman. It was quiet and kinda peaceful when he asked my Grand-Dad if we should maybe tell the whole town about the Hungry Teeth. My Grand-Dad didn't answer right away.

Then he turned to us and said, "Whatever is going to happen may not happen to everyone in Bridge Crossing."

I asked him what he meant by that. What about the innocent people who went missing over the years? What about that little girl Cecelia? Didn't the Hungry Teeth dead people get them?

"What happened to all those people—Cecelia, the transients who were hoboes, and others—was a terrible thing. Horrible to say the least. But the words in the book, the words spoken by that dying soldier stated: '*We will have our revenge against those who tortured our bodies and our souls.*' And that may not mean that they're seeking revenge on everyone in Bridge Crossing."

"I don't get it, Mr. Hopper. Aren't the Hungry Teeth guys comin' to get *all* of us?"

My Grand-Dad looks out into the yard for a long time before he answers. Then he says something really strange.

"The sins of the father are to be laid upon the children."

"Huh?" Kev looks from my Grand-Dad to me. I just shrug 'cause I have no idea why he's quoting something.

"It's a line from Shakespeare's play, *The Merchant of Venice*. You boys will have the pleasure of reading it in high school. That particular line means that if one's ancestor has done something horrible to another person in the past, their modern day descendants— people living today—must atone or pay for

144

that wrong even though it was many years ago. They are responsible for the actions of their ancestors so to speak."

"You mean like Billy Sarlewski's family? 'Cause the real name of Captain Death was Sarlewski, right? Are the Teeth comin' for them, Mr. Hopper? Boy will Billy be surprised when the Hungry Teeth get him!"

My Grand-Dad suddenly turns towards Kev and I'm surprised when he raises his voice. "Kevin! I don't want you or Chris to say anything like that to Billy, do you understand? You are to say nothing about this! All we have is a statement, an angry threat, made by a rescued soldier, a man who was dying of starvation and disease. He may have been delirious; we just don't know. Do not say one word of what we've talked about tonight to Billy, is that clear?"

I'm so surprised by him practically yelling at us, that a couple of minutes pass before I can say something.

"Gosh, Grand-Dad, what makes you think we ever even *talk* to Billy?"

"Yeah, Mr. Hopper," Kev says in a scared voice. "We never really talk to that creep Sarlewski. He's always lookin' to make fun of us or get us to do stuff we don't want to do."

My Grand-Dad sighs and passes his hand over his face. "I am sorry for that unnecessary outburst. Forgive me boys. I didn't mean to raise my voice. I just want it understood that you'll say nothing to anyone about what we've discussed tonight." He turns to Kev. "Not even your parents or your brother Jeremy, Kevin."

"No sir, Mr. Hopper. I won't say anything to them, honest!"

"Thank you, Kevin. No need to worry them or anyone else over what might just be a fluke in some odd weather patterns. There are some strange things happening around here, yes, that's true. Supernatural? I don't know but I think it's best if I to look into this situation before we create mass panic."

"But what about what you and Jonesey talked about the other night, Grand-Dad? What he said Mr. Hobart's old uncle said about teeth and everything. Jonesey sounded pretty sure that all the bad things, all the missing people and all that stuff, had to do with The Plot."

"Missing people, strange sounds—it's possible there's a rational explanation for all those things. Even old Uncle Pete's story may be somewhat of an exaggeration of a tale meant to scare a young boy. Maybe Jonesey, Mr. Hobart, and I, well maybe we're just all imagining the worst. Just tell me that you will keep what we've talked about tonight between ourselves, Jonesey, and Mr. Hobart. Agreed boys?"

We both answer, "Yes, sir" and carry the empty glasses into the kitchen to put into the dishwasher.

* * *

"You thinking about what my Grand-Dad said?" I ask.

"Yeah, I am. Chris, what he said made me feel kinda better—not *all* better but a little bit better—about all the weird stuff goin' on. What he said about the Hungry Teeth not comin' to get everyone in Bridge Crossin'? It made sense in a way."

"You mean about the name Sarlewski from back then and Billy's family now? Maybe they're the ones the Hungry Teeth are after?"

"You got it my man. Like the Sarlewski family owes something to the Hungry Teeth dead because of all the cruel stuff that Captain Death did to those Union soldier captives."

"Yeah, Kev, you're right. Not everybody's ancestors were like Billy's. There were some good people back then; there had to be some good ones. But the people who did those cruel things, I guess their families living here today have to pay for it. I think that's what my Grand-Dad meant when he quoted that line from that guy Shakespeare."

"Yup. And like Old Man Hobart keeps sayin', a score's gotta be settled. Jeez!"

We talk for most of the night and then we must've fallen asleep at some point because the next thing I know, Kirby is scratching at my bedroom door to go out to the backyard to do his business. As I get out of bed I glance towards my window. There're heavy dark clouds just hanging in the hot air. No breeze, just air that seems to be staying in one spot, not moving at all.

Like the day is waiting for something bad to happen.

chapter

32

Even though it's dry and hot, the clouds look so heavy with rain that we decide that we're going to leave right after breakfast to go to Old Man Hobart's store and avoid getting caught in a storm. The sound of distant thunder makes the day even scarier. Kev grabs bagels and puts lots and lots of cream cheese and butter on them while I pour lemonade from a pitcher into two tall glasses and get paper plates from the pantry.

We carry everything out to the deck where my Grand-Dad is sipping his coffee. He only takes half a bagel and, after a few bites leaves most of it on the plate. Kirby comes back from messing up on my Grand-Mom's flower bed and sits as close to my Grand-Dad as he can. Like he's protecting him.

The three of us don't talk much. Me and Kev just answer questions about how we feel, how we slept, and how we need to be ready to leave for Hobart's in about an hour. The sky seems so low with the clouds hanging heavy and full of rain. The clouds look like they could touch the ground. There's a steady rumbling sound of thunder which sounds like empty trash barrels rolling down the street. The air feels thick. Flashes of lightning inside the dark clouds make us jump as they flash really fast over the shed and near the fence.

"Let's get inside, boys. I'm not comfortable with this lightning."

Kev grabs the plate with the bagels and I take the glasses as we rush inside to the sound of thunder and the flash of lightning. It's getting scary outside.

* * *

"Never seen anything like it. Nope, never in all my years. My arthritis is acting up something fierce so I know rain *should* be coming. Thunder and lightning doing it's damnedest to start a storm, but no rain. Hot, dry air, but no rain. Thick low-lying clouds, but no damn rain. When the clouds do decide to open up, there's gonna to be some helluva torrential rain. Maybe we'd best start building an ark, professor. Damn infernal heat and no rain!"

At the mention of dry heat, Kev looks down at his sneakers, the expensive ones he puked on and my Grand-Dad washed off with the hose. Kev was so afraid he'd ruined them but thanks to the dry heat, they look like new. I guess the 'damn infernal heat' did some good.

The old air-conditioner rattles and both overhead fans plus three standup ones on the floor are keeping the store pretty cool. I watch Old Man Hobart grimace as he limps over to where the coffee pot sits and pours himself a cup. He holds the pot toward my Grand-Dad to ask him if he wants a cup but my Grand-Dad shakes his head no. Old Man Hobart walks slowly back to his chair and sits down with a loud thud and a mumbled curse.

"That damn Warren Sarlewski has been having meetings all over town, Will. Telling everybody who will listen that their property taxes will be lower if they agree to invest in a mall built on Dansbury Plot. Says the stores there will bring in a 'high revenue' that will pay for a lot of things our taxes pay for now. Wants to have the 'measure', as he calls it, put to a vote at the next township council meeting. Well, you know how I feel about this and if—"

"Where's Jonesey?" interrupts Kev looking at the empty covered plate that usually holds the doughnuts and other gooey goodies. Kev loves food but he's skinny like me 'cause he's so hyper and active that his mom says he "burns up all the calories before they get a chance to settle".

"Be back in a bit, young Mr. I-Want-Doughnuts-Lingle. Went out for the usual, pastries, milk, coffee. Hey!" Old Man Hobart yells a warning to Kev who's bumped into a table near the coffee pot. "Careful over there. You almost made the vase fall. Jonesey picked them flowers early this morning."

I look at the calendar hanging on a nail on the back wall. It's Friday. Flowers for Elizabeth day. I guess even with everything going on with The Plot, Jonesey will still pick up flowers for when he goes to have tea on Elizabeth's grave. I feel sad for him.

Hobart shifts and grunts in his chair as he turns towards my Grand-Dad and says with a laugh, "He'll return with your favorite chocolate filled

148

doughnuts soon enough, Kevin."

The book—the one I really wish I hadn't read, the one written by Old Man Hobart's old relative—is on a small table near his chair. Hobart reaches inside his shirt pocket, grumbling that he has "to put my specs on to read anything nowadays", picks the book up and turns to the pages my Grand-Dad has bookmarked. My Grand-Dad is looking at some old newspaper articles Old Man Hobart got from Jonesey's room in the back of the store.

Me and Kev wander around the store looking at the stuff Old Man Hobart sells. There's not a whole lot 'cause he doesn't really make money on what he sells. Like I said he owns the building so he gets rich on the rents I guess. The shelves with the cat, dog, and rodent food are the newest and neatest probably 'cause they're the best sellers. My Grand-Dad buys Kirby's food here and he told me he always looks for the sell-by and use-by dates printed right on the labels so he knows it's fresh.

After a few minutes of checking stuff out, we decide to go outside to wait for Jonesey. We both know that Old Man Hobart and my Grand-Dad are going to talk about stuff in that book and we just know that they don't want us to be there when they do.

It's too hot to do anything outside so we just sit on the steps of Hobart's store and wait for Jonesey to come back. The heat makes the sidewalks shimmer so that they look like they're alive. It's spooky.

I'm glad Kev is here with me. I know that he's always got my back and will always be there for me. Look at how he bit Billy Sarlewski in the gut to save my life when Billy was drowning me? That's a real, true friend all right. He's funny and a little nutsy too, especially when it comes to his pet rat Louie-Louie, but that's probably something that's really good to have in a best friend. He loves animals and so do I.

From Hobart's front steps I can see up and down the street clearly. Just like all the streets we saw coming here this morning, this street is decorated in red, white, and blue streamers and what Old Man Hobart calls 'bunting' for the Fourth of July celebrations. There are people putting up open tents and carrying chairs and tables inside, getting ready for the food and game places. Big metal steamers to cook hot dogs and large grills for hamburgers and sausage and peppers are being hauled up to be placed outside a couple of the food tents.

I used to love the Fourth of July celebrations in Bridge Crossing, but now I'm afraid of what's going to happen on that day this year.

We see a car coming down the road. It's Jonesey and we watch as he turns to go park behind the store. Tomorrow every street will be closed to traffic so people can walk from one end of town to another ending up near the bridge to watch the fireworks at night.

Kev jumps down from the steps and races past me yelling, "Let's go help him carry stuff in. Especially the doughnuts!"

I follow him slowly. It amazes me how Kev can be so terrified one day about what we read about in that book that he barfs all over his new sneakers. Terrified that the Hungry Teeth are coming back to get revenge, terrified that they might eat us the way they ate all those people who disappeared over the last one-hundred-twenty-five years.

But then, after he goes nutsy—or what my Grand-Dad calls ballistic—he can think about food and put any fears he has about other stuff in the back of his mind. I wish I could do that, but once I have a scary thought it stays with me for a long time. Like that snap I heard at The Plot and those dreams with Kirby talking to me. Food, even my favorite ones, can never make me put them completely in the back of my mind. No, sir.

Jonesey is taking bags out of the car and Kev grabs the big one with the pastries. I reach in to take a bag and, on the front seat, see a cloth sack, a blue clay pot, a folded white table cloth, a thermos, two mugs, and kinda hidden under the tablecloth, a small paper bag from the pastry shop that probably has just two doughnuts in it. Later he'll put all of this in the sack, get the fresh flowers from the store, and take everything to Elizabeth's grave so they can have tea together. He never misses a Friday sitting on her grave and reading that book to her. I guess that's what people call undying love 'cause even if the other person is dead, you still love them.

chapter

33

"We got two days until the Fourth of July, Kev. What're you thinking of doing?"

"Runnin' away."

We're back sitting outside and it's hot as anything. Kev lifts his shirt, wipes the sweat off his face and looks at Hobart's store where my Grand-Dad and Old Man Hobart are talking. Jonesey left about a half hour ago to drive up to the cemetery to have tea with his wife Elizabeth. Before he left he brought out a box of pastries and two cans of ice tea for us and said that Old Man Hobart and my Grand-Dad were almost finished talking. Then he carried that old sack of his to his car and drove away.

"Your parents are lucky, Chris. They don't even know that the whole town is in danger."

I tell him that my Grand-Dad told me not to tell them anything when they call me. Nothing about what's happening or what Old Man Hobart said about Bridge Crossing

"He kinda said that they had enough on their minds without worrying about what's happening here."

"What about your grandmother? Shouldn't she know?"

"My Grand-Dad said that she's busy in New York City and that's where she wants her to be right now so I guess he doesn't want her worrying either."

Kev shakes his head. He told me that he decided that he wasn't gonna tell his parents or his big brother anything either after my Grand-Dad asked him not to tell. He said it's kinda like Batman not wanting to worry people when he knows The Joker is planning something bad. No use scaring everybody until you really have to.

I don't say anything to Kev, but I think the real reason my Grand-Dad doesn't want my parents or my Grand-Mom knowing anything is so they don't decide to come back to Bridge Crossing. I guess he wants at least some members of this family to be safe and away from all this. But I can't tell Kev this 'cause his parents and brother are right here, right now. They're not away from anything that might happen.

* * *

Kev's eaten two big chocolate doughnuts and downed a can of ice tea. I just finished a glazed doughnut that we call a bowtie 'cause it looks like a big bowtie guys in old movies all seem to wear to weddings and fancy restaurants. Kev lets out a loud burp and I do the same. Usually this burping contest makes us laugh but not today. Today is a serious day.

"Anyway, there's still gonna be a celebration with food and music and that hot dog contest," I say, trying to make Kev forget about all the crap that just might happen. "It's great the way those guys can stuff their faces, huh?"

"So we're gonna go to the Fourth of July celebrations and stuff, right? Nobody will really be all that interested in anythin' but what that real estate guy wants to do with The Plot. We're gonna be forced to listen to Mr. Sarlewski talk about buildin' stores and all on The Plot. What a helluva day that's gonna be! *AND...*, we have to be careful about dead people, comin' outta The Plot and maybe eatin' everybody! Boy, this Fourth of July is gonna suck big time."

"Yeah, you're right about Sarlewski and that real estate guy talking. But I think people are either gonna be thinking about making money from The Plot or else they just want free beer. Me and you gotta be on the look-out for anything strange and scary like lightning and stuff. We gotta stay close to my Grand-Dad and Hobart."

"And Jonesey," Kev reminds me. We both look up the hill toward the cemetery. "Don't forget Jonesey."

"Yeah, him too. All of us have to be prepared. We're like the only ones around here who
know how much danger the people in this town are really in."

"Kinda like Batman and his butler Alfred." Kev's quiet for a few minutes, wiping the sweat off his face with his shirt again. He looks out at the street then turns to me. "You know what, Chris?"

"What?"

"I will be so God-damn happy when it's July fifth."

* * *

About twenty minutes later my Grand-Dad comes to the door of Hobart's and asks us to come inside where it's cooler. He tells us to sit down and listen to what he and Old Man Hobart have to say about the Fourth of July and what they've read in the book and what Jonesey had to say.

"Now, boys," begins Old Man Hobart, "I can understand that you're concerned about something happening on Dansbury Plot. Your Grand-Dad told me about you reading the book and listening to him talk with Jonesey. Things you shouldn't have done but, right or wrong, what's done is done and so now you're aware of things that should never have entered your minds. So I'm guessing that you're scared and, believe me, you have the right to feel that way. God knows it's scary and I'm a bit skittish myself." He turns to my Grand-Dad. "Will?"

"We understand and acknowledge that there *could* be some truth to the stories in that book we've read and to the ones Jonesey told us. People have disappeared but there can be many reasons for that. And Cecelia? We don't really know the absolute truth. All we have are stories passed down from one generation to the next and what was written in that book."

"What about waking up the Hungry Teeth dead, though? Remember that surviving soldier said that they would wait to be awakened?"

"Hobart and I have come to believe there can be two things that can happen. One, all the horror that we expect may just actually happen and so we've got to be alert to any danger and be prepared. Two, nothing happens and we just have a Fourth of July like we've always had. Perhaps nothing will happen that wakes the dead.

"But that being said, we both still feel that we should be extra cautious and watch out for anything strange happening. And no, we shouldn't alarm anyone else with our worries. Yes, terrible, inhumane treatment was given out by a cruel, sadistic commander one-hundred-twenty-five years ago. That's a fact. But, as far as a real curse happening, well, as I've said before, it may be nothing but the delirious ravings on the part of a tortured, dying soldier."

"And the book written by my ancestor?" Old Man Hobart leans forward and fixes us with a stare. "He may have taken some tales he was told and blown them all into fantastic stories with only a bit of truth in 'em. Like the

Cecelia story. Took a story about that little girl gone missing and added the dead human teeth part to make it more interesting.

"Maybe my Uncle Pete inherited his wild imaginings and story-telling from his great-grandfather. He sure was a spinner of tales all right. Probably scared the be-jesus outta poor Jonesey that night when I left him alone with Pete. He was just a boy, same as me, and whatever Uncle Pete told him that long ago night, well, sometimes a scary story grows with imagination and gets scarier in our memories. I wouldn't put too much stock into what Jonesey may believe Uncle Pete said."

Me and Kev look at each other for a long minute. Jeez, is there even a chance that everything we know is just crazy made-up stuff? Are we just imagining all the scary things we think are going to happen? There's a look in Kev's eyes of hope that everything might just be okay.

"So, again," continues my Grand-Dad, "we will say nothing about what we know or *think* we know to anyone."

"We will tell no one. Understood?" Old Man Hobart looks first at Kev and then at me.

We both shake our heads yes.

"That's good, boys," says my Grand-Dad. "People react strangely when they fear something and think there's real danger near them. We don't want people to panic because when panic sets in, they act in a dangerous manner that could lead to serious trouble. Now, we'll all go see the festivities for the Fourth of July, hoping for the best." He pauses and I hear him sigh. "Hoping for the best, but—being prepared for, well, just being prepared. That's always a good thing to remember for every situation."

Old Man Hobart nods his head slowly but doesn't meet the look I give him.

* * *

Me and Kev walk outside to wait while my Grand-Dad is grabbing a bag of dog chow for Kirby. As we cross over to the door, I hear Old Man Hobart say something under his breath.

Outside, Kev seems to be all happy and relaxed. He takes a baseball out of his pocket and begins tossing it into the air and catching it. Then he tosses it to me.

"Hey, Chris? You think that maybe they're right, your Grand-Dad and Old Man Hobart, that nothin' bad's gonna really happen? Like maybe they didn't want to say it but they think that Jonesey is kinda crazy and so was Old Man Hobart's Uncle Pete? Maybe all the stories about The Plot just kinda got scarier each time they were told?"

I catch the ball easily and lob it back to him. Kev looks so eager and willing to believe that nothing bad is going to happen so I almost don't want to say what I say next.

"I think everything we know about The Plot, Cecelia, and the Hungry Teeth and the dead soldiers, and waking up the dead guys are real and something bad *is* gonna happen on July Fourth. I don't think Jonesey is crazy at all or imagining stuff. He heard Uncle Pete all right and I think Jonesey is telling the truth. *And* I think Old Man Hobart and my Grand-Dad are saying that nothing bad's gonna happen 'cause they're just trying not to scare us"

"What? Why do you think that?"

"Because when we were leaving I heard what Old Man Hobart said while he was getting the bag of dog food. He said, 'We'd be damned fools if we weren't prepared for the hellish shit storm that's gonna hit in two days' time, Will. Damned fools!'

"Did your Grand-Dad say anything back to him?"

"Yes. He said under his breath, 'I know, God help us, I know.'"

chapter

34

"It's good to have this meeting tomorrow on July Fourth," Mr. Sarlewski says to the people gathered around him outside the bank. He's standing in that stupid way he has with his legs apart and his arms folded across his chest, like he's a big deal or something.

"Independence Day can mean *independence* from high property taxes for us all. Building stores and offices on Dansbury Plot will rake in money and free us from rising property taxes. We all need to invest our money to get even *more* money. Yes, sir! Once we build on that plot of land which has stood empty for so many years we will see money from the rents and services making a big difference in individual taxes."

Me and Kev are sitting up on the low branches of an old leafy oak tree across the street from the bank. We're like the best tree climbers in Bridge Crossing. We came to see the tents and stuff being set up for tomorrow but when we saw a group of people gathering around Billy's father, we climbed the tree to get a better view and hear what he's saying.

"Come around to hear me talk about what's best for our town and join all the festivities. There'll be games and food, including my own *Mrs. S's Simply Sensational Cookies.*"

I smirk and nudge Kev when Sarlewski says that crap about cookies. Yeah, right, like *he's* making the cookies.

"And Mark Colbert here? Well, his real estate agency is happy to supply beer to all the people who come to the ball fields to hear us speak about building on Dansbury Plot. I like that idea. Beer, yes sir."

Some of the people in the small crowd laugh at that remark.

"Mark and I will be handling the finances for the mini-mall so you know your money will be in good hands. So—we'll see you all tomorrow, folks. Remember, six-thirty on the dot. Make sure you get your beer before the meeting!"

Mr. Sarlewski and Mark Colbert walk away from the crowd of people and cross the street. As they pass under the tree where we're hidden, Sarlewski looks around to make sure no one is close to them. Then he leans in close to the real estate guy and says—

"Make sure to keep that beer flowing Mark. People are always willing to invest money in something when they've got enough alcohol inside them. Make damn sure there's a lot of beer. Maybe that'll make them forget those old stories about that piece of land being, well, being cursed or whatever story that old kook Hobart is putting out."

"Do you believe that Warren? That it really is cursed?" Mark Colbert stops walking. "I heard the so-called legends when I first came here. Personally I don't believe it but, sometimes it's hard to make people who grew up here hearing those stories forget things like that."

"Bullshit! You get enough beer in these people, make them think they're going to get money, and they'll forget those old stories soon enough." He looks around. "Just remember that I get a cut of that money these morons are going to invest in that mall your real estate agency is so keen on building. Got it Mark?"

Me and Kev look at each other, our mouths open in surprise. Boy, what a money hungry creep Mr. Sarlewski is!

"How could I forget *your cut* of the money, Warren? You remind me of that fact every day," says the real estate guy sarcastically.

When they walk down the street and go inside the real estate office, me and Kev climb halfway down and then jump to the sidewalk, bending our knees to land just right. We give each other high-fives and turn to ride our bikes over to the Dairy Barn where they're setting up tables for the hot dog eating contest. If we help them with the chairs and stuff, Kev thinks that maybe we can get a couple of hot dogs for free, maybe even zoupies.

Just as we get on our bikes, a loud bang makes us fall into each other and drop our bikes on the sidewalk. We smell something like burning tires and look down. On the ground close to our feet are pieces of a firecracker called a Boom-Rocket. They're small but boy do they make a loud noise and smell really bad. My Grand-Dad told me the smell comes from the black powder that's inside fireworks to make them explode. He also said that they're illegal for anyone to own. They've got to be handled by experts like the firefighters in town and not just anybody.

"Hey, Rat-Boy!"

Billy Sarlewski is standing in the street holding another Rocket in one hand and a book of matches in the other. He's laughing his head off at us. "Ooooo, did something scare you babies?"

"Yeah," says Kev picking up his bike, "your face." Good ol' Kev!

"You *should* be real scared, Lingle. My father says there's a rats' nest hidden under The Plot. Before they start building anything they've got to get rid of them all. They're gonna smoke 'em out and kill all of them, they're gonna bash their heads in when they run out of the ground, just like *your* rat should be killed. He's nothing but a dirty, disgusting, disease carrying rodent. Hey, Rat-Boy! I know where you're staying and I'm gonna break in, get your rat, and bash his head in like all the others will get their heads bashed in."

What Billy said to Kev was the worst thing he could've ever said. He threatened Louie-Louie's life. Kev drops his bike again and charges at him like a crazy man, yelling curses and everything. Billy runs toward the train station parking lot but Kev is a faster runner and he catches up with Billy in a heartbeat. He shoves Billy to the graveled ground, sits on his chest, and kneels on his arms, his fists ready to smash Billy's face into a bloody mess. I start to run to the parking lot when I hear someone yelling Kev's name.

"Kevin! No! No! Don't do it!"

I turn and see Jonesey running across the road toward Kev and Billy. He drops a bag he's carrying and a bunch of peaches tumble out onto the dirt. I start running too, and get there two steps after Jonesey who's panting like crazy. He bends forward, takes a deep breath, and puts his hand on Kev's back.

"C'mon, son," Jonesey says still trying to catch his breath, "he's not worth it."

"But what he said about Louie-Louie!" Kev is screaming and his face is all red. "Did you hear what he said? He threatened his life! *His life*! I'm gonna smash Billy's face into raw meat!"

"He's just a big-mouth bully, all talk. He's not worth your time, Kevin."

Me and Jonesey each grab one of Kev's arms and pull him up off Billy. We back him up a little bit away from Billy before we let him go.

"You son of a bitch, you sewer shit!" Kev screams at Billy. "You God-damn bastard!" He's so angry spit flies out of his mouth along with all the curse words and I'm waiting for him to use the word I heard grown-ups call the F-bomb. That would be something all right. Saying that word right out in public.

I'm standing next to Kev kinda holding him back again and am surprised to see Jonesey get closer to Billy. He stands over him and prevents him from getting up. Billy looks scared. Jonesey is saying something to Billy and I tell Kev to stop yelling so we can hear what he says.

"Get up, Billy, and go home. If you say anything about what happened here, I will call the police chief and report you for having illegal fireworks. The only fireworks that are allowed here in Bridge Crossing are the ones that will be set off tomorrow night by the fire department. If I report you, you'll go to the juvenile detention center in the state capitol and believe me that's a wicked, wicked place to be." He leans down so he's almost face-to-face with Billy. "I know boys who were sent there and horrible things were done to them. They never came back and nobody knows what happened to them. So you will not say anything to your father or your mother or anyone else or the police chief will make damn sure that you get sent there."

Wow! I've never heard Jonesey talk so tough and Kev is so surprised he's stopped cursing.

"You get up and you go home and you keep your mouth shut. Do you understand me?"

Billy shakes his head yes and sits up. Then he whispers something to Jonesey and points to us. Jonesey looks over to me and Kev and then back to Billy.

"Those boys won't say anything about this to anyone especially the police chief. I can promise you that. I know them and I trust them." He looks over at us and says, "Right boys? What happened here ends here."

We both nod yes, and he turns back to Billy. "Now give me that firecracker and go home."

Billy hands the Boom-Rocket to Jonesey and gets up slowly. Then, when he's on his feet, he turns and runs away from us as fast as he can. Jonesey watches him until he's almost out of sight and then walks over to where he dropped his bag of peaches. We go over to help him pick them up.

There must be about a dozen peaches in the dirt and we pick them up and examine them one by one. A couple have pebbles stuck in them but most are just dusty from the parking lot. Jonesey cleans each one off by rubbing them on his pants leg and puts them back in the bag. Without saying a word to us he starts walking toward the center of town.

Kev clears his throat and takes a few steps toward him. "Um, Jonesey? *Jonesey?* Do you *really* know boys who were sent to that kids' jail place who never came back?"

"Maybe, Kevin, maybe," he says without stopping. "As long as Billy believes that I do."

I guess Jonesey says a lot more things than I thought he would ever say. Anyway, he sure knew what to say to Billy to make him keep his mouth shut.

chapter

35

We wake up on the Fourth of July to a hot and humid day. A hot and humid day isn't really a surprise in Bridge Crossing in the month of July but somehow this sweaty heat feels different than other times. The clouds are covering the sun and they seem to be just hanging over everything. Holding the area in a grip of heat and moisture that feels like it just might explode. Like the balloon water bombs that Billy likes to throw at girls who have come out of the changing rooms at the pool and are all dressed up to go out somewhere. He does it when the lifeguard isn't watching and laughs like crazy when the balloons hit the girls and explode, getting them soaked and pissed as hell.

The clouds feel like that, like those water-filled balloons—heavy and just waiting to hit us and explode.

I didn't sleep all that good because of a strange dream where Kirby is talking again. While we're getting dressed I tell Kev about my dream last night.

"It was scary, Kev. Kirby was sitting on my bed just staring at me, waiting for me to wake up. Then, when I was awake and looking at him, he said really calm and everything, 'Be careful. They tasted your blood. Your blood. They might want more.'"

Kev just kinda nods his head and looks out the window for a really long time. Then he says, "We've gotta be really careful, Chris. I mean it's a dream, but we gotta be extra careful. I'll watch your back and you watch mine."

We solemnly shake hands like we've seen grown-ups do when something really serious is about to happen, and then finish getting dressed.

Me, Kev, and my Grand-Dad each grab bagels as we head out the door to the car. It's ten o'clock and we're meeting Old Man Hobart and Jonesey down by the Dairy Barn in half an hour. Then we'll probably walk down the main street and see all the tents that are set up. I guess we'll be walking kinda slow 'cause Old Man Hobart has that stiff knee and has to stop every few steps but maybe that's a good thing. The slower we walk, the better it will be to look out for anything bad that might be happening. Later, around six o'clock, we'll go over to the Little League fields and wait to listen to that blowhard, Mr. Sarlewski. Old Man Hobart called him a blowhard and I looked it up in the dictionary. It means 'an arrogantly and pompously boastful or opinionated person; a braggart, a windbag'. That's Billy's father all right. I wrote the word and the definition down in my special notebook.

Kev's awfully quiet and he doesn't even finish his bagel, just wraps it up in one of the paper napkins we took with us. I can tell he's scared about what might happen. When his mom called last night and said she and his dad would see us later by the hot dog eating contest, I thought he was going to cry. Before he hung up he told his mom that he loved her and I guess she thought something was wrong 'cause most guys our age never say I love you to our parents like that just out of the blue. She must've asked him if everything was all right because I heard him say, "Yeah, everything's good, Mom. Me and Louie-Louie are okay."

My Grand-Dad parks on the street four blocks from the Dairy Barn. Cars are already lined up on the streets and we can't park any closer. The lot at the Dairy Barn is set up with long tables and an outdoor cooking area for the hot dog eating contest and, even though it's early, I can smell the chili and onions for the zoupy sauce cooking in a big pot. The smell almost makes me want to cry because I remember the last time I had a zoupy when we came here after the *Batman* movie. We were laughing and joking and the most important thing on Kev's mind then was why nobody ever knows that Batman and Bruce Wayne are the same guy. We sure as hell weren't worried about people with dead teeth coming out of the ground.

We meet up with Old Man Hobart and Jonesey over by where the hot dogs will be grilled later and then we begin to walk the main street. I hear music being played over by the small merry-go-round they set up every year near the bank. Joey, Brad, and Sal usually head there early to check out the new paint job on the wooden horses and the other wooden animals on the ride. I ask my Grand-Dad if we can go over there. He gives us money for rides and snacks and says me and Kev can run ahead a little but not to get too far away.

"You can stop at each stand and tent. Just check back with us every once in a while. Just stay in the general area of the fair. Let's try to make this as pleasurable a day as it's always been in past years."

We're nowhere near The Plot so I guess he feels it's okay for us to go see things and all. Anyway it's better than walking real slow with Old Man Hobart. Even though I thought walking slow would make us be more alert to any scary things, I changed my mind. Walking slow is one thing but with the way Old Man Hobart walks, we're almost standing still.

* * *

If I didn't know about the Hungry Teeth and the missing people, and little Cecelia, I'd probably look forward to enjoying the celebrations today just like I always do on July Fourth. But this year is different. Everything I know might happen keeps me from really having fun. Kev isn't his usual goofy self, running from one food stand to another and making sure he saves a front row seat for the hot dog eating contest just so he can be up close to see if someone barfs. Nope. Today he's quiet and watching everything, like *he's* Batman or something. We buy a roll of tickets for rides and food and then head out to find our friends.

After checking out the merry-go-round and riding it twice, we leave Joey, Brad, and Sal to go get some lemon ice. They're going over to try their luck at the ring toss and try to win one of those big stuffed monkeys for Brad's little cousin.

Before they leave, Sal tells me that the hole in his yard is being inspected to see if it really can be filled with cement and that one of the inspectors found two really old buttons in the dirt near the hole.

"Like maybe somebody who was burying a treasure had them ripped off when he was digging in the backyard." He turns to Kev. "Remember you said that maybe someone robbed gold and diamonds from a jewelry store and buried it in my yard? Well, maybe those are his buttons and they can get his, you know DNA off them, and now after all these years, the cops will know who robbed the store! Maybe there's still a reward for information and we'll be rich!"

Kev doesn't get all excited about that robbery story like he usually would. And he doesn't say a thing about the gold tooth I have in my underwear drawer. He just says, "Yeah, maybe. You might be right about that Sal."

"Yeah and you know what else? There's a funny smell coming from that hole. It started after those inspectors began sifting through the dirt."

"What kind of smell?"

"Kinda like moldy food. Like, remember the time I left my lunch in my gym locker for a whole week? That kind of smell. Really gross!"

I tell them we'll see them around the rides and then me and Kev leave.

On the way to the lemon ice stand I ask Kev if he's worried about leaving Louie-Louie in my bedroom. I tell him that I was kinda worried about leaving Kirby at the house but figured the house is pretty far from The Plot so he was safer there than with us.

"No, Louie-Louie's safer at your grandparents' house 'cause, like you said, it's pretty far from The Plot. I'm still mad about what Billy said about knowing that me and Louie-Louie are stayin' with you but I think Jonesey scared him about that kids' jail. And besides, Kirby will bark his head off if anyone steps even a big toe on your Grand-Dad's property, forget about even tryin' to get into his house. Kirby's fierce."

"Yeah, ol' Kirbs is a barker all right. His bark scares some people 'cause it's so loud."

"Yeah and that's good. That creepy little slime-ball Billy is afraid of all dogs."

chapter

36

"If those clouds get any lower, they're going to cover all of Bridge Crossing! Ain't never seen anything like this. You?"

"They're filled to the brim with rain is all. Makes 'em look heavy. Only thing is, once they let loose, we just might have to swim for our lives!"

Two of the old guys from the pool are sitting on chairs by the Ferris wheel talking about the weather. They're taking tickets from anybody who's going on the ride. They get paid by the town to do it so I guess it makes them feel important. We see Joey, Brad, and Sal over by the Ferris Wheel and we walk over.

"Hey there, sonny," one of them says to me. "How's your Grand-Dad? Did he come here today? Good man your Grand-Dad."

I answer that he and Mr. Hobart, and Jonesey are walking around Main Street.

"Going on the wheel are you?" says the other old guy.

Now we talked about this, me and Kev, and he knows how I feel about heights so, because he's my best friend, we're staying over by the bumper cars while the other guys go on the Ferris wheel.

"You're smart, you two," says the old man after I told him we're going on the bumper cars. "You sure don't want to get stuck up in them clouds now,

164

boys. They can suck you right up! Say goodbye to your friends." He points to Joey, Brad, and Sal. "Suck'em right up!"

The two old guys laugh like crazy until one of them starts coughing from all that laughing and spits into the street.

Sal and Brad and Joey get in a car and the operator slams the cage door shut and makes sure it's locked. Me and Kev watch the wheel slowly rise up. It stops every few seconds to let some people off and then other riders get in the empty cars before going up again. When the cars are full, the operator pulls a switch and the wheel begins to go faster. They'll go around four times before they have to get off, one car at a time.

I watch the car my friends are in and when the ride stops it at the top of the wheel, the car and the people in it really do seem to disappear into the clouds. I hold my breath—it *does* look like the clouds sucked them up. I can't see them!

Then the car comes out of the clouds and I see Brad waving to me. They go around three more times and each time I watch them disappear into the dark clouds I feel my stomach tighten. I am so glad when their car finally comes down and the operator opens the caged door to let them out.

"It was wacko spooky, Chris," says Joey as the three of them walk over to us. "Once we were up at the top, we couldn't see anything but the clouds. And it had a funny kind of hot wind that almost made you think people were whispering."

"Yeah," agrees Brad. "But it wasn't really whispering, right? It was only the wind."

Sal shakes his head and says, "I dunno, I could swear I heard people whispering. Like when you're in the library and you have to whisper so you don't get kicked out. It was words all right. I heard them, honest! Spooky is right!"

"Nah," says Joey. "It was only the wind, Sal. You didn't hear words. It's really windy up there by the clouds and you just heard the wind is all."

Kev looks at me and I see that look in his eyes that he had the day I told him about the snapping sound I heard the day I almost fell on The Plot with my cut hand.

Old eyes, knowing eyes like the old guys down at Hobart's.

* * *

We ride the bumper cars, killing time before the hot dog eating contest. The bumper cars are okay. Usually me and Kev are a lot more into bumping each other but today is different and it isn't even all that much fun. When we get off, Kev asks me if I want to go check out the ball field where Mr. Sarlewski is going to talk about building on Dansbury Plot later. He wants to see the stage that's being set up and the beer kegs being hauled in. It sounds really good considering that the hot dog eating contest is two hours from now.

I look around for my Grand-Dad and see him over by the Ferris Wheel talking with the guys from the pool. He's there alone so I guess Old Man Hobart and Jonesey are stopping at one of the other parts of the fair. I tell Kev that maybe we should ask my Grand-Dad about going to the ball field.

"We're just goin' to the ball field, yeah, but—maybe you should ask him. You know, just in case he wants to know where we are."

I run over to my Grand-Dad just as Old Man Hobart and Jonesey walk up. Hobart sits down on a bench near the Ferris Wheel and looks like he wants to talk to my Grand-Dad so I start talking first.

"Grand-Dad? Kev wants to go look at the beer kegs and stuff at the ball field where they're putting up a stage for Mr. Sarlewski and his dumb speech. Is it okay if we go?"

"Kevin wants to do this, hmmm?"

"Yes, so can we?"

He smiles at me but hesitates before he answers. "All right Christopher. I'll say yes if you promise that you'll stay away from Dansbury Plot."

"Gosh, Grand-Dad, I sure don't want to go over there and Kev doesn't either. Believe me, we're not going anywhere near The Plot. We just want to see the beer kegs."

My Grand-Dad turns to Jonesey and asks him if he minds going with us to the ball field. Jonesey smiles his sad smile and says he'll go with us.

"All right, Christopher, as long as Jonesey here goes with you, I'll say yes. I imagine a lot of the townspeople are over there anyway." He looks at the large clock across the street on the bank. "Let's say you meet us over by the Dairy Barn in about thirty minutes. Here's my watch."

I promise we'll be back in thirty minutes 'cause how long does it take to check out beer kegs? Then I take the watch and run over to where Kev's waiting.

"He said okay." I show him the watch. "We've got thirty minutes and then we'll meet by the Dairy Barn."

Then we run ahead of Jonesey toward the ball field feeling an excitement that's part fear.

chapter

37

There are some people on the ball field when we get there, a few people from town, not a whole lot. Mostly there are workers checking to make sure the stage is up and not wobbly and decorated with that bunting stuff. The stage is smack on the corner of the ball field right across the street from The Plot. It scares me to see it so close to that dead piece of ground.

Mr. Sarlewski and Billy are there but, once Billy sees Jonesey, he looks scared and turns away and pretends like he doesn't know us. I'm betting that he didn't tell his father anything about the Boom Rocket or being knocked on his butt and almost being clobbered by Kev. Probably remembered what Jonesey told him about that kids' jail.

As soon as his back is turned, me and Kev run over to the clubhouse far away from Dansbury Plot and sit on the back steps away from the sight of father and son Sarlewski. Jonesey stays near the stage. Even from where we're sitting we can still hear Mr. Sarlewski's big, booming voice telling the workers what to do.

"Make sure that microphone is smack in the middle of the front of the stage. I want to be facing the people who come to hear me. Put those chairs over by the side. Put that sunshade over where I'll be standing, did you hear me or are you deaf?"

He's not even nice about telling them, he's just rude and nasty like he's a king or something. The workers look pissed as anything.

I peek around the side of the clubhouse and see a truck pull up. It's carrying the beer kegs and big ice containers to put them in so they stay cold. I hear Mr. Sarlewski tell the guys hauling them off the trucks where to put them. Then I hear him say to the guys finishing the stage, "My wife can't be here today. She's still finishing up the cookie platters. I told her to make them herself, adds a personal touch to my business. I like it that way. Too bad she won't see my speech here but she knows she's working to help us get this business deal going."

"Wow, Kev! Now he's saying 'my business' as if he is the one who started it and does all the work. It's like Mrs. Sarlewski is just some woman who works for him. Boy, Old Man Hobart was sure right when he called him a blowhard!"

"He's an asshole, a blowhard asshole plain and simple," says Kev. He's been cursing a lot since this whole thing about The Plot started. I guess it's like with grown-ups—when they're mad and stuff, or really upset about something bad, they sure curse up a storm. Maybe it makes them feel better, I don't know. I just nod and agree with Kev. Mr. Sarlewski *is* a blowhard asshole.

We hear a car pull up and then hear Mr. Sarlewski say, "I'll be back later to make sure you've done your jobs. Make sure that beer stays ice cold and the stage looks exactly the way I told you. If everything's not the way I want it to be, you won't get paid a cent. Come on Billy."

I hear two car doors slam and I turn to Kev. "They're leaving now, Kev. As soon as the car drives away, we can check out those beer kegs."

When the car leaves we walk over to where the kegs have been dropped. The guys who are still working on the stage are pretty nice to us and let us look at the big kegs of beer sitting in the huge tubs filled with large blocks of ice. The ice and the kegs are really cold and you can feel the chill when you walk near them. My arms have goosebumps on them. I look at my Grand-Dad's watch and tell Kev that we have to head back to the Dairy Barn now. Our thirty minutes are almost up. Jonesey is waiting for us over by the fence near home plate.

"Hey, kids," says one of the workers stopping us as we walk away. "Let me ask you something. Is there a food garbage dump around here? There was a strong smell of rotten eggs in the air early this morning. You got any food places that dump food out every night?"

Kev shakes his head. "No, sir. Right Chris?"

"No dumps, no. There's the Dairy Barn but they dump their food in a trash compacter and put sand in it so it doesn't smell. And the pizza place and pastry shops do the same thing. They make sure that they do it every night 'cause if there's any garbage left out, the raccoons will come and make a mess with it all over the place."

"Oh yeah? How do you know all this?"

"My friend's brother told us and he knows that stuff 'cause he has friends who work at those places. And he worked at the Dairy Barn last summer until he got a job in a book store."

Kev nods his head. "Nope, no old food left around here at all. I think you gotta pay a fine or somethin' if you dump food."

"Yeah? Well, a couple of hours ago, something smelled like rotten eggs around this ball field and that's usually the smell of spoiled meat. No idea where it came from that rotten egg smell. It's gone now but it was just hanging in the air for a while. Rotten eggs, phew!"

Rotten eggs. That awful smell. Me and Kev look at Dansbury Plot and I know what we're both thinking. That girl, little Cecelia—the teeth marks on her body smelled like rotten eggs until the day she died.

chapter

38

The hot dog eating contest, the band playing old songs, the food stands—everything is just something to do while we're waiting to go to see Mr. Sarlewski's big deal speech and to see if something bad is gonna happen or not. Even the hot-dog contest guy who puked on another contestant wasn't enough to take our minds off of what could happen. Kev didn't even laugh like he always does.

Old Man Hobart is talking in a low voice to my Grand-Dad and Jonesey. I can't hear what he's saying but I do see Jonesey shake his head like he's saying yes. Finally, my Grand-Dad calls us over and brings us to the side of the Dairy Barn, away from the crowd of people, so he can talk to us. He bends towards us and looks at us to make sure he has our full attention.

"Before we walk over to the ball field I want to ask you something. Remember what we talked about down at Mr. Hobart's store a few days ago? About what might or might not happen today? Do you remember what Mr. Hobart and I said?"

Kev nods his head and says really fast, "Yeah, you told us that we've got to be alert and prepared for stuff that might *not* happen but *could* happen. We got that."

"That's right and what else?"

"We shouldn't scare other people by tellin' them what we *think* might happen 'cause we might have a riot when people go nuts about the curse and the dead guys."

"That's correct Kevin. Very good." My Grand-Dad looks at me. "Chris?"

"Okay," I take a deep breath. "So you said the curse might just be crazy talk from a tortured, dying soldier. And Mr. Hobart said that maybe the book his ancestor wrote was a big exaggeration, kinda like he took the truth and made it a whole lot scarier by adding made-up stuff. He also said that maybe his Uncle Pete made things up too, just to make the story about little Cecelia sound more interesting."

My Grand-Dad bends toward the ground breathing deeply like he's just finished a tough game of tennis and has finally won. He straightens up and says, "All right boys, good."

Then he looks at us both for a few seconds and his look is very serious, like it was when I fell off my bike two years ago and broke my wrist. Serious and grateful that I hadn't been hurt more.

"Christopher, Kevin I want you two boys to know how very proud I am of you. A lot of what you've heard and read is very frightening for an adult and I can't imagine what it's like for young boys your age. But you've both proven that you're strong and resilient."

"What's res-il-, what you said," asks Kev and my Grand-Dad laughs.

"It means, young man, that you are capable of recovering quickly from something unpleasant. In this case, recovering from fear of the unknown."

"Yeah that's us all right. Reslint, right Chris?"

"*Resilient* and I guess we are."

Old Man Hobart and Jonesey come over to us and Jonesey asks if we're ready to go to the ball field.

"Might as well get this shit storm over with and hope that we'll all still be here tomorrow. Debt's gotta be settled and who knows who will settle it?"

Hearing Old Man Hobart's words, I don't feel so resilient any more.

* * *

The ball field is pretty crowded by the time we get over there. We had to walk real slow and everything 'cause of Old Man Hobart's bad knee. The bleachers are almost full but my Grand-Dad manages to find a seat for Hobart. The rest of us stand as near to the stage as we can get. I see Mr. and Mrs. Lingle who wave at us and also Jeremy with some of his buddies.

There's a table setup with a sign that says *Mrs. S's Simply Sensational Cookies* and some people are lined up to grab the few that are left. Some guy is handing out sheets of paper with a lot of stuff typed on them. Jonesey takes two of them and hands one to my Grand-Dad and one to Old Man Hobart. My Grand-Dad lets me and Kev read his paper and it's all a lot of crap about money and a new mini-mall and how everyone's gonna get rich by investing in it.

A lot of people have cups of beer in their hands and there's lots of loud talking, like you hear sometimes when there's a party or barbecue going on and grownups are having beer and wine. There's a lot of loud talking then too, that's for sure. People who are drinking always get kinda loud.

The people from the bank are there and so is Mark Colbert who's looking at his watch. I don't see Billy or his father and it's already almost six-thirty but I guess Mr. Sarlewski wants to make a big deal entrance like he's somebody important. And make sure that people have had a lot of beer to drink before he makes his big deal speech.

The sky over The Plot is grey and heavy with clouds. It's hot and humid. Nobody goes off the baseball field. We're all crowded together and that kinda makes it hotter. I feel as if I'm holding my breath waiting for something to happen so I take a deep breath and try to breath normally.

"Hey." Kev nudges me and points to a fancy car parking on the edge of the ball field. A man gets out of the driver's side and goes around to open the back door. Ellen and Billy step out from the car into the street and then go wait by the front of the car. After a few minutes, Mr. Sarlewski comes out.

"Jeez," says Kev. "He's got his own Alfred the butler type driver."

Some of the loudest talking beer-drinkers let out a cheer when they see him. I hear Old Man Hobart curse under his breath and my Grand-Dad says to him, "They're like sheep following blindly to the slaughterhouse. He's made them think that somehow they're going to get rich by building on Dansbury Plot."

"They're damn fools, Will, damn fools with too much beer in them."

Mr. Sarlewski walks to the stand waving at everyone like he's some kind of a king. Some man walks up to him, beer cup in his hand and says loudly, "You're the best, Sarlewski. You're helping all homeowners who pay taxes through the nose. Bringing in a money-making mall to lower our tax bill. You outta run for governor!"

"That guy's sloshed," says Kev. I look around. There seems to be a lot of sloshed people. I guess Mr. Sarlewski was right when he told the guy from the real estate office to keep the beer flowing. I guess he figures that the more they drink the more they'll agree with his crazy ideas. Mr. Sarlewski walks up the two wooden steps to the stage and over to the microphone. He stands there while some of the men cheer him.

My Grand-Dad leans over toward me and Kev and says, "Boys, I want you to remember this moment, remember it all. What you are seeing is man who is able to convince others, by lying and exaggeration, to follow him in a scheme that they don't even understand. He doesn't care about these people. All he cares about is getting what he wants. You are seeing greed corrupt the minds of these men and women. They are not thinking for themselves. It's called a mob mentality. That means that instead of making their own decisions and choices, they're just following what everyone else is thinking and doing. He's promising them that they will have more money and money can make some people do strange things. Do you boys understand what I'm saying?"

Kev nods his head. "Yeah, I get it Mr. Hopper. Kinda like zombies following their master, right? They're zombies and Mr. Sarlewski is the zombie master."

"No, Kev," I say, "it's more like a kind of wacko mass hypnosis I think. Like Mr. Sarlewski has used the beer and his talk about how everyone who supports his plans to have the mall built will have more money 'cause their taxes will be so low. He's hypnotizing them so they can't think for themselves. Grand-Dad?"

"In a strange sort of way, you're both right. It is like a mass hypnosis and they do seem to be zombie-like in the way they're simply following along with what Sarlewski is telling them."

"See?" says Kev nodding again. "I knew they were like zombies."

Mr. Sarlewski smiles and waves at people and taps the microphone to see if its's on. Then he leans toward it and says, "Everyone having a good time? I heard all the cookies are already gone. Well, no worries on that score. We got more *Mrs. S's Simply Sensational Cookies* coming soon. My wife is hard at work making them. And the beer will keep flowing!"

Big cheer from the crowd when he says that about the beer.

"Yes, sir, we're going to do it. We are going to put the sleepy little town of Bridge Crossing on the map by investing in a town mini-mall! In doing so, your property taxes will be lowered and you will be able to keep more of your hard-earned dollars. The stores that will be built on Dansbury Plot will be a blessing for this town. Not to mention more money in your pocket when tax time comes around!"

More cheers. Sarlewski raises his hands to quiet the crowd and smiles at them.

"That's right. You'll be able to hold onto more of your hard-earned money and not give it away in town property taxes. That small investment you make to build shops on Dansbury Plot is a necessity for us all. I'm a hard-working man, just like you are, and believe me I will damn well enjoy keeping more of my money."

The beer drinkers near the stand let out a whoop and then start cheering again. I hear Old Man Hobart shout, "Hard-working man my ass!" as he gets to his feet and faces the stage and Mr. Sarlewski. The crowd turns toward Old

Man Hobart.

"Sarlewski, what do you know about hard work? The hardest work you ever did was scheming money from people. First from your sick, elderly parents, then from your long-suffering wife—Lord knows *that* woman understands hard work. I heard that she's working so hard today that she can't even come out and enjoy the July Fourth celebrations. You sure as hell scammed that poor woman. Now you're making false promises to your fellow citizens and trying to scam them outta *their* money."

Mr. Sarlewski looks down at Old Man Hobart. "What are you blabbering about you senile old coot."

Hobart laughs and says, "Old? Well, damn right, I am old. But senile? Nope. I got my senses in first rate condition, better than yours will be at my age. You're a scam artist, a sneak, and a dirty schemer. You know about Dansbury Plot. How nobody ever walks on it—hell people will go out of their way to avoid being near it.

"Kids playing on this here field? No way do they ever go over to The Plot, no sir, not even if they hit a ball onto it. The land is cursed. Nobody will be building anything for profit on Dansbury Plot, not you nor nobody. You've heard the old stories same as we all have."

He spreads his arms wide toward the people on the field and I see a lot of them nod their heads yes, like they know about all those old stories passed down from one generation to the next. "A score's gotta be settled for the evil wrongs done there. It's got to be settled, Sarlewski."

Mr. Sarlewski's face gets beet red and he shakes a finger at Old Man Hobart. "What the hell are you talking about you damn old fool? What stories, what score? You really are senile."

Old Man Hobart takes his time then slowly walks closer to the stage until he's standing directly in front of Mr. Sarlewski.

"You're a damn fool, Sarlewski if you say you don't know about the old stories surrounding The Plot and the reasons behind those stories. I'm talking about the prison-of-war camp the Confederates built on Dansbury Plot and the atrocities inflicted on the poor prisoners here. The dead are hungry for revenge."

chapter

39

Sarlewski laughs and says, "If there *was* a prison-of-war camp on this land, then those who were imprisoned here deserved what they got. They were enemy prisoners, how the hell should they have been treated? Revenge? From what? The dead?! From what I know the dead can't hurt anyone. You want to know why, you old fool? Because they're *dead*!"

There's a little bit of laughter but most of the people standing on the ball field suddenly look like they're not really sure if they should laugh or not. Maybe they think laughing about the dead is bad luck or something. Boy, I sure do.

Thunder crackles overhead and everyone looks up at the sky. Sparks of lightning are sprinkled through the clouds.

"Dansbury Plot is sacred ground. A score's gotta be settled for what happened there," says Old Man Hobart looking up at the clouds hanging over The Plot. "The dead will have their revenge, believe you me. Men, good men, suffered horrible tortures and died there."

"And they're *dead,* old man. Get it? *Dead* and *rotted* in that bullshit sacred ground! They're not settling anything, Hobart. You're crazy if you think the dead can come back for revenge. *Dead* is *dead*."

I hear more thunder and see a quick lightning flash. The weather is changing kinda quickly. People are looking up at the cloudy masses overhead and a few hold their hands out to see if there are any drops of rain coming.

But there're no raindrops—just a hot and humid wind that seems to suddenly kick up from nowhere. It's not *real* windy, just like a steady small wind that doesn't stop. Kev jabs my ribs and points to The Plot. Small swirls of dust seem to be moving from the wind, just swirling in circles but only on The Plot, nowhere else. The dirt circles seem to be getting bigger and higher as I watch.

"Sarlewski, I can almost pity you but I won't because my pity would be wasted on you. All you have in your heart is greed. You have no feelings for anybody but yourself. I tell you what happened on Dansbury Plot has haunted this town for one-hundred-twenty-five years and unless we settle the score, all hell will break loose in Bridge Crossing."

"Listen to him Mr. Sarlewski. Please listen to him," says a soft voice. "We can't, we just *can't* build on The Plot. It's a sacrilege. You don't know the horrible things that will happen if you don't listen to Hobart."

I turn to the side and there's Jonesey standing at the edge of the stage, looking at Mr. Sarlewski with a look that is sad and almost desperate.

"Well, well, well. Look at the town nutcase telling me what I should do."

He bends towards Jonesey with a look of real hatred in his eyes. Jonesey doesn't back up or anything, just keeps looking at Mr. Sarlewski. He doesn't even blink from Sarlewski's hate-filled look.

"You should've been locked away in a looney bin years ago when that wife of yours died. Everyone knows that you're not all there." He points to his head and makes circles with his finger like Jonesey is a crazy man. "Why don't you go back to Hobart's and make coffee and put out doughnuts? That's all you're good for anyway. I'll tell you something though, the coffee sucks and the doughnuts are stale. Get lost you crackpot."

Sarlewski laughs and turns to the crowd expecting them to laugh too but nobody is laughing. The crowd of people is so quiet it's almost as if there's nobody even here. Even the beer drinking guys are quiet. Just about everybody knows Old Man Hobart and Jonesey. They all know about what happened after Jonesey's wife died and how Old Man Hobart helped him. They all know Jonesey's a sad, quiet guy who doesn't bother anyone, takes care of Hobart's store, and is nice to kids and the old guys down at the store. And Old Man Hobart, jeez, just about everybody in town has been down to Hobart's and had free coffee and doughnuts, and listened to his stories—not just the old guys and us kids—everybody.

"Sarlewski overplayed his hand," whispers my Grand-Dad to me and Kev. "He went too far with what he said to Jonesey."

Jonesey is still standing there, not saying a word. Old Man Hobart walks over to Jonesey and puts his hand on his shoulder. I guess he's letting him know that Mr. Sarlewski is what my Grand-Dad calls an anal perforation, which, like I said, is his nice way of saying ass-hole.

Mr. Sarlewski looks at the people standing there. For a couple of minutes, he doesn't seem to know what to do. Everyone is looking at him. Then he clears his throat and says, "We all know that there are people in this town who would like to stop any new construction, stop anything that would make our town more modern, more in step with the other towns around us. They're old-fashioned in their way of thinking, afraid of change. They'll say the most ridiculous things to keep this town from moving forward and keep us from paying less taxes. Are you going to listen to them and live in the past or are you going to make an investment in your future? What will be built on Dansbury Plot will benefit us all. More money for the hard-working people in Bridge Crossing! More money in your pockets!"

He seems to have gotten people's attention again. Some of them are listening to him. Like my Grand-Dad says, it's the promise of money. Money can make you do strange things.

"Who is with me on investing a small amount of money now to reap more money in the near future? Helluva deal, my friends, helluva deal!"

"That's right! More money in our pockets. It *is* a helluva deal Sarlewski!" shouts one man in the crowd.

The beer drinkers are nodding and you can tell they're agreeing with him. Mr. Sarlewski walks over to where they're gathered at the corner of the stage and begins to laugh and joke with them like they're old buddies. He knows who's with him on this deal all right.

Kev looks at the beer drinking guys and says, "I guess they're not afraid of dead guys, Chris, or curses and stuff. Boy are they stupid! They're not listenin' to anybody but Sarlewski! Jeez!"

"Yeah," I say.

I look at the people standing around and listening to that blowhard Sarlewski. I look at Billy and his sister Ellen standing in that corner of the stage with their father. Billy looks bored. Ellen seems embarrassed by her father and looks like she wants to be a hundred miles away from here so she doesn't have to listen to his bull crap speech. I look at my Grand-Dad, Jonesey, and Old Man Hobart talking quietly together and looking worried. I think about everything I read in that awful book and I think about what Jonesey told us about little Cecelia and people who went missing over the years. I think about The Plot and that snapping sound when my hand dripped blood on it. Finally, after taking three deep breaths, I make a decision.

"C'mon, Kev. We *gotta* do this."

"Huh? Do what?"

"Let everyone know what *we* know about Dansbury Plot and the Hungry Teeth dead and, and…everything!"

Before he can say anything else, I grab his arm and we walk up the steps, right past a totally surprised Billy and Ellen, and stop in front of the microphone. Kev stands there looking a little scared but ready to be there for me, his best friend. He's loyal like that, that's for sure. I reach up and grab the mike out of its holder.

"Hey, everybody. Listen up for a second. I'm Chris Hopper and I've lived in Bridge Crossing all my life. This is my best friend Kev Lingle and he's lived here all his life too. Me and Kev, we know a lot about Dansbury Plot and all the stories told about it. You gotta believe Mr. Hobart and Jonesey when they tell you that we can't build stores on The Plot. Something awful and terrible will happen if we even *try* to build anything. Please don't listen to Mr. Sarlewski! He only wants your money. He's even getting a cut of any money you give to the real estate guys—honest me and Kev heard him tell Mr. Colbert not to forget about his cut. He doesn't care what horrible thing will happen to you! Something bad is gonna happen today if you don't stop talking about it and making plans to disturb The Plot. It'll happen right today!"

Suddenly, Kev grabs the mike from my hand. "Listen, Chris is right, really bad things are gonna happen here if you try to build stuff on The Plot. Me and Chris know about that, we know because we read a really, really old book about things that happened here in Bridge Crossing that nobody can explain. People goin' missin', a little girl bitten all over her body just 'cause she walked near The Plot after gettin' scratched up by berry thorns and the Hungry Teeth smelled her blood, crazy crap that happened and no one ever can explain it 'cause it's, it's—crazy, crazy stuff!"

I'm looking at Kev in total surprise. He's all hyper and just saying everything that comes into his mind which is a lot of things. Then I look at the crowd and see that people are kinda talking together and nodding their heads like they've heard some of the stories Kev's talking about. Like maybe, just maybe, they might believe them.

"And there were alive soldiers in that prison that was on The Plot eatin' dead soldiers 'cause the commander of the prison was this mean, really cruel guy who put them in holes in the ground and starved them—they were so hungry they even ate some guys who were kinda still livin'! Yeah, really, listen to Old Man, uh, I mean, Mr. Hobart and Jonesey. You know them. They won't lie to you. Believe me the dead guys are comin' back. They're the Hungry Teeth dead guys and they're comin'. The book said they would come back in one-hundred-twenty-five years and that's now! Right now, today, on the Fourth of July! They're just waitin' for somethin' to wake them up and then all horrible stuff will happen. Please don't wake them up!"

"What the hell do you think you're doing? Stop this bullshit right now. You boys have no business being on my stage. Get the hell off now!"

chapter

40

Mr. Sarlewski comes stomping across the stage right towards me and Kev and he looks as mad as hell. He moves straight past me and tries to take the mike from Kev. But Kev hangs onto it and back steps away from him. I search the crowd for Kev's parents and his big brother Jeremy and see them way in the back trying to get closer to the stage. I see my Grand-Dad and Jonesey trying to get to us too and even though they're closer to the steps they can't seem to move through the crowd. Everybody is so tightly packed around the stage that they're having a hard time reaching us.

I step right next to Kev. I remind myself that Mr. Sarlewski is just a bully like his son Billy. Older and bigger, but still a bully. And you gotta stand up to a bully even if it's just with words like my Grand-Dad did at the pool.

"Tell them the truth, Mr. Sarlewski," I say facing him and trying hard not to look scared. "Like Mr. Hobart said, you heard the stories. I mean, even if some of them are just kinda exaggerated made-up stories, others are really true. Like the fact that no one ever even walks on The Plot or that when a baseball is hit onto Dansbury Plot during a game, the coaches tell us to leave it and they get another ball for the pitcher. Nobody walks their dogs near it either."

"Yeah," Kev chimes in, "The Plot would be a great place for a dog to poop but they would never ever go near it even if their owners pulled them there. Nope, no way. Dogs are smart."

"Get off my stage, both of you!" screams Mr. Sarlewski, his face all red and a purple vein bulging in his neck. "Get the hell off it now!"

Kev drops the mike and we both back up fast. "But you don't understand Mr. Sarlewski," I say. "You can't build on The Plot, you just can't. Talking about building stuff on The Plot will wake them up! You gotta stop talking about it."

"Yeah, you can't build on The Plot. The Hungry Teeth won't let you, believe me. They're gonna come after everybody if you don't stop tellin' people to build a mall and stuff."

Kev's getting really hyper and I can hear him breathing super hard.

"Who the hell are you talking about?"

"The dead guys with their teeth, the hungry dead guys!"

Mr. Sarlewski looks at Kev and then he starts to laugh. "The hungry *dead guys*?! You're as screwed up as Hobart. Hungry dead guys!"

"No, really, I know what I'm sayin'. Those soldier prisoners died horrible deaths in those holes in-the-ground prison on Dansbury Plot and they're comin' back with their Hungry Teeth to get even."

"Listen to me, kid," Sarlewski says, his face leaning closer toward Kev. "Like I told that old coot Hobart, if there *was* a prison-of-war camp on Dansbury Plot—and nobody knows for sure that there *was* one—and those prisoners died horrible deaths in that underground prison, I am positive the bastards deserved it. They were *pri-son-ers*, prisoners, do you understand? They were there because they were the enemy and they got what they deserved. Starve the bastards? Why not? Torture them? It's part of war you stupid kid. And the dead aren't hungry *because* they're dead! They're not coming back *because* they're dead! Do you understand me? You can't wake the dead, kid. They're gone forever! There is no way they're coming back today or any other day."

When he says that a terrible rumble of thunder crashes right over our heads and lightning streaks through the dark, heavy clouds. I look around for my Grand-Dad and see him and Jonesey getting on the steps to the stage. I see Jonesey turn and help Old Man Hobart up the steps. They're gonna come help us.

"But Mr. Sarlewski, please," I say desperately, waving toward my Grand-Dad, "they're gonna come and settle a score like Mr. Hobart says. My Grand-Dad will tell you. They're gonna come! They said one-hundred-twenty-five of them died here and they'd wait one-hundred-twenty-five years and return to get even. The dead are coming back! Today! We gotta get away from here so we don't wake them up!"

Mr. Sarlewski just looks at us, like he's trying to understand what we're

180

saying. Maybe what I said finally got through to him. He seems to have stopped talking and for one moment I think that maybe, just maybe, things will kinda be all right. Maybe he'll understand why nobody can build on The Plot. Maybe there's nothing to be scared of anyway. If I get through to Mr. Sarlewski everything might just be all right after all.

But boy, oh boy, was I ever wrong on that one!

chapter

41

It all started with the Boom Rocket that Billy threw onto Dansbury Plot. Early that day, I really wanted to believe that maybe the stuff we read in that old book that said the dead prisoners were coming back to settle a score on Independence Day one-hundred-twenty-five years later was just some guy's wild imagination. I even was starting to believe that what my Grand-Dad said about the rescued soldier who said that stuff really was crazy from all the starving and living under ground in those cells. Going nuts from all that was maybe the reason he said all that stuff about Hungry Teeth returning. I told Kev that maybe it really was true that Uncle Pete was a looney bird making up stories and that Jonesey believed him and made the stories worse each time he told them. Kev shook his head and said, "Maybe" and he had looked at me like he really hoped that everything was gonna be okay too.

And then, even after we got on stage and had that big thing with Mr. Sarlewski and then saw Billy making faces and stuff at us, I still kinda had hope that nothing would happen. Especially when Mr. Sarlewski seemed to have nothing to say about the Hungry Teeth dead guys. Like he really was starting to believe us and change his mind.

But Billy had to go throw that firecracker on Dansbury Plot and, when Old Man Hobart saw him do that I heard him say, "Now's when the shit really hits the fan."

Out of the corner of my eye I saw Billy making faces at me and Kev. He was holding something and my stomach hurt when I saw what it was in his hands.

"Hey, Rat-boy! Watch this!" Billy yelled just before he threw the firecracker. He was standing on the stage by the corner of The Plot. Even though he's not at all that good at throwing a ball, he was close enough to throw the Boom-Rocket and have it land on the dead dirt that was on the corner of Dansbury Plot.

He lit the Boom Rocket, took aim, and swung his arm up. I heard someone yell out, "No!" Maybe it was Jonesey yelling it but I don't know for sure 'cause the thunder was so loud.

I watched the Boom Rocket fly up into the air, curve and land on The Plot. And then, as Old Man Hobart said, the shit really *did* hit the fan.

The thunder and the lightning kicked up and big charges of electricity started striking The Plot. Billy jumped down from the stage and ran like crazy in the direction of the Dairy Barn. The lightning and thunder were so bad, people started screaming and running for shelter. The ball field got empty pretty fast. Soon there was nobody there except me, Kev, my Grand-Dad, Jonesey, Old Man Hobart, and Mr. Sarlewski and his daughter Ellen, standing on that stage near The Plot. And all of a sudden, the seven of us were inside a horrible nightmare.

The stage rose up and shifted sharply over the wide street toward Dansbury Plot just like it was lifted up by some giant's hand. The force flung us high up into the air and we all landed on that terrible plot of dead earth! My Grand-Dad grabbed me and Kev as we fell toward him and we smashed together landing on The Plot. Old Man Hobart cursed loudly as he fell forward and I saw him and Jonesey just lying in the dirt trying to get up. Mr. Sarlewski fell hard on his face and Ellen slid right into Kev and knocked him down again. We all struggled to stand up.

And then something else happened that scared me even more if that's even possible. Along with the lightning and thunder, a strange fog began rolling in and surrounded everything outside of The Plot. All we could see clearly was the cursed land that was Dansbury Plot. I heard Kev's mom and dad and his brother Jeremy calling his name but I couldn't see them. And the smell that came with the fog was even worse. Rotting eggs. The smell was awful. Nobody but us really saw what was happening because nobody else could get near The Plot with that heavy fog.

Inside the fog an eerie light began to glow. The ground rumbles, the swirls of dust on the ground rise higher, and I see large pieces of dirt rise up out of The Plot. Except it isn't dirt. Kev grabs my arm and points.

"Holy shit, Chris! Look!"

I look but I don't want to believe what I see. Oh man. I really don't want it to be real. What I first thought was dirt are nothing more than skeletons, some with flesh and skin hanging on them, dressed in the rags of Union Army uniforms. And they keep rising out of the dirt, still coming, there are so many of them! I feel like I'm in a nightmare and pinch myself hoping I'll wake up. But I *am* awake all right and looking at this group of skeletons coming out of the ground.

The hollow sockets where their eyes once were seemed to be able to stare as if they could still see. And what they were staring at, what they saw, was us. But it was their teeth that were the scariest, scarier than those staring eye sockets. They were long, yellow, and sharp, and I could hear a snapping sound when they looked at us. That same snapping sound I heard when my cut hand bled on the corner of The Plot. Snap. Snap. Snap. I feel like I can't breathe.

I see a half skeletal boy about my own age standing there, holding a rusty and bent bugle. There's a kid's army cap on his skull. He looks straight at me with those empty eye sockets, I swear, and slowly, so slowly, nods his head. It's a scary feeling and it makes me feel cold all over, because that nod—it's almost as if he knows me! My heart pounds and I feel my body shake. Kev sees it too and I hear him say, "Holy shit!" again.

We sure can't run anywhere because we're trapped by the fog. Another skeleton looks right at me, ripped skin hanging from his face and arms. I can't move. He takes one step toward me but is stopped by the large bony hand of another skeleton who seems like he's in charge of the dead guys coming out of the ground. I hear him say—

"No. Not this boy."

The skeleton who was moving towards me quickly steps back.

The one in charge speaks again. His voice is deep and scary and his words seem to echo in the air around us almost like we're in a tunnel.

"Heed my voice any who would *dare* to defile this hallowed ground solely to put money in your own pockets! You who would wish to profit from land that is the burial place of tortured men!

"We the dead, who have no rest and who have waited for more than a century, have come to exact payment for wrongs done to our comrades-in-arms. I swear to you the terrible things that have been done here will be avenged. They will be *avenged!* We have had nothing but time, the endless time of the dead. Today we will have our revenge."

The skeleton, skin hanging from his face, turns and looks at us one by one.

"We seek a member of the family descended from one Albin Sarlewski whose cruel and inhuman treatment caused anguish, unbearable pain, and death to my comrades-in-arms. That person must be sacrificed to us.

"Albin Sarlewski, Captain Death, escaped our vengeance by running away like the coward he really was, but his descendant *must* settle the score we were unable to exact from him. Our Hell has a price. We have waited long enough. If we do not have this sacrifice, we will unleash horrible deaths on *all* the residents of this town, even the innocents! We will destroy all who are living here the same as we were destroyed."

"Atrocities occurred here, cruelties were deliberately committed," says Old Man Hobart shaking his head and breathing hard. He's leaning against Jonesey and trying to move his stiff knee. "Like those old Bible stories Jonesey and me used to hear in Sunday School. Death and destruction, revenge on their enemies were what the victims wanted from their God and they got it too."

"I believe you're right Hobart. Settling *this* score is a lot more Biblical than I thought," said my Grand-Dad.

The light and the fog have us locked-in and I know there's no way to escape from this. The Hungry Teeth want a Sarlewski and the only Sarlewskis here are Warren Sarlewski and his daughter Ellen. She's hanging onto her father, crying and scared as hell. Mr. Sarlewski's eyes are bugging out of his head and he's looking all around for some escape but the thick fog makes that impossible.

The skeleton points one bony finger toward us and asks, "A descendant of Albin Sarlewski must come forth now. We know you are here."

When no one moves he raises his voice, and it seems to boom louder than the thunder in that small space. "I ask again! Come forth now. You must pay your debt for our torment."

A slow, circling hot wind kicks up again, blowing across Dansbury Plot and over to where we stand. No one is moving.

"One last time I ask you to come forth and pay the debt of your ancestor!"

The skeletons march slowly forward and surround us in a kind of semi-circle. Kev barfs right where he stands, he doesn't even bend over. Pieces of hot dog and lemonade spill all over his shirt.

Mr. Sarlewski is moving back, away from the Hungry Teeth. He has his hands on Ellen's shoulders and he shakes her a little. I thought that maybe he was trying to take his daughter and make a run through the fog to save her. Boy was I wrong again!

"You want a Sarlewski?" he screams at the Hungry Teeth. "This girl is a Sarlewski!"

He shoves Ellen toward the skeletons who snap their teeth as she falls toward them. But she gets up quickly and grabs her father's arm.

"No, Daddy, no! They want to eat me, please, Daddy, help me!" screams Ellen.

185

My Grand-Dad turns to him, shouting over the hot wind blowing across Dansbury Plot,

"You'd sacrifice your own daughter for this ritual? What kind of a person are you, Sarlewski?"

"Daddy! No, please!"

Mr. Sarlewski turns Ellen around to face him and smiles this wacko kind of smile. Then he talks to her in a strange soft voice that's almost as scary in its sound as the skeleton's booming voice.

"Ellen, Ellen, I'm sorry Ellen. Please understand. It has to be this way. It will be your great sacrifice to your family. You understand? Your mother needs me, your brother needs me. I am a prominent, important man in this town. You will be remembered by everyone in Bridge Crossing as a brave young girl, a heroine who saved her family, saved her town by sacrificing herself. You must understand why it has to be you and not me!"

"No! Daddy, no!"

She tries to pull away from him but he's got her in a strong grip. He shoves her hard toward the Hungry Teeth but my Grand-Dad steps forward, catches her, and pulls her over by Jonesey.

He turns and stands near Mr. Sarlewski as the skeletons begin to close the circle. The head skeleton in his torn and ragged clothes looks at my Grand-Dad and says in that horrible voice louder than thunder, "Do not interfere in this Will Hopper!"

Kev looks at me and I know what he's thinking; the skeleton knows my Grand-Dad's name! How does he know his name?

"This debt is not yours, Will Hopper. You and yours are free. But there is no mercy for this man Sarlewski as his ancestor showed no mercy to us. Since we do not have Albin Sarlewski, this man, not the girl, must pay the price for what has been done. Keep back!"

I close my eyes as the Hungry Teeth snap, snap, snap their way to surround us. The air smells of rotten eggs and the hot wind blows faster. I hear that snapping sound so close to me.

"No! No!"

The scream makes me open my eyes and I see the skeletons reach past me toward Mr. Sarlewski. He turns to my Grand-Dad.

"Will, have mercy, help me for the love of God, help me. They're going to eat me alive! Will, please, Will!"

My Grand-Dad reaches for Mr. Sarlewski and me and Kev yell for him to stop. Suddenly he pulls back really quick. I look at his arm. There are the marks of teeth on his skin but no blood. No blood! The Teeth didn't break the skin so he won't end up like little Cecelia! Just kinda put their teeth on his arm as a warning to stop trying to save Mr. Sarlewski and let them have their revenge.

"Ellen! Ellen save me! Save your father!"

But Ellen just stands there like she's turned to stone or something. She looks like she doesn't even know where she is. She stares and stares, I guess just like that little girl Cecelia from so long ago.

I see Mr. Sarlewski being pulled away from us toward the center of Dansbury Plot. He's still reaching his hand towards my Grand-Dad begging him to help. One of the Hungry Teeth clamps down on that hand and bites half of it off. Mr. Sarlewski screams and screams as the skeletons' teeth began to tear the flesh from his body.

"Will! Help me! Please help me!" His voice fades to a horrible shriek. The skeletons sink their teeth into Sarlewski's flesh and shake their heads back and forth like a dog playing tug-of-war with a toy, ripping and pulling on his body.

My Grand-Dad's face is a sickly white and he steps forward and calls out to the skeleton who had spoken to us before. "Is there no other way to have this debt paid? A human sacrifice doesn't have to happen, does it? Please tell me. There *has* to be some other way."

The skeleton answers, "This human sacrifice must be so that this plot of earth can be free. After today, there will be no need to fear us, the dead, any longer. The townspeople are fortunate that one life for many lives will suffice and will satisfy this debt owed us. There is no other way. You cannot be a part of this. You cannot save him." He faces my Grand-Dad. "Look inside the cover of the old book you have, Will Hopper. See the pictures hidden within it."

"Pictures? I-I don't understand."

"You will understand."

He turns to follow the others then turns to my Grand-Dad. His voice is low and respectful. "Sir, you are a gentleman and so I would ask a promise of you. I ask that you make of this hallowed ground a memorial, a sacred place where we who died will always be remembered. Erect a memorial stone with the names of all one-hundred-twenty-five of the brave men who died here so we shall not be forgotten."

My Grand-Dad nods and quietly says, "I promise you that you will not be forgotten."

The skeleton raises his bony hand in a salute, then turns and walks away.

* * *

Mr. Sarlewski's screams are awful! I cover my ears with my hands but I still hear them. They echo around the fog as his body is pulled under the ground of Dansbury Plot. I think I'm gonna hear them for the rest of my life.

My grandfather tries to follow Mr. Sarlewski in some crazy attempt to maybe save him, but the hot wind blowing hotter than before stops him and he falls to his knees. Jonesey and Old Man Hobart drag him back towards me and Kev.

When there are no more screams to be heard and there's nothing but silence, the hot wind slowly stops blowing. The army of skeletons seems to have faded away and the fog begins to disappear. We can almost see the ball field and the streets leading to town.

Old Man Hobart looks around for a long time and finally says, "Come on. Let's get out of this hellish place and find Kevin's parents so they know we're all okay."

Boy, I think, okay doesn't even half cover how we are. We're more than okay, we're alive! Which is more than I can say for Mr. Warren Sarlewski.

Quickly Jonesey leads all of us away from The Plot, me and Kev helping Old Man Hobart as he limps toward town. My Grand-Dad and Jonesey take Ellen's hands, making her walk with them. She doesn't say a word, just stares straight ahead and kinda stumbles when she walks.

"The Hungry Teeth got what they wanted, Chris," whispers Kev to me.

"Score's finally been settled, that's for sure," says Old Man Hobart sighing. "Debt's been paid."

As we walk, the clouds seem to burst open and a slow steady rain begins cooling the air and wiping away that horrible smell. I glance back and see that the rain's falling on Dansbury Plot too. The ground is getting soaked and there are even small puddles on the ground.

The rain starts falling harder but not one of us seems to mind getting wet at all, no sir. We don't hurry to get out of it or anything. Me and Kev even turn our faces up and let the rain fall on us.

It feels so damn good.

chapter

42

Things have kinda settled down since the awful night of the Fourth of July. It was the scariest night of my life and I never, never want to go through anything like that again. I saw the Hungry Teeth come out of the ground and drag Warren Sarlewski into their circle on Dansbury Plot where they ate him alive. It was the most horrible thing I have ever seen or could ever imagine. The lightning, the deafening thunder, a horrible smell, a fog, and dead soldiers.

Kev keeps saying that Billy really started it all by throwing that Boom-Rocket onto The Plot.

"He woke up the dead, Chris. Woke 'em right up out of the ground. That's what he did all right."

I think he's right because until Billy threw that Boom-Rocket, the night was quiet—a little spooky with the sound of distant thunder and just a couple of flashes of lightning and Mr. Sarlewski yelling at us on that stage—but still kinda quiet.

Since no one really saw what happened on Dansbury Plot — except me, Kev, my Grand-Dad, Jonesey, Old Man Hobart, Mr. Sarlewski and Ellen—because everyone was running for shelter from the lightning storm, the story was told that Mr. Sarlewski had a massive heart attack, after being attacked by some rabid raccoons who were hiding on Dansbury Plot. He died from the shock and his wounds. His wife was told that Mr. Sarlewski's remains were taken to the county morgue and that she didn't have to deal with anything and that 'his friends' would take care of the service and burial arrangements. She seemed okay with that.

My Grand-Dad convinced Mrs. Sarlewski not to see good ol' Warren's body—good thing too said Kev 'cause there *was* no body to see anyway—so a closed coffin with some heavy dirt and rocks in it was supplied by Old Man Hobart who's richer than God. He told Mrs. Sarlewski it was the least he could do for her and her family after having known Warren for such a long time.

"That woman's been through enough being married to him. She's a victim too," said Old Man Hobart. "No need to know the truth about how Sarlewski really died."

My Grand-Dad agreed and said, "The truth doesn't necessarily set you free. You're right Hobart, there's no need for her to know the truth of how Warren died."

So Mrs. Sarlewski never knew the truth and—after a church service which almost nobody went to—had Warren Sarlewski buried in the local cemetery where Jonesey's wife Elizabeth is buried. It's not near Elizabeth's grave or anything—it's actually pretty far away from her grave on the hilltop— but Kev asked me if I thought Jonesey ever thinks about the fake Sarlewski coffin buried there when he goes to have tea with his dead wife every Friday. I thought about that for a few minutes and then I told him that I bet he doesn't think about it at all because Sarlewski isn't really there.

The strange weather and that fog were explained as a 'weather anomaly'. I looked up the word and it means an unusual change of weather, rain, temperature, or fog over a region. "A strange but completely natural occurrence," said the weather guy on our local TV station. Nobody ever said anything but we all know there was nothing natural about what happened on The Plot at all that day.

Mrs. Sarlewski left town with Billy and his sister Ellen. Mrs. Lingle heard that she's opening her cookie business in a small town in Pennsylvania where her brother lives. I guess she still makes the best cookies ever and she can make them in Pennsylvania the same as she made them here in Bridge Crossing. Mrs. Lingle also said that she thought Mrs. Sarlewski was kinda relieved to be rid of her husband Warren. He was a mean demanding man who had no love or respect for his wife. She said that if she was Mrs. Sarlewski, she would have left him years ago. Their house is up for sale although why anyone would want to buy it is a mystery to me and Kev.

"Yeah, Billy's sister is in that catnip state your Grand-Dad talked about. She doesn't talk at all just sits and stares. My mom heard that she's in some hospital out there in Pennsylvania.

"*Cat-a-ton-ic,* Kev, not catnip. Yeah, she is catatonic and nobody knows if she'll ever come out of it."

"Kinda like that little girl Cecelia, right Chris? Boy, imagine never talkin' again? Wow!"

It's a sad thing to think that pretty Ellen Sarlewski will never talk again. I feel awful but then for no reason I can ever explain, all of a sudden I start laughing because I can't help it. It's one of those laughing fits that you sometimes get in a school assembly when the principal is talking about something serious and important and you're supposed to be quiet. I'm laughing because I'm imagining Kev never talking again! Jeez!

* * *

The day after the whole horrible thing at Dansbury Plot took place, my Grand-Dad takes out the old book written by Old Man's Hobart's ancestor and me and Kev sit with him on the deck. He reads a few pages and shakes his head then gently peels back the front cover. All three of us stare at what is hidden inside.

In the cover of the book are five old wrinkled photos, sepia-toned ones taken by a photographer before the men went off to war. The author of the book, Old Man Hobart's ancestor, must have gotten them from some old photographer's studio and placed them in the cover so they wouldn't get lost. Me, Kev, and my Grand-Dad look at the photos. There they are in their brand-new Union army uniforms and shiny new boots, serious-looking men and one boy.

"Look at them, Chris and Kevin. Young men and one bugle boy, a boy about your own age, setting out to win the Civil War." My Grand-Dad's voice is soft and sad.

"Wow, Mr. Hopper. Why'd they let kids be in the army?"

"It was a tradition, Kevin. Young boys have been bugle and drummer boys through many wars down through the centuries. During the Civil War they were usually poor boys from small farms. Many times the money they earned in the military was their families' only source of income."

There are names written on the backs of the pictures. "Thomas Miller Hansom, Josiah Baxter Isaac Kellen, Timothy Harris Ford, Aaron Marlon Fens."

A hand-written note is attached by some sort of sticky stuff to the picture of the bugle boy. I turn the picture over and read the note out loud to Kev and my Grand-Dad.

"This boy, this bugle boy is the youngest victim of that horrible camp on the Dansbury

Plot. It has been said that he was captured along with the soldiers and sent to Camp Death. When, weeks later, while cleaning out the privies, he heard one of the guards say that Union troops were near, he tried to escape to tell the troops where they were in the hopes of having his fellow prisoners rescued. But he was captured and Albin Sarlewski had him put in one of the hot holes without food or water where he died of starvation. This boy is named William Christopher Hewitt Hopper and he died a hero's death." J.P. Balif

"Chris!" Kev grabs hold of my arm. "That must've been the bugle boy skeleton! The one who nodded at you kinda like a hello or somethin'!" He turns to my Grand-Dad. "Both your names, that bugle kid has both your names! Wow, Mr. Hopper, wow!"

My Grand-Dad looks closely at the picture of the bugle boy and I see tears in his eyes. Then he smiles sadly and says, "Wow indeed Kevin, wow indeed."

* * *

My Grand-Dad did some research into what he calls historical archives by contacting a couple of universities and found out that what the skeleton said about Albin Sarlewski running away after the Civil War ended was true. He was never prosecuted because no one could find him after the South lost the war.

The books in the archives said there were some rumors about what happened to him and one of them was that he hid out in Mexico in some small town and lived there until he died at the age of ninety years old. Another rumor said that he stowed away on a ship going to England, changed his name, and worked as a gravedigger.

But the truth is, nobody really knew back then or even knows now what happened to him. That's why the Hungry Teeth took Mr. Sarlewski. Someone had to pay for all the horrible things Albin Sarlewski did and if they couldn't get him, well, Warren Sarlewski had to take his place.

As Old Man Hobart said, "Given the right circumstances Warren Sarlewski would have been just as cruel to innocent people as Albin Sarlewski was. He had to be sacrificed to settle the score. No doubt about it in my mind."

Old Man Hobart also told me and Kev something real interesting about Sal Minella's backyard too, the place where I found that gold tooth.

"That there hole in your friend's Sal's backyard? Well, boys, it was examined by some engineers who were hired by a fancy Delaware historical society. After a whole lot of digging around and examining the dirt, and with the help of an old map from around the Civil War time, they're saying that the

Minellas' backyard was exactly on the path those prisoners-of-war took when they tried to tunnel out of those hell-holes and the tunnel collapsed on them. They found the remains of a few prisoners and now they're declaring it a historical site."

Old Man Hobart sits in his chair and sips his coffee, and nods at me and Kev. We came in so's Kev can buy some fresh straw for Louie-Louie's cage. I nod back at Old Man Hobart and remember what Sal told us. The society is offering to buy the land and are offering his parents a ton of money to move to another house. Sal's mother said that they'd be 'God-damned idiots' not to take the offer and she already has her heart set on one of the houses in a new development near the high school. There're tape and markers around Sal's property so that nobody can go on the land. It must be pretty cool to have stuff from the Civil War buried in your backyard. I feel bad for the soldiers who died there though. Dirt falling on top of you and burying you there scares me nuts especially since I fell in that hole and that could have happened to me.

Anyway, about that gold tooth I found in the sinkhole? I still have it and my Grand-Dad never said that I had to give it back to Sal. That's good because I'm gonna keep it in my underwear drawer forever.

* * *

Me and Kev grab a doughnut, say good-bye to Jonesey and Old Man Hobart, and walk out to where our bikes are by the front steps of Hobart's pet store.

My parents are coming back from Hawai'i at the end of next month. My mom is going back to work because, as she told me when she called, that that is what she needs to do to 'feel good about herself'.

I'll be going to *The Willin' Cate* book store every day after school next year. Kev's parents said it's fine if Kev comes with me. My Grand-Dad says he needs us to keep an eye on the store if he and my Grand-Mom have to go anywhere. He's gonna pay us each ten bucks a week. We'll take Kev home when the store closes at five o'clock. Kev's happy and nutsy about it all. He loves my grandparents and he loves money.

My dad told me that he's expanding his business in a couple of other towns and he'll be busy as hell traveling going to them all. He also told me on the phone that he'll be sleeping back in their old bedroom.

"Your mom and I are really working on this Christopher and, with some major changes in our lives, we'll do our damndest to make it work. We just need more time."

Maybe the Hawai'i trip really did help.

I don't know exactly what's gonna happen with my mom and dad but I do know that, when they do return, I'll be living with my grandparents for a while. That's until my parents can settle into what my Grand-Mom, who's coming home from New York in two weeks, calls their 'new life'.

"People make changes in their lives all the time Christopher," explained my Grand-Dad one night when me and Kev were sitting on the deck with him and Kirby. He'd just come outside after having gotten off the phone with my Grand-Mom. I know they were talking about my parents and stuff. Me and Kev kinda listened in by the back door.

"Sometimes the old way of living a life doesn't work anymore—it becomes stale and unexciting, boring and not satisfying. That's when we have to adjust our lives, find out what's important to us and what will work to make our lives more fulfilling. We need to feel good when we wake up and not dread the day ahead."

Kev nods. "I get it Mr. Hopper. It's like I feel all good when I wake up now because the Hungry Teeth are gone for good. I don't have to be afraid of them anymore. That old way of bein' scared sure wasn't workin' for me."

My Grand-Dad smiles and says. "Well, that's as good an analogy as anything that can be said about what happened and what's now behind us Kevin."

"What's ana- what you said?"

"A good comparison, Kevin, a good comparison."

Epilogue: One Year Later

Grass is growing on Dansbury Plot—almost everybody still calls it The Plot—where it sits on the very edge of the Township of Bridge Crossing, across a really wide street from the Little League field. A lot of flowers are beginning to bloom there too. It's really kinda pretty

My Grand-Dad kept his promise to that skeleton leader of the Hungry Teeth and convinced the township council to use their eminent domain rights to claim The Plot as a Civil War site and to honor those soldiers who died there by building a memorial. Old Man Hobart was the first person to walk on The Plot to prove to everyone that it was no longer a danger to anybody. He got his picture in the town's weekly newspaper and everything so me and Kev think that makes him kinda famous.

A narrow brick pathway leads to the center of The Plot where there's a big, fancy white stone with all one-hundred-twenty-five names and ranks of the men who died there carved into it. It took my Grand-Dad almost four months of contacting historical societies to find out the names of all the prisoners who died there but he finally found every single one of them. On one side of that stone there's a large wreath with real live red, white, and blue flowers, which a florist changes every week so there's always a fresh one, and on the other side is an American flag. It looks nice.

There's no fence around Dansbury Plot. No one walks on The Plot, though, but it isn't because they're afraid anymore or think that it's cursed. Nope. My Grand-Dad told me that no one walks on it out of respect for the dead who lie buried there. He says they're at peace now and their rest shouldn't be disturbed.

I think about Jonesey putting flowers on his dead wife's grave stone every Friday. He walks on the ground where people's dead relatives are buried.

"Aren't all those dead people buried here somebody's long dead relatives and all though, Grand-Dad? I know there's a flower wreath here but maybe

195

someone will want to put their own flowers on the ground, right? It's kinda a cemetery when you think about it."

"In a way it is, Chris, but it's not like a regular cemetery where people can walk on the grass to put flowers on the individual graves of their loved ones. No, Chris, this is a memorial on sacred ground that shouldn't be disturbed, that should not have foot traffic tramping on it. Not allowing people to walk on it, well—the town council made the correct decision." He looks at Dansbury Plot and nods his head. "It was the right thing to do."

I nod. I guess that's why there are white signs on the four corners of The Plot. From the ball field where we're playing catch, me and Kev can read the signs, "*Civil War Memorial Site. Do not walk on the grass. Please Be Respectful.*"

My Grand-Dad's right. It is sacred ground.

We put our baseball gear into our duffel bags and sling them over our shoulders then ride our bikes from the Little League field over to Old Man Hobart's store. When we get there, before we go inside and get a couple of doughnuts for the ride home, we stop and look across the street at a small park. It's brand-new.

Everybody in the town chipped in to build this park and make it really nice. There was even a humongous fundraiser at the Dairy Barn. It's really another memorial if you think about it. There're two benches on either end of the park and smack in the middle of the park is a statue of a little girl standing next to a real flower garden where yellow and pink flowers have been planted. It's quiet and shady and nice. Some ladies planted what they call butterfly plants in the park. I guess the butterflies must like the plants a lot 'cause there're always some of them flying around the statue. The town named it Cecelia Park.

Me and Kev talk a little about how the park was named after that poor little girl whose life was changed after she went berry picking so long ago. Kev looks at the statue for a long time, like he's studying it.

Finally, he turns to look at me, his eyes all serious and wise-looking and says quietly, "The town came up with the perfect name for this park don't ya think, Chris? Cecelia Park. I like it."

I think about it for a minute. "Yeah, Kev, I like it too. It sure is the perfect name for the park." Then I nod my head and say, just like my Grand-Dad said about Dansbury Plot being sacred ground and that's why the town put up signs so nobody would walk on the land—

"It was the right thing to do."

Notes from the Author

Though this book is a work of fiction and fantasy, during the Civil War there were actual prison-of-war camps where soldiers were housed in horrific, inhumane conditions suffering under enemy commanders notorious for their deliberate cruelty to the prisoners-of-war. One of the cruelest of these commanders was Henry Wirz who was the commander of the infamous Andersonville Prison camp. The character of Albin Sarlewski is based on this man.

Unlike the fictional character of Albin Sarlewski who fled the country after the war ended rather than face a trial for his inhumanity to the prisoners, Wirz was brought to trial. Maj. Gen. Lew Wallace, later the best-selling author of the biblically inspired novel *Ben Hur,* presided over the 63-day military tribunal which lasted from August 23 to October 18.

Thirteen separate charges were leveled against Wirz, alleging such acts as the *"inciting, and urging of ferocious bloodhounds to pursue, attack, wound, and tear into pieces, soldiers belonging to the U.S. Army, and the intentional murder of a prisoner (name unknown) upon whom Henry Wirz did feloniously and with malice aforethought, inflict a grievous wound from a pistol. Wirz refused to have the man attended to by the company doctor and, after six days of suffering, the soldier died."*

Henry Wirz was hanged on November 10, 1865, in Washington, D.C., the only Confederate officer executed as a war criminal.

Besides Andersonville, two of the worst prisons were Libby Prison and Fort Delaware.

The *Official Records of the Civil War* cite a total of 127,000 Union soldiers who endured the privations of being prisoners-of-war in these camps. These privations ranged from inadequate shelter and clothing, poor hygiene, to outright starvation, intentional cruelty, and harsh summary justice with severe penalties. More than 22,580 prisoners died in captivity. 18 percent of Union captives never returned from incarceration.

Libby Prison, was a Confederate prison at Richmond, Virginia, during the American Civil War. The Confederates took over the land from the original owner and made it one of the worst places of the Civil War and it quickly gained an infamous reputation for the overcrowded, disease-ridden, and harsh conditions under which officer prisoners from the Union Army were kept. Prisoners suffered from disease, malnutrition and a high mortality rate.

Fort Delaware is located near the fictional Township of Bridge Crossing. The fort was originally devised as a harbor defense facility in 1859. It is located on Pea Patch Island along the Delaware River. During the Civil War the Confederates had control of Fort Delaware and used it as a prison to house captured Union prisoners of war. The fort itself was a horrible place to be but what was even worse were the 'punishment cells' outside the fort, similar to those described in the book's Dansbury Plot. There were 'hot-holes', cells that were underground with only a small grated window above the cell. Union soldiers, starved and it has been documented that they were sometimes forced to eat their own dead and dying simply to survive.

My reading about the horrors of the above named prisons, and the infamous Henry Wirz, inspired this book. There are many legends about the ghosts* who haunt the camps and Civil War battlefields. All were woven together to create this story.

*Many Civil War sites have legends of ghosts and strange happenings. However, the story of Little Cecelia is purely from my own imagination and one, I hope, that adds to your reading enjoyment. ~KH

www.ingramcontent.com/pod-product-compliance
Lightning Source LLC
Chambersburg PA
CBHW050843180626
46814CB00007B/2601